SYNOPSIS

Surviving the South Side of Chicago feels like a war to many. Every day, residents battle the constant threat of violence to protect their families and themselves. Tough, fearless, and street-smart, they've adapted to a brutal reality. But can they survive the undead, creatures more terrifying than any street rival?

When the undead rises, Chicago becomes a living nightmare. The South Side is ground zero, sealed off by the government as the infection spreads like wildfire, trapping survivors in a hell they never imagined.

Fable, a streetwise hustler, is determined to save the woman he's loved since high school, Niyah. But as danger closes in, protecting her becomes more than just survival—it's a fight for the love he's always wanted. As the two battle relentless hordes of the undead and ruthless scavengers, their fiery connection grows amidst the ruins. But will it be enough to keep them alive?

Paris is in love with Salem, but his emotional distance has

become unbearable—especially now, in the chaos of the apocalypse. She needs his comfort more than ever, but Salem is so fixated on survival that he's blind to the fact that he's losing her. Meanwhile, his brother August offers the softness and understanding she craves. An undeniable attraction simmers between them, but they both bury it deep, refusing to betray Salem despite the pull that grows stronger each day.

Pier 31 is a pulse-pounding tale of suspense, horror, and forbidden romance where survival demands sacrifice, and love may be the most dangerous risk of all. As food runs low, alliances shift, and danger lurks around every corner, the real question emerges: Can their grit and resilience save them from a horror they've never faced before?

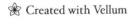 Created with Vellum

ABOUT THE AUTHOR

National Best Selling Author, Jessica N. Watkins, was born on April 1st in Chicago, Illinois. She obtained a Bachelor of Arts with Focus in Psychology from DePaul University and a Masters of Applied Professional Studies with a focus in Business Administration from the like institution. Working in Hospital Administration for most of her career, Watkins has also been an author of fiction literature since the young age of nine. Eventually, she used writing as an outlet during her freshmen year of high school as a single parent: "In the third grade, I entered a short story contest with a fiction tale of an apple tree that refused to grow despite the efforts of the darling main character. My writing evolved from apple trees to my seventh and eighth-grade classmates paying me to read novels I wrote about kids our age living the lives our parents wouldn't dare let us".

In September 2013, Jessica's novel, Secrets of a Side Bitch reached #1 on multiple charts, which catapulted her successful career in the Urban Fiction book industry and labeled her a national best-selling author. Since, Watkins' novels have matured into steamy, humorous, and realistic tales of African American Romance and Urban Fiction.

Jessica N. Watkins is available for talks, workshops, or book signings. Email her at authorjwatkins@gmail.com.

FOLLOW JESSICA ON SOCIAL MEDIA:
Instagram - @authorjwatkins
TikTok- @authorjwatkins
Twitter - @authorjwatkins
Facebook - @jwpresents
Facebook Group -
https://www.facebook.com/groups/femistryfans

PROLOGUE

D errick and Slim approached the old, rundown warehouse on the edge of the industrial district. Derrick couldn't shake the uneasy feeling crawling up his spine. He glanced over at Slim, who was so excited that he was practically bouncing.

"Man, we about to come up," Slim said, grinning ear to ear. "Can you believe these prices? This dude, Dmitri, is offering kilos at prices like it's the eighties. We about to make some real bread."

Derrick remained quiet as his eyes scanned the warehouse. Something felt off. He couldn't figure out why a Russian guy like Dmitri, who none of the hustlers had even heard of, would just show up out of nowhere offering prices for kilos of heroin so low it seemed unreal. Prices like his didn't exist anymore in this game. A week ago, when Dmitri approached them in their hood, he'd said that he was recommended to them because they were known for moving product fast. But something about this smelled wrong.

"You sure about this?" Derrick pressed. "I mean, prices like this... they ain't been seen in decades. And now this dude just shows up with all this weight to unload? I don't know, Slim."

Slim rolled his eyes, already walking ahead toward the warehouse entrance. "There you go again, overthinking shit. We about to get paid, bro. *Paid*. Ain't nobody gonna sell it faster than us. That's why we got the recommendation."

Derrick slowed his pace, watching as Slim reached the heavy metal door and tugged it open. "You don't find it weird that we don't know who recommended us? That a Russian dude is selling weight like this to niggas like us?"

Slim stopped, turning around with an annoyed glare. "Look, this is how the drugs and guns got in our neighborhoods in the first place. Some white motherfucker showed up with some product and made a deal for us niggas to sell it. We either get in here and make this money, or we sit outside and let somebody else take the opportunity. You heard Dmitri. He said we the best on the South Side. Now stop worrying and let's get this paper."

Derrick sighed but followed. His instincts were screaming that something was off about this. But Slim was right; they were about to make some real money off this deal if things went according to plan.

Still, as they stepped into the dimly lit warehouse, Derrick's hand lingered near his waistband. His fingers brushed the cold steel of his gun as he rested his hand on it just in case.

Slim was already inside, greeting Dmitri with a slap on the back like they were old friends. Derrick hung back slightly. His eyes narrowed as he watched Dmitri's calm, composed demeanor. When Dmitri smiled at Derrick, something about it felt rehearsed. Something about this whole setup felt too good to be true.

⚜

A FEW HOURS LATER, THE SUN HUNG LOW IN THE SKY, washing a block that many people would deem filthy in a beautiful, warm, orange light. It was August, and the heat was relentless. A gentle breeze rustled the leaves on the trees lining the street, but despite the beautiful weather, the air on the corner was filled with desperation.

Derrick and Slim stood by the old convenience store. Its neon "Open" sign flickered weakly as people hustled in and out for blunts, cigarettes, snacks, and lottery tickets. One dope fiend after another approached Derrick and Slim's corner boys, eyes wide with hunger.

Slim watched as their corner boys handed off small bags of heroin with practiced ease. The dope fiends took the bags eagerly, nodding in thanks or mumbling incoherently before scurrying off to shoot up. Some disappeared into a nearby alley to get high immediately.

Derrick casually leaned against the brick wall of the two flat they stood in front of, scanning the street lazily with sharp eyes that stayed on point.

"Damn, they hungry today." Derrick grinned as he looked toward a scrawny man who was already stumbling toward the alley with the bag of dope clutched in his shaking hand.

Slim snorted. "They always hungry, bro. That's why we ain't never out of business. And they love Dmitri's product."

As they laughed and made small talk, business continued. Dope fiends came and went like clockwork, their movements twitchy and frantic.

Derrick cracked a joke about one of the junkies—how fast he'd sprinted off like a rabbit—and Slim doubled over in laughter, slapping his knee.

"Man, he was gone! Looked like he was runnin' from the police!" Slim howled.

But their laughter was interrupted by a sharp, piercing scream that was full of terror.

Derrick straightened up. He squinted with focus as he glanced toward the alley. The scream resonated again, more frantic this time.

Slim squinted in the same direction but quickly shrugged it off. "Crazy ass fiends probably in the alley fighting over dope."

But a figure emerged from the alley. A familiar, neighborhood dope fiend, Lester, moved slowly and awkwardly, like he couldn't quite get his limbs to cooperate. His clothes were filthy, and his skin was pale and sunken. But none of that was unusual. Dope fiends walked like zombies every day on this block.

Derrick chuckled, crossing his arms. "Yo', look at this nigga. Lester straight up looks like the living dead."

Lester stumbled closer. His eyes were wide and bloodshot, but there was something... *off* about him. His mouth hung open, drool slid down his chin, and his breathing came in ragged, gurgling gasps. Derrick's eyes narrowed more as he focused on the bag in Lester's hand that he had just sold him. He hadn't even smoked it yet. And as he shuffled towards them, Derrick noticed the oozing bite mark on his neck.

"Ugh, fuck is wrong with this nigga's neck?" Derrick asked himself, frowning.

"Yo', Lester," Slim called out, waving his hand dismissively. "You already got yours, so back the fuck up."

Lester didn't respond. Instead, he came closer with jerky movements. His eyes locked on Slim like he was zeroing in on prey.

"Yo', for real, get the fuck on!" Slim snapped, taking a step back. Derrick chuckled, but Slim was starting to lose his patience. "Back the fuck up!"

But Lester didn't stop. His eyes were wild and unfocused. Then, before Slim could react, Lester lunged.

It happened so fast that Slim barely had time to defend himself. Lester's mouth opened impossibly wide, revealing yellowed, broken teeth, and then those teeth sank deep into Slim's forearm.

The sound of the bite was grotesque. It was a wet, tearing noise, as flesh and muscle ripped beneath the pressure of Lester's jaws.

"*Arrrgh!*" Slim bellowed out in pain.

Blood sprayed from the wound, splattering the pavement as Slim screamed in shock and agony. Lester gnawed at him, teeth grinding against bone. The whites of his eyes rolled back into his head as he sank deeper into Slim's arm like a wild animal.

"Yo', what the fuck!" Derrick shouted, eyes wide with horror as he watched, frozen in disbelief.

The busy corner erupted into chaos as people witnessed the gruesome attack. Junkies who had moments ago been lining up for a hit scattered in all directions, some screaming. Others were paralyzed with fear, their eyes wide with disbelief. A woman near the convenience store dropped her soda, backing away slowly before breaking into a sprint. The regulars who normally ignored the violent happenings on the block now found themselves panicking, unsure of whether to run or intervene. The sound of Slim's agonized screams mingled with gasps and shouted warnings, as bystanders watched in horror, assuming that the bite was part of some drug-induced madness.

Slim thrashed violently, trying to push Lester off, but his grip was like iron. His jaw clamped tighter, ripping through the muscle, skin shredding as Lester growled—a low, guttural noise—before jerking his head back, taking a chunk of Slim's flesh with him. Blood dripped from his mouth as he chewed it, his lips smacking hideously.

Slim staggered backward, clutching his mangled arm. Blood

poured between his fingers. His face warped in horror and pain, as his breath came in ragged gasps.

"Argh! Fuck! My arm!" Slim screamed.

Lester stood there with blood smeared across his face, eyes still glazed and empty. Then he started to move toward Derrick.

As Lester advanced on him with the same jerky, unnatural movements, Derrick's hands trembled as he fumbled for the gun tucked in his waistband.

Derrick raised the gun and squeezed the trigger. The deafening crack of the shot echoed through the block as the bullet hit Lester in the chest. Lester staggered as a spray of blood misted the air, but he kept approaching Derrick, as if the bullet had only pinched him.

"Shit!" Derrick exclaimed.

"Shoot him again!" Slim called out, still holding his arm in agony.

Derrick did just that, but this time, shooting Lester in the head. Finally, he collapsed to the ground. Derrick barely had time to catch his breath before a chilling growl rose from the alley. His eyes snapped up, and his stomach dropped as more dope fiends emerged—five, maybe six of them—stumbling forward with twisted limbs and glazed eyes, their mouths gaping as they zeroed in on him.

"Shit!" Derrick yelled, turning on his heels and sprinting down the block.

Panic spread like wildfire as people who had been frozen in shock moments ago now ran, screaming, in every direction. The sound of feet pounding the pavement filled the air, mixed with the terrifying, throaty growls of the approaching horde who was now running after them.

The dead were walking.

THE FLASHING BLUE AND RED LIGHTS FROM THE POLICE cruisers danced chaotically as detectives and officers swarmed the area in front of the convenience store. Lester's body lay sprawled on the sidewalk. His clothes were soaked in blood. His eyes were wide open in a frozen expression of horror. The crowd that had gathered around whispered among themselves, chattering with fear and confusion. A few witnesses tried to approach the yellow tape, but officers quickly pushed them back.

Detective Brooks knelt beside the body, glancing over at his partner, Detective Ramirez, who was flipping through a small notepad.

Brooks shook his head with a grim expression. "Looks like a dope fiend that got too close to a hustler," he muttered, squinting at Lester's wounds. "Probably attacked the wrong guy and ended up catching a bullet."

Ramirez nodded in agreement as he scribbled a few notes. "It happens all the time. Junkie gets too high, thinks he's invincible, and goes after the wrong dude. Doesn't look like much of a struggle, though. The assailant must've shot him quick."

"Detective!" a woman in the crowd yelled. She pushed forward despite the officers trying to hold her back. She was frantic with wide terrified eyes. "You don't understand! It wasn't just him! There are more! They came outta the alley like they was crazy, like zombies! I saw it!"

Brooks sighed as he stood up and turned to the crowd. His eyes scanned over the nervous faces, but his patience was already thin. "Ma'am, we're handling this. It's probably just a bad batch of dope making these fiends act wild. You should go home and let us do our job."

"No, *no*!" The woman's voice rose with frustration. "I know what I saw! They weren't just high, they were..." She paused as she searched for the right words. "They were different! They weren't acting normal! They were growling and stumbling around like dead men walking!"

Ramirez rolled his eyes while stepping toward the woman with a tired look. "Lady, these dope fiends are always out here doing some crazy shit. We got it under control."

Another man in the crowd chimed in, shaking his head vigorously. "Nah, man, she's right! They came outta that alley, all messed up, like... like they was dead or something. Then they started attacking people. One of them bit one of the hustlers, then that hustler started acting weird too! His body started twisting and shit, and he started chasing people, like the rest of them were!"

Brooks exchanged a humored glance with Ramirez. Both of them were clearly unconvinced. "Look, I get it," Brooks said dismissively, wearing a taunting smirk. "These streets are rough, and you all see a lot of crazy stuff out here, but this is just another case of a junkie losing it. We've got it handled."

Another voice from the crowd shouted, "You need to listen to them! It's not normal, man. Ain't nobody ever seen them act like that before. They looked like... *zombies*!"

Brooks groaned under his breath, rubbing the back of his neck in frustration. "Enough with the zombie talk. Ain't no such thing, and you know it. Y'all been watching too many movies. *Go home*. We'll take care of this."

The crowd murmured, still uneasy, but slowly began to disperse as the police officers pushed them back further.

Brooks crouched again, looking at Lester's body one more time. He examined the torn flesh on Lester's neck and shook his head. "Crazy junkies. Must be some new shit they're mixing in the dope."

Ramirez nodded while flipping his notebook shut. "Yeah, and

whatever it is, it's making these fiends lose their damn minds. Let's get this body bagged up and outta here before another one of these witnesses tells us they saw aliens too."

They turned away from the body, completely dismissing the fear that lingered in the air.

TWO DAYS LATER

PIER 31

JESSICA N. WATKINS

with
JAMES D. GAVINS

PARIS

I sat next to Salem on Meesha's couch, tucked up under his arm. He had one arm lazily draped over my shoulder. His fingers grazed my skin, but his eyes were stuck on the TV. My mind wasn't on the movie, though, or even the sounds of the rest of the crew joking around in the room. My thoughts were on me and Salem, on how we had been off lately, and how I wasn't sure how to fix it.

"Salem," I called quietly.

His arm tensed, like he already knew I was about to go there. We'd been together almost ten years now, so we knew each other's moves before they even happened.

"Yeah?" he answered, not looking at me.

"We need to talk."

Bothered, he sighed and didn't even turn toward me. That was the problem. Over the years, he had grown hard and carried this cold exterior into our relationship. His hustler mindset had invaded every part of his life, especially our relationship.

"What about?" he bit.

"About us, Salem. You know we ain't been right." My eyes

searched his face, hoping to see some hint of emotion there. Instead, I got the same blank look I always got when we talked like this.

"We good, Paris," he said. "We just goin' through some shit. It happens."

I leaned back, feeling my frustrations starting to simmer. "Nah, it ain't just 'some shit.' It's *you*. You bring that same hard-ass energy you have in the streets into our relationship. I ain't one of your boys, Salem."

He ran a hand over his face, rubbing his light brown beard. "I know you ain't, but this is just me. You know what you signed up for."

I didn't respond. I just let my eyes wander over to August, who was in the kitchen grabbing something to drink. He was only eleven months younger than Salem. They were so close in age that people called them "ghetto twins." They looked damn near identical. They were both tall with basketball builds, and brown skinned with light greenish-gray eyes that made them look like mystical gods. Even their beards were the same, full and perfectly lined, just a shade lighter than their skin.

But despite their physical similarities, August was so different on the inside. He had a way about him that made everything feel softer. He was caring in ways Salem never quite managed to be. He was affectionate and never hesitated to offer a comforting touch or a playful nudge to lighten the mood. A simple smile from him made my stomach flip. I craved that warmth, that tenderness. It was so different from the hard edges of survival I was used to with Salem. In August's presence, I could breathe a little easier, even if just for a moment. It was the softness I yearned for. Every smile, every caring word drew me closer to him, leaving me caught between what I wanted and what I knew was right.

I opened my mouth to respond to Salem's tired-ass

comment, "*You know what you signed up for*," but before I could say a word, the front door swung open hard, nearly crashing into the wall. Cane, DeShawn, and Fable came barreling in, both wide-eyed and breathless.

Something was wrong—*real* wrong.

"Cane!" Meesha screamed, jumping up from the couch.

I gasped when I noticed the blood dripping from a gaping wound on Cane's arm. He was clutching it as his expression tangled in pain.

"Shit! What happened?" Kecia gasped. She rushed toward him with Navon close behind her. August, Salem, and I were right behind them as the whole room burst into chaos.

"I'm good! I'm good!" Cane tried to insist, but his voice was shaky as he stumbled into the middle of the living room.

Navon curiously stared at the blood dripping down Navon's arm. "You don't look good."

"I just got bit by some crazy-ass dope fiend."

The energy in the room shifted from panic to suspicion real quick. Everyone froze for a second. Kecia stopped in her tracks, eyes wide, and Navon was the first to pull back slightly. "Wait... Bit by *who*?"

"A dope fiend," Cane repeated, frustrated. "Y'all don't start actin' like them crazy motherfuckas online with that walker shit."

I peeped Fable nervously scratching the back of his head, as if he wanted to say something. Meesha put her hands over her mouth. Her eyes bounced from the blood on his arm to his face, then back again.

"You sure it was *just* a dope fiend?" Meesha asked.

Cane glared at them, pissed now. "Y'all really about to believe that conspiracy theory shit? Walkers? Man, c'mon! It's just a bite. I need to get it patched up." Disappointment and hurt blanketed his eyes as he stared at all our continued hesitation. "Wow. Y'all trippin'."

"Cane," I called his name gently, trying to calm the energy down in the room. "We're not trying to insinuate anything. We just—"

"Just what?!" he snapped.

"Chill," Salem quickly interjected.

"Nah, fuck that," Cane spit. "I'm good." He glanced around the room, shaking his head in disbelief. "I'm goin' home. Niyah can patch me up. I ain't got time for this bullshit."

He reached into his pocket, fumbling with his keys. The whole room was still watching him, frozen between worry and fear.

"Cane, wait up," Fable tried to stop him.

But Cane was already heading for the door, shaking his head. "I'm good!" he barked back at us. "I'll be fine. I'm going home to my girl."

He didn't look back as he stormed out, slamming the door behind himself.

CHAPTER 1

NIYAH

I was sitting on the couch, scrolling through my phone while Neveah was in the dining room doing some TikTok dance with her Air Pods in, completely ignoring the rest of the world. She'd been cutting up lately. She was in typical, disrespectful teenage rare form, and Cane and I agreed one of us needed to keep an eye on her at all times. So, while he was at the kickback, I stayed home.

I swiped over to Instagram, checking stories from everyone I knew was at Meesha's house. Part of me wished I was there, turning up with them, but Neveah was acting so wild lately that I didn't trust her to be home alone, though she was sixteen.

I tapped on Meesha's story, and the video played, showing everyone laughing, playing spades with drinks in their hands. It looked like a good time. I could hear Cane's loudmouth in the background, joking about how he was killing it at cards.

Then the camera panned to Fable, sitting across from Cane, grinning.

"That smile," I swooned.

Damn, that smile could make you forget your own name.

I bit my lip, tapping the screen to pause the video for a second just to take him in. He was still so beautiful. He'd always had that bad boy look, with his own street edge that made him stand out even more. He had smooth, caramel skin that looked like it soaked up the sun perfectly. His eyes were this warm, golden-brown color that always had this quiet intensity behind them, like he was thinking five steps ahead of everybody else. His jawline was sharp, and he kept his beard lined up perfectly, not too thick but just enough to make you look twice. And his body was cut, but not in a way that felt like he was trying' too hard. He had that lean, athletic build. He could just throw on a hoodie and still look fine as hell. His tattoos peeked out from his neck and arms, giving him that bad boy vibe that stole everybody's attention, mine included.

Back in high school, all the girls were on him. I used to think he was so far out of my league, so I never told anybody. He was my little secret I kept to myself.

Then Cane came into my life. When he approached me at Homecoming, all I thought about was Fable. But, I knew that Fable was just a fairytale, while Cane was trying to fulfill my fantasies in real life. Cane was cool, attractive, and made me laugh. So, before I knew it, we were together. Then I was pregnant with Neveah. Life got real fast, but I was happy. I loved Cane, but every time I saw Fable that feeling I had back in high school resurfaced. There was something about him always drawing me in. He had that edge, that swag that just made him stand out and made him different from everybody else.

I was still staring at Fable's smile on my phone when the sound of screams cut through the house, loud enough to pull me out of my head. I groaned, wondering what the hell could have been going on now. Though we lived in a decent neighborhood, fights and domestic altercations were frequent since a problematic family had moved in a few months ago. I stood up, frowning, and went over to the window, pulling the curtain back just enough to see what was happening.

Down the block, a group of kids were running towards my house like they were trying to escape something. Panic was all over their faces. I looked behind them and saw two older boys chasing after them.

At first, I thought it was just some older kids messing with the younger ones, but then I noticed how the older boys looked. They were dressed like the young boys did nowadays; tight jeans, but still sagging, with hoodies with the hood over their heads, despite how awfully hot it was. But they were filthy, like they hadn't seen a shower in weeks. Dirt was caked on their skin and clothes. Their faces looked inhumane, and their eyes were wide but hollow. Something dark was smeared around their mouths. I squinted, and my stomach turned as I realized it looked like blood, dried *and* fresh.

"What the hell?" I mumbled.

My motherly instincts kicked in. Without thinking, I let the curtain drop and rushed to the front door. I flung the door open, stepping halfway outside. "Hey! Leave those kids alone!"

The boys stopped dead in their tracks, which was weird as hell. One second, they were running, and then, suddenly, they were just... *still*. So still that it was creepy. Watching them, my stomach tightened.

They turned to face me, both of them moving at the same time, like something out of a nightmare. And when I locked eyes with them, something cold crawled up my spine. Their eyes were empty and lifeless. I'd never seen anything like it before.

Before I could process it, they *sprinted* toward me.

I screamed as I slammed the door shut. My hands were shaking so badly I almost couldn't lock it. I was fumbling with the locks, screaming, "Neveah! Neveah!"

My heart raced as loud, angry fists slammed into the door,

and something that sounded like growling, deep and unnatural, came from the other side.

I finally managed to twist the locks, and just as I backed away, Neveah took out one of her Air Pods, looking at me like I was losing my mind. "What's wrong, Ma?"

I couldn't even speak. My mouth was dry, and my heart was thudding so loud I thought it might burst out of my chest.

"What the fuck did I just see?" I breathed.

Outside, the distant screams were getting louder. The banging on the door was relentless. My whole body was shaking, and I couldn't catch my breath.

Neveah's face bawled up with confusion. "Who's at the door?" She moved to head toward it like she was about to open it up and see for herself.

I snapped out of my shock just in time. I grabbed her arm with trembling hands. "No! Don't go near it," I gasped. "Just stay back!"

Neveah pulled away slightly, but she didn't go for the door again. "Is it those drugged-out kids?" she asked. "I saw people online talking about some new drug that's making people go crazy and bite people."

I swallowed hard, trying to keep my voice steady. "Yeah... maybe. I don't know," I stammered, still unable to catch my breath. "Just stay away from the door, Neveah, please."

She hesitated as she looked toward the window where the screams outside were getting louder.

"Ma, what is that?" Neveah's voice was quieter now with a tremor in it.

I backed away from her with my legs barely able to hold me up. "I need to call your dad."

But when I grabbed my phone and dialed, the line just rang and rang.

"Pick up," I whispered under my breath. "Please, Cane, pick up."

But there was no answer.

The banging on the door was still there. Whoever—or *what*ever—was out there wasn't giving up.

PARIS

The room was still after Cane stormed out, slamming the door behind himself. Everybody was just standing eerily still, like they didn't know what to do next.

My eyes narrowed as I inched towards him. "What the hell happened out there?"

Fable rubbed the back of his neck, still baffled and disturbed by whatever had gone down.

He finally sighed and looked back at me. "We saw a guy attacking some girls. We stepped in, and he bit Cane. Shit was crazy, Paris."

"Yeah, but it's nothing," DeShawn was being way too cool for what had just happened. "Y'all need to cool out. Cane's good, and Niyah's got him. She'll patch him up." He waved his hand like he was brushing off the whole situation and headed for the card table. "Ain't no point in stressing over it. Let's get back to this game." I raised an eyebrow, watching him as he sat down and gestured to Fable. "Fable, you my partner now," he said, tapping the table. "Paris, Salem, y'all get in on this game."

But even though DeShawn was trying to act all nonchalant,

everybody in the room was still moving slow, like we weren't so sure the situation was as simple as Cane was trying to make it seem. Even Fable, who was fearless and a beast in the streets, had an eerie, unsettling look in his eyes.

DeShawn laughed, trying to force the mood back to normal. "Come on, y'all actin' so scary. It ain't that deep." He picked up the deck, shuffling the cards with a shaky hand.

I watched him, noticing how the cards kept slipping through his fingers. "You good?" I teased, leaning back against the couch. "You're telling us to calm down, but you're looking real frazzled yourself."

DeShawn 's eyes flicked up at me, and he chuckled, though it wasn't as confident as before. "Girl, please. I'm chillin'."

But he wasn't, and I could see it. His hands shook while he tried to shuffle the deck, and his jaw stiffened every few seconds like he was trying to force himself to get it together. He was frontin', trying to make it seem like he wasn't scared, but clearly, he was.

"Yeah, alright," I said, smirking a little.

He ignored me, finally managing to deal the cards, but the energy in the room still felt off.

Salem nudged me. "Come on, let's play this game."

Sighing discreetly, I followed him to the table. We sat across from each other, and Fable sat across from DeShawn, who was still trying to play it cool, but I noticed something was off with him.

Meesha, Kecia, and August were still hanging around, glancing at the door like they were waiting for something else to happen. Eventually, they wandered over to the couch. August cracked open another bottle of Patron and poured another drink.

"Pour me up too," Navon told him.

Legion grunted. "Yeah, me too, shit. I need a shot."

After DeShawn dealt the cards, I picked mine up and glanced at Salem. "What are you thinking?" I asked, scanning my hand.

Salem's forehead wrinkled as he thought for a second. "I can do four. You?"

"Three. Let's go seven then."

Fable looked over at DeShawn. "Yo', how many books you got?"

But DeShawn didn't answer. He just sat there, staring at his hand with the oddest look in his eyes. His skin looked pale, almost ghostlike.

"DeShawn, you good?" Fable asked.

DeShawn still didn't respond. His breathing was getting louder, heavier, and then he leaned forward, pressing a hand to his stomach like he was about to puke.

"Man, quit playin'," Legion said, laughing, though nervously. "You tryin' to scare us or somethin'?"

But DeShawn wasn't playing.

Without warning, DeShawn doubled over and started coughing hard. Then blood—dark and thick—shot out of his mouth, splattering across the table and hitting Fable in the face.

The room froze. Then suddenly the sound of everyone's screams filled the room as we all stared at DeShawn, who was shaking with a mouth full of blood.

Fable jumped back, pushing his chair away from the table. He wiped the blood off his face with the bottom of his shirt, revealing his abs in the process.

"Shit!" Fable yelled, backing away.

Salem leaned over and began frantically searching DeShawn. His hands moved fast like he was trying to find something that could explain what the hell was happening. DeShawn was shaking as his eyes rolled back. Then Salem pulled up DeShawn's shirt and froze. There, just above his waistband, was a deep bite mark, oozing something thick and dark, almost black. It was swollen and pulsing like it was alive.

Salem jumped back, asking Fable, "He got bit?!"

Fable blinked owlishly. "I didn't see him get bit, but we were tussling with the dude. He must have bit him then."

DeShawn's body started to jerk violently, making us all frantically stumble away. Salem grabbed my arm and pulled me back further from the table.

"Get back!" he ordered, pulling me with him as he stood between me and whatever was happening to DeShawn.

Suddenly, DeShawn's eyes shifted to Fable, and that's when I knew something was *really* wrong. His face had gone slack. His skin was now almost gray, and his eyes weren't human anymore. They were dark, glassy, and completely hollow like there was nothing behind them. His mouth twisted into a snarl. His lips curled back, revealing blood-stained teeth. His body started twitching and jerking like he was fighting against something inside him. His movements were sharp and unnatural, like every muscle in his body was malfunctioning at once.

"DeShawn?" I whispered, but it wasn't DeShawn anymore. Whatever he was now wasn't human.

In a flash, he lunged across the table. He moved so fast and violently that it didn't even seem real. He leaped at Fable with an animalistic force. His arms were stretched out as his fingers clawed for Fable's throat.

"Shit!" Fable shouted, jumping back just in time. DeShawn missed and hit the floor hard, but he didn't stay down. His body contorted as he pushed himself up from the ground. He was growling and his mouth foamed. His eyes—those black, empty eyes—locked onto us. They looked so hungry and vicious.

That was all it took. Everyone ran. Screaming. Chairs crashed to the floor, cards scattered, and we all bolted for the door. I could barely think as Salem yanked me along, pushing through the doorway and out into the night. Behind us, I could still hear that inhuman growling, the sound of DeShawn —whatever he had turned into—trying to get to us.

We ran like our lives depended on it. Salem, August, and I were right on Fable's heels as he sprinted toward his car. It felt like I could barely breathe, and my legs were burning, but I didn't stop. The second Fable unlocked the doors, we all piled in, slamming them shut behind us. I could barely catch my breath. My hands were trembling as I fumbled with the seatbelt. Fable was just about to pull off when I heard pounding on the window.

All of us let out terrible screams and hollers.

"Oh shit!" August bellowed.

"Let me in!" Kecia screamed. Her fists hit the glass like she was fighting for her life.

Relieved, I reached over and pushed the door open. Kecia jumped in so fast she literally landed on top of me. Her legs were tangled with mine as she tried to find room. Before I could push her off, Fable floored the gas, tires screeching as we sped away.

My heart was pounding in my ears, but when I looked back at the house, I saw DeShawn. He was coming out of the front door, sprinting like he wasn't human any longer. My stomach dropped, and I felt sick. His movements were fast and jerky, like he had turned into some kind of monster.

"Where the hell is Navon, Meesha, and Legion?" I cried, frantically scanning the street. I spotted them just as they were getting into Navon's car. But DeShawn saw them too.

"Shit!" I yelled, my eyes wide as I watched in horror.

DeShawn ran toward them. Legion was struggling to shut the passenger door, but before he could get it closed, DeShawn was on him. We could hear Navon, Meesha, and Legion's screams of terror even with Fable's windows rolled up. DeShawn grabbed Legion and yanked him out of the car. His body slammed onto the ground. Then, without hesitation, DeShawn bit down on

Legion's face, tearing into him like an animal. Blood sprayed everywhere.

"God damn!" Fable shouted with disgust as he slowed the car, unable to look away.

"Oh my God, oh my God!" Kecia was shaking on top of me. Her hands gripped my arm so tight it hurt.

Salem's face was contorted in horror. His eyes locked on Legion's body as DeShawn continued to tear him apart. August wasn't saying anything, just staring out the window, frozen in shock.

"Drive!" I screamed, grabbing Fable's shoulder. "We gotta go!"

Fable snapped out of it, slamming on the gas again. The car lurched forward as we sped down the street. None of us could stop looking back, watching as DeShawn tore into Legion savagely.

CHAPTER 2

PARIS

F able gripped the steering wheel as he sped through the streets. His eyes darted between the road and the madness happening outside. Kecia's face was pressed up against the window with one hand covering her mouth in horror. August and Salem were both staring out in silence. Everywhere we looked, people were running, screaming, or being chased by *whatever* the hell these people had turned into.

The scene outside was pure chaos. People were running in all directions with terror all over their faces as bloodied figures chased them down the street. A man sprinted down the middle of the street, but he didn't make it far before one of those creatures tackled him, sinking its teeth into his shoulder as he screamed. Another one, its clothes torn and covered in dirt, was gnashing its teeth at a woman who was desperately banging on a door, begging to be let inside. Sounds of screams, frantic shouts, and the eerie growling coming from the monsters running wild was excruciating to listen to. It looked like the world was ending, and the streets were turning into Armageddon.

"Look at them," Kecia's voice trembled. "They're biting people. Oh my God, they're *biting* people!"

I turned to see what she was looking at—a woman sprinting down the sidewalk, screaming for her life, with one of those creatures—those *things*—right behind her. He caught up to her, tackled her to the ground, and without hesitation, sunk his teeth into her neck. Blood sprayed across the pavement, and I had to look away as my stomach folded in knots.

"We're almost there," Fable muttered, barely blinking as he pushed the car faster. His house was just a few miles away, but every second felt like a lifetime. As we got closer, it didn't get any better. More of those *things* were running wild, chasing people down like prey, biting and ripping at their flesh.

When we finally pulled up in front of Fable's house, it was chaos. A few of the infected were running up and down the street, tearing after anyone they could catch.

Fable pulled the car to a stop, but nobody moved. The engine hummed quietly. My pulse was in my throat, and I could feel the thick and suffocating fear in the air.

"We-we-we can't get out," I stammered breathlessly. "We shouldn't. We should just stay in the car until... I don't know, maybe they'll go away."

Salem looked over at me. "We can't stay here, Paris. We'll be sitting ducks. We have to get inside. Now."

I opened my mouth to argue, but I knew he was right. We weren't safe here, and waiting around would only make it worse.

"Y'all got your guns ready?" Salem asked August and Fable.

"Yeah," Fable lifted his shirt to reveal his piece tucked into his waistband. August nodded, already checking his gun, making sure the safety was off.

"Okay, we get out, and we move fast," Salem instructed us. "No stopping. We head straight inside, and if any of those things come at us, shoot them. Paris stay with me. Kecia stay with Fable. Hold on to our belt loops and do *not* let go."

Me and Kecia nodded quickly with wide, frantic eyes. My hands were shaking, and my mind was screaming to stay put. But Salem pushed the door open. He stepped out of the car with his gun already in his hand. Fable and August followed, guns drawn, their eyes scanning the street.

I hesitated for a second, my heart pounding violently. But then I took a deep breath and followed close behind Salem as he instructed.

We rushed toward Fable's house. I didn't know that I could run that fast. I held onto Salem's belt loop, keeping close, while Kecia did the same with Fable. Every time I glanced over my shoulder, it felt like the whole city was collapsing behind us. Up ahead, we saw a man wrestling with one of those creatures. His screams echoed down the street.

Fable was in front, leading us forward.

"Hurry up, y'all! We're almost there!" I yelled, but my voice was barely loud enough to be heard over all the madness.

We made it to the gate surrounding Fable's house, and he immediately dug into his pocket for the keys. His hands trembled as he fumbled to unlock it. "Fuck!" he barked.

"Come on, come on," August muttered under his breath as his panic visibly rose.

Salem, calm even under this amount of pressure, placed a hand on Fable's shoulder. "Relax, bro...But hurry the fuck up."

Just as Fable started to steady himself, Kecia's scream ripped through the air. "*Shit*!! They're coming!"

I looked up and felt my stomach drop. Three of the infected were sprinting toward us. It was such an odd sight to see. Two of them were women, dressed in their finest Fashion Nova type fit like they were getting ready to go out on this once beautiful summer day. There skimpy outfits exposed curvy bodies with tiny waists, flat stomachs, and breasts that had to have been bought recently. But they looked horrific. Their faces were pale and gaunt, and blood was smeared across their mouths like they'd been feeding recently. Their eyes were black and soulless, like empty pits, and their clothes hung off them, torn and soaked with grime. One of them had skin peeling away from her face, exposing bone, while another had chunks of flesh missing from its arms, revealing raw muscle beneath. The other was a guy dressed like money. He was decked out in a Louis Vuitton short set, the kind that cost more than what most people make in a month. But it was covered in rips, dirt, and dried blood. Around his neck was a thick, gold chain with a massive medallion still glistening, though it was smeared with gore. His wrists had gold bracelets, one of them with diamond studs that still caught the light, if you could see past the congealed blood and dirt. His kicks were Balenciagas, but they were barely holding on, with one sole flapping off every time he dragged a foot. The hat he wore was a fitted cap with a Chicago logo, but it had been knocked askew, exposing patches of his rotting scalp. His face, once probably clean and lined with a trimmed beard, was now twisted into an awful snarl. His eyes were hollow and yellowed, but still filled with a strange, eerie hunger.

"Fable, hurry the fuck up!" I screamed, loud and hysterically, while Kecia cried out next to me.

August and Salem didn't wait. They aimed their guns and started firing. The shots were deafening because they were so close. Two of the infected dropped instantly, but the third took a bullet to the arm and just kept coming. It didn't slow down at all, its dead eyes locked onto Kecia.

It slammed right into her, knocking her back. She screamed, her hands flailing, trying to push it off, but the thing was too strong, too fast. Before I could even react, Salem lunged forward, grabbing the infected and using every bit of his strength to throw it to the ground. His face was covered with rage as he pummeled it with his fists. His hits landed with violent force. The infected's head snapped back, but it still clawed at him, teeth gnashing in the air.

Salem pulled out his gun and shot it in the head, the sound of the shot ringing out just as Fable finally got the gate open.

"Inside! Now!" Fable shouted.

We all rushed in. Kecia stumbled as she slammed the gate shut behind us, making sure it was locked tight. Fable fumbled with the keys again, unlocking the screen and front door just in time.

"Go, go, go, go!" Kecia desperately chanted as we rushed inside.

We all barely made it inside, and everyone was still catching their breath when we heard the screeching of tires that cut through the chaos outside. We all turned and saw that it was Navon's car. He and Meesha hopped out fast. We could see the terror written all over their faces. They sprinted toward the gate, and as soon as they got to it, Navon started to pull it, realizing it was locked.

Meesha's eyes went wide with panic. Her hands slammed against the gate, shaking it.

"Come open the gate! Let us in!" she screamed, looking up at us with this desperation that made my chest ache.

I glanced past her and saw what she was running from—a mob of about ten of those things were sprinting down the street, tearing after them like they were on a mission.

Kecia was in front, closest to the door, and I could see her freeze, contemplating. She hesitated, her body stiff with fear.

"Move!" Salem barked, pushing her to the side. Without hesitation, he lifted his gun and started firing at the mob.

Watching Salem handle himself so fearlessly had me feeling some type of way. The man was pure strength, moving with this quiet authority that left no room for fear. Seeing him take charge like that, gun in hand, saving us without flinching, had me turned on in a way I couldn't even explain. It wasn't just that he was strong—it was how protective he was, how I knew that no matter what, he'd make sure I was safe. Seeing him like that, fierce and in control, reminded me exactly why he was mine, and I felt so proud.

Salem yanked the gate open and Navon and Meesha came flying in, not even looking back. Salem slammed the gate shut behind them just as the mob got close. Salem, Navon, and Meesha rushed inside, barely shutting the door in time.

Once the door clicked shut behind us, the sound of the infected's growls, their footsteps pounding on the pavement, faded. But the image of them running after us stayed with all of us, burning into our minds like a nightmare we couldn't wake up from.

I glanced back one last time, looking through the glass decorating the door. The mob of the infected was trying to climb the gate, their bony fingers curling around the metal.

CANE

I had already missed a call from Niyah, so when she called again, I made sure I answered, despite the complete mayhem that was unraveling outside. "Yeah, bae?" I answered, trying to mask my fear and worry.

"Baby, please come home *now*! It's some crazy shit happening outside. I'm so scared!"

"I'm pulling up right now," I assured her.

"Oh," she breathed with relief. "Good. Please hurry up, baby. And be careful. Some of those drugged out people are outside. Some of them tried to get in the house!"

My eyes widened even more than they had been. "Shit. Okay, baby. I got you. I'm pulling up right now."

"Okay."

I hung up, flying down the street.

When I pulled up to the house, I was barely breathing and my whole body was on edge. The rumors had been right. Something was happening, something I couldn't even wrap my head around. People were getting bit left and right, straight up wildin' like animals.

I could hear the faded screams of terror in the distance. I slowed the car down, staring through the windshield as I saw a woman lying on the ground, bleeding out. Then, outta nowhere, she started to twitch. First it was just her fingers, then her legs jerked like she was getting electrocuted. Slowly, she pushed herself up, like she was being pulled by an invisible force. I blinked, trying to convince myself I wasn't seeing what I was seeing.

"*Yooooo'*, what the *fuuuuck?*" I spoke low and slow, in complete disbelief of what I was seeing.

Her face gnarled, and her eyes went black. Her teeth bared, and her skin started to pale until it didn't even look human anymore. Her body came back up like a demon. I'd never seen anything like it.

I froze, my mind stuck on one thing....

I got bit too.

I looked down at my arm. The bite was still burning. My whole body shook, thinking about what I just saw. I wondered if that was going to happen to me. As I wondered if I was about to turn into one of those things, my heart started to beat out of my chest and the world felt like it was tilting.

But I couldn't believe it. I couldn't let myself believe it. No way this was real.

I waited, breathing hard, keeping my eye on the block. It was clearing up, whatever that thing was had hobbled further down the street.

I quickly opened the glove compartment, grabbing my gun, feeling its cool metal in my hand. I got out of the car and ran to the door, unlocking it with trembling hands. But when I tried to push it open, it wouldn't budge. I already knew Niyah had the security bar on. She always used it when she was home alone and scared. And with all the chaos happening outside, I knew she was terrified.

"Niyah!" I yelled, banging on the door with my fist. "Niyah, open the door!"

No answer.

"Niyah! It's me, Cane! Open the damn door!" I kept hitting the door, each bang louder than the last. "Niyah!" I shouted again. "Please, baby, open the door!"

NIYAH

Me and Neveah were clinging to each other on the couch, both of us shaking and crying. We stared at the doorknob turning. The distant screams from outside kept piercing through the walls, and I could feel Neveah's grip tighten every time we heard a new one.

Then I heard Cane's voice calling out, desperate and loud. "Niyah! Niyah, open the door!"

Relief hit me so fast, I almost collapsed.

"Oh, thank God!" I breathed.

"Daddy!" Niyah exclaimed with relief.

I let go of Neveah and rushed to the door. My hands were trembling as I pulled off the security bar and flung it open. Cane practically shoved his way inside. His face was filled with fear and frustration. He was breathing hard, like he'd been running.

"What the fuck, Niyah?!" he snapped, charging past me. "Why the hell you got the security bar on? You knew I was pulling up! You almost got me killed out there!"

"What else was I supposed to do, Cane?! You see what's goin' on outside?! There's drugged-out people trying to get in the house!"

Neveah clung to my side, still trembling. "Mama's right," she told Cane. "They were banging on the door and windows. I'm so scared."

Cane's demeanor softened as I comforted Neveah. "I know, baby," I said, brushing her hair back. "It's just that new drug. It's making people lose their minds."

Cane reached for Neveah, lovingly pinching her cheek. "I'm sorry for yelling. I probably freaked you out more."

"It's okay," Neveah muttered.

Then Cane started pacing, still attempting to catch his breath. "It's gotta be that new drug. Ain't no way this is anything else. Walkers ain't real."

"*Walkers?*" Neveah asked, her voice getting higher.

"No, baby," I reassured her quickly, even though my own voice wasn't as steady as I wanted it to be. "This ain't a movie. People just out here straight trippin' from that new stuff."

Cane ran his hands over his head with frustration clear in his tone. "Look, we gotta stay calm. We can't start believing all that walker bullshit. This is just like that flakka stuff from a few years ago, but worse. They are just infected or something."

"Exactly," I added, trying to convince myself as much as Neveah. "It's just drugs, not... not the end of the world."

Neveah looked between the two of us, clearly not convinced. "But... what if it's not? What if it's something else?"

Cane stopped pacing with his eyes lovingly on her. "Listen, I know it looks bad, but we're safe as long as we stay in here. We just need to keep the doors locked, and we'll ride this out."

I shook my head, urging, "We need to leave before one of those people manage to get inside. We can't stay here, Cane."

He shook his head, pacing the room. "Nah, we ain't goin' nowhere. It's mayhem out there, Niyah. You should've seen it.

There's no way we're safer outside than in here." He looked at me with a stern glare. "We stay put. At least in here, we can lock the doors."

I stood there, staring at him, my body still trembling from the fear of what I'd seen.

Cane's phone buzzed, tearing through the tension and fear in the room. Looking at the screen, he muttered, "It's Fable," and swiped to answer. He lifted the phone to his ear, and that's when I saw his arm. My heart sank at the sight of the deep bite oozing with something dark.

"Cane!" I gasped. "What happened?!"

But he didn't answer me. He was too locked in on whatever Fable was saying. I could hear the urgency in Fable's voice. He was talking so fast, and his tone sounded frantic, but I couldn't make out his words.

My gaze stayed glued to that bite as Cane ended the call. His expression was terrifying. It was blank and distant, like all the blood had drained from his face. I'd never seen him look so frightened before.

"Cane?" I asked timidly. "What's wrong?"

He didn't answer at first. He just stared at the wall like he wasn't really there. Then, suddenly, he pulled the gun from his waistband and tossed it to me. It was so unexpected that I caught it awkwardly. I stared at it in my hands, confusion clouding my mind.

"Don't let me hurt y'all." Cane's voice was so flat and dead, and his eyes were still far away.

It took me a minute to comprehend what he said, what his words meant. "What?" I whispered shakily.

He took a breath, but it wasn't steady. "I was bit. So was DeShawn." He spoke softly, almost like he didn't want to say it. "Fable just told me that uh... that DeShawn ... he ... he changed."

"*Changed?*" The word barely made it past my lips.

43

But suddenly, Cane's body jerked. Me and Neveah yelped out in worry. His phone hit the floor. His muscles seized up violently, and I gasped, backing up into the wall, frozen with fear.

"Shoot me," he managed to force out as his eyes rolled to the back of his head. Then he let out a low, rasping growl as his body convulsed again, harder this time.

This wasn't real. This *couldn't* be real. My heart pounded in my ears as I watched his face contort with a warped combination of pain and something darker. My legs felt heavy, like they were rooted to the spot, unable to move even though every part of me screamed to run.

Neveah grabbed my arm, squeezing it tight. "Momma, oh my God." Her voice was a terrified whisper, but her eyes were wide with horror. I could feel her shaking, her hand clinging to me as if I were the only thing keeping her from being swallowed up by the nightmare unfolding in front of us.

I couldn't find words. I couldn't even think straight. Cane's skin began to gray. His veins darkened beneath it like ink spreading through water. His jaw clenched so tight I thought his teeth would break. Then he snapped his head towards us. His eyes were wide, black, and lifeless. He growled, loud and terrifying, like some kind of animal.

Neveah's voice was shaking, but she didn't flinch. "Shoot him, Momma. Shoot him now!"

I couldn't move. My body was frozen in place, staring at the man I loved, the father of my child, as he became something else, something *unhuman*.

"No, Neveah. That's...that's your *father*."

"That ain't Daddy anymore!" she screamed back, panic rising in her voice. "Shoot him!"

But I couldn't. My hands trembled so bad I almost dropped the gun. My mind couldn't make sense of what was happening. Cane was convulsing. His face was contorting, and his mouth was pulled back in a snarl as more growls erupted from his throat. His eyes continued to dart back and forth between us, locking onto me and Neveah like we were prey.

I gasped, fear stealing the breath from my chest. Neveah moved faster than I could. She snatched the gun from my hands. Her fingers gripped it. I could see the overwhelming fear in her eyes, but there was determination in them too.

She handled the gun so well, just like her dad had taught her and I when we took our frequent trips to the gun range.

Then she aimed and fired, breaking my heart.

"*Nooooo!*" I screamed so loud and raw that my throat hurt.

The shot rang out, ringing through the house, louder than anything I'd ever heard. Cane's body jerked as the bullet pierced his head. His growls ceased as he collapsed to the floor.

I continued screaming a howl that ripped from deep in my soul. My knees hit the floor as I sobbed. Neveah stood there, the gun still trembling in her hands, tears streaming down her face.

I couldn't breathe. I couldn't think.

Cane was gone, and now, my world had shattered.

CHAPTER 3

NEVEAH

"Why did you shoot him?! Why did you shoot *your father*?!" Momma was freaking out. Tears were pouring from her eyes. She couldn't stop staring at Daddy's body lying on the floor, lifeless, blood pooling around his head.

I couldn't believe what I had just done. I didn't want to do it. I really didn't. But I'd watched enough *Running Dead* to know what was about to happen if I didn't stop him. My dad wasn't my dad anymore; he was something else, something dangerous. The moment the shot rang out, my whole world shattered. My mom's scream tore through me like a knife.

I would never forget the way my mother was looking at me with such betrayal behind her tears.

"How could *yooooou?*" she sobbed. "Why did you do it?!"

I swallowed hard. My hands were still quivering as I held the gun. "Because... that's how you gotta kill them in the movies. In the head or the heart."

Momma screamed at me with her whole body still trembling. "This ain't the movies, Neveah! That was your *dad*!"

"*No*, Momma!" I snapped back. "He was a *walker*."

"Walkers are *not* real!" She screamed to the top of her lungs to the point that her face began to turn red.

The room went silent, except for the sound of her sobs. She crumbled to the floor, kneeling beside Daddy's body. Her hands shook as she hovered over him like she could somehow bring him back. But he wasn't coming back.

I just stood there. I was too scared to move. My body felt paralyzed by what Dad had become. His once warm, familiar, handsome face was now ugly. I couldn't bring myself to touch him. I could hardly even look at him. My dad was gone. He had been replaced by something monstrous and unrecognizable. Every instinct in me wanted to reach out, to hold him one last time, but fear kept me in place. Instead, I wrapped my arms tightly around myself.

I felt cold inside, like I had been snatched from reality. It didn't even feel like it was me who pulled the trigger. It felt like I was watching someone else do it. But I *had* to do it. I couldn't let him bite us and turn us too.

Momma didn't want to believe what was happening, but what I had seen Daddy turn into wasn't human. She was wrong, this was *just like* the movies.

"Call 9-1-1," Momma's voice cracked. She didn't even look at me. She just stared at Daddy. "Call 9-1-1, Neveah!"

I stood there for a second, staring at her, feeling this weird numbness creep over me. Then I shook my head. "It's no use, Momma. No one's coming."

She jumped to her feet and darted across the living room, stepping over Daddy's body. She leapt towards the couch and scrambled for her phone. "What are you talking about? We have to call someone!"

She dialed with trembling fingers. But a moment later, she pulled the phone from her ear. Her eyes were wide in disbelief.

"It's... busy."

"I told you," I said, stepping closer to her. "Do you hear any sirens outside? Did you see any cops outside? Nobody is coming to help us, Momma."

She blinked long and slow, like the world just crashed down on her. She opened her mouth to argue, but nothing came out.

I looked around the room at the blood and my dad's body. I listened to the distant sounds of chaos on the other side of the windows. I knew we couldn't just stay in the house scared.

"We gotta go, Momma. We need to hit the grocery store before everyone else figures out what's happening."

Her eyes darted towards me. "What are you talking about? We can't just leave!"

"Yes, we can. And we have to." I squared my shoulders, trying to sound more confident than I felt. "I watch *Running Dead*, remember? This is just like that. The first thing people do is hit the stores and grab everything they can. We need to stock up, *now*, before the whole city figures out what's going on. Even if you don't believe that there are walkers out there, that its just drugged out people, they are everywhere, so we can't go outside anytime soon."

She stared at me like I had lost my mind, but I could see in her eyes she knew I was right. She just didn't want me to be.

"Momma, if we're stuck in here for days or even weeks, we have to be prepared," I told her. "Ain't no Uber Eats or Door-Dash coming if there's walkers outside."

Momma just stared at me for a second, her eyes glassy, like she couldn't even process what I was saying.

Finally, she sighed and nodded, but her voice was still shaky. "Alright... alright. But you're not coming with me, Neveah. You're going to hide in the basement."

I watched her grab her keys from her purse on the dining room table and slip her shoes on. The tears kept falling quietly down her face, and every time she glanced at Daddy's body, her breath caught like she was choking on her grief. I felt a lump rise in my throat, guilt washing over me for what I'd done, but I had to push it aside. We didn't have time to grieve.

As she turned toward the door, I couldn't stay still. "I'm going with you."

Her head whipped around so fast. "Neveah, I said no!"

"You need two sets of hands, Momma! We need to get as much as we can. I'm coming with you."

She looked down at the gun still in my hand and inhaled sharply.

"We need this," I insisted.

Her lips tightened, and for a moment, I thought she was going to snap at me again. But instead, she looked at me with those tired, tear-filled eyes and didn't say anything.

Instead, she moved to the front door and peeked out of the peephole with her fingers gripping the knob. "I don't see anyone," she whispered. She turned back to me and grabbed my hand, squeezing it harder than usual. "Stay close to me, Neveah. Don't let go."

I nodded as my own fear bubbled up while we crept out of the house. We paused at the screen door, and both of us scanned the block. The street wasn't quiet. We could hear screams from the corner, some people shouting, others honking their car horns like they were trapped in traffic. A porch that was a few houses down the way was full of chaos, people running around, yelling and fighting off walkers.

"Now!" Momma whispered, pulling me. We bolted down the porch, our feet hitting the pavement as we sprinted toward the car, hands still locked together. I could hardly catch my breath. Every sound felt like it was getting louder, closer, and every shadow made my skin crawl. When we finally reached the car, we threw open the doors and hopped in, slamming them shut.

We sat there for a second, breathing hard, looking at each other, both of us relieved but still terrified. It felt like a small victory, making it to the car, but deep down, I knew we weren't even close to the end of this nightmare.

This was just the beginning.

FABLE

We were all pacing, freaking out, trying to make sense of what the hell was happening. Navon sat on the couch, rocking back and forth, his hands in his lap like he couldn't get a grip. Meesha was near the kitchen, talking too fast, and Kecia was right next to her, crying into her hands. Paris just kept shaking her head, repeating, "This *can't* be real. This *can't* be real."

But it was. We were in the middle of a real-life nightmare, something none of us ever thought we'd ever see. This shit was supposed to be on TV, not on the fucking South Side of Chicago.

Salem stood by the window, looking out of it silently.

"Man, this some fucked-up shit," August said, pacing back and forth. "Is this really happening?"

Navon spoke up, shaking his head. "Nah, this can't be real. People don't just turn into walkers. This gotta be that drug. We ain't in no damn apocalypse."

Meesha's voice shook with fear. "You saw what we saw, Navon! They ain't on no drug. People don't run like that... or *bite* people!"

"It's the drug. People on acid trip like that all the time," Navon tried to convince her.

Paris looked like she was on the verge of losing it. Her hands were shaking as she stood in the middle of the room.

"We gotta figure something out," Salem said quietly, finally speaking. "We can't stay here forever."

I ran my hands over my face, trying to think. But I felt DeShawn's blood on my face.

"Fable, you good?" Paris asked, breaking through my daze.

I blinked, trying to focus. "I still got DeShawn's blood all over me." My voice sounded distant, like I wasn't fully present. Without another word, I headed to my room, needing to wash it off. I couldn't think straight, not with that on me.

I made it to my master bathroom and stripped off my clothes after closing the door behind myself.

As I ran the hot water, all I could see was DeShawn, my boy, changing right in front of us. That wasn't DeShawn. That wasn't the nigga I grew up with. Whatever he became in those last moments was something else, something I couldn't explain but I knew in my gut wasn't him. The vision of him growling, his body convulsing, as he turned into something else was haunting me.

I stepped into the shower and the hot water hit my skin, but it didn't bring the clarity I needed. I watched the blood swirl down the drain, still not believing any of this was real.

Nothing made sense.

I leaned against the tile with my hand braced against the wall. My mind kept running back to what I'd seen outside, the way DeShawn changed right in front of us, like something straight outta *Running Dead*. But this wasn't TV. This was real life. I didn't know what to do or how to process it.

The voices from the living room cut through my thoughts.

"We can't just stay here and wait to die," August was saying. "We need to find a way out."

Meesha sounded scared as hell. "And go where? Every where's probably like this."

Paris chimed in, "We can't just sit here, but we can't go out there either. It's suicide."

I rinsed the last of the soap off and shut the water off. I stepped out, feeling the cool air begin to dry my skin.

I grabbed a towel off the hook and started drying off when I heard the doorknob turn. The door creaked open slowly, and Kecia peeked in. I scoffed, shaking my head with a dry chuckle. She'd been feeling me for the last two years. She and Meesha met then, when they started working together. When Meesha started bringing her around the crew, she was always throwing the pussy at me, and I finally gave in a few months ago. It wasn't anything serious—at least not to me—but the girl was getting clingy as hell.

"Do you think this is really happening? An apocalypse?" she asked. She sat on the counter. Her long, thick brown legs were wide open as her eyes scanned my body.

I shook my head slowly as I continued to towel dry. "I don't know what to believe. It sounds crazy, but I know what I saw."

She blew a heavy breath. "This is insane."

"It is."

"I can't take this."

Then she looked up at me, biting her lip as she reached for my dick. She started to slowly massage it from the base to its tip.

I deeply chuckled. "Really, Kecia?"

"You need to relax." Her voice was too casual for everything going on outside. "*We* need to relax. Let's just forget about all this... what we've seen, what's happening. I need to forget for a few minutes."

I stared at her for a second, knowing where she was going with this. Part of me wanted to brush her off, tell her now wasn't the time, but honestly, I needed the distraction, too. This whole thing was too much, and I was tired of thinking about it, tired of the fear gripping me. So, I let out a breath and gave in. I closed the space between us, stepping between her legs. She started to press gentle kisses to my jaw and neck. I pulled her body flush against mine as her soft lips explored my neck. My dick started to rock up as her tongue soothed my stress. Her warm soft fingers were still wrapped around my dick, stroking it. I lowly moaned and shifted my hips, encouraging her to do more.

"Tell me what you want me to do," she whispered, teasingly running her fingers around the head of my length.

"I want you to suck this dick."

She grinned into my neck. "Good."

I stepped back as she hopped down off the counter and dropped down to her knees. She licked my balls, gently sucking them into her mouth one by one. I growled low in my throat, and she grinned, looking up at me, making eye contact before she quickly took the head of my dick into her mouth and sucked. I moaned, grabbing a handful of her hair. I moved it out of her face so I could watch as she took my length as deep as she could into her throat. I could see the outline of my dick as it slid down to the back of it.

I pressed down on her head, forcing my dick past her gag reflex into her warm throat.

"Fuck yeah," I encouraged her.

I released her head and let her come up for air. While she caught her breath, she swirled her tongue around the tip, meeting my eyes.

Without warning she took my dick back into her warm mouth, moving past her gag reflex on her own this time. She bobbed her head up and down with my hand in her hair. Her eyes watered as she took me deeper with every stroke.

"Stand up," I told her as I stepped back.

My dick fell from her mouth. She stood eagerly with a small, pleased grin. She pulled down her yoga pants and her big, beautiful brown ass fell out. She bent over and suddenly it was in the shape of a heart.

I rammed into her pussy, causing her to gasp at the way I filled her up with one thrust. She cried out, but she arched her back. I started to slide in and out with slow, long thrusts, pulling nearly all the way out and slowly pushing back in. They were teasing, gentle, sensual, full strokes.

She moaned, clenching her pussy around my dick.

I began thrusting harder, hitting spots inside of her that most niggas couldn't reach. Both of my hands gripped her hips, pulling her back onto my dick with each thrust.

"*Yeees*, Fable. Fuck me," Kecia encouraged me.

I lifted her shirt so that I could watch her titties bounce in the mirror. She cried out in pain *and* pleasure.

Suddenly, I could hear Meesha screeching out in disgust from inside my room. "Are y'all fucking?! How could you freaky ass niggas fuck at a time like this?!"

CHAPTER 4

PARIS

"They are so fucking nasty," Meesha muttered as she stormed out of Fable's room.

"They wild," August added with a small chuckle.

I didn't find anything funny, however. I couldn't believe it —*none of it*. Though I had seen DeShawn turn right in front of my eyes, it still felt unreal. It felt like I was going to throw up every time the vision came to mind. And then, on our drive here, we saw more people being ripped apart. Some were changing right in front of our eyes. It was like some sick, twisted nightmare, except I knew I wasn't asleep.

My breath started hitching, coming out in these short, panicked bursts. I clutched my chest, feeling my heart race faster than it ever had before. It felt like it was slamming into my ribs, each thud more frantic than the last. I couldn't catch my breath. Everything got blurry, my vision narrowing like a tunnel. My skin went clammy, like a cold sweat just broke out all over me. My head started spinning, and I swore I was about to pass out.

"Paris! Paris, look at me!" I heard Meesha's voice, but it felt distant, like I was hearing it underwater. I couldn't focus; all I could think about was that I was going to die violently. My chest ached, my head pounded, and my entire body shook uncontrollably. I tried to scream, but no sound came out, just a strangled gasp.

"You're having a panic attack. You're going to be okay," Meesha gently comforted me as she grabbed my hands and squeezed them. But I could barely feel her touch. My mind was lost in a whirlwind of terror, a void where all I could think about was those things outside, the way they moved, the way they attacked, the way DeShawn ate his own homeboy.

"Get it together, Paris!" Salem's voice boomed over Meesha's, cutting through my panic. His tone was harsh, not comforting in the least. He grabbed my shoulders, shaking me roughly. "Man up. You can't be falling apart like this!" His grip was hard, and his eyes were cold. There wasn't an ounce of softness there, only impatience.

Tears spilled over my cheeks. I felt so small and so damn scared. "I... I can't," I gasped.

But there was no sympathy in his eyes. Just frustration, maybe even anger. He looked at me like I was weak, like I was a liability. "You *have* to," he said through clenched teeth. "You wanna end up like DeShawn and Legion? Like those people out there?"

"No," I cried.

"Then get your shit together."

"I can't get it together, Salem! Get the fuck away from me!" I screamed. Tears blurred my vision as I shoved him back, but he didn't move an inch, just stared down at me with those cold, disappointed eyes. "Just get away from me!" I yelled again, my voice shaking with desperation.

I felt like I was drowning in fear, gasping for air that just wouldn't come. And Salem's hard stare, his impatience, made it worse. It was like he was looking at me like I was the weakest link.

Before I could break down even more, August stepped in, moving Salem back. "Back off, man. She's going through it," August told him with a quiet authority that held the compassion I needed.

August wrapped his arms around me, pulling me close to his chest. His embrace was warm, solid, and I collapsed into him, sobbing uncontrollably. "It's okay, Paris," he whispered softly. "I got you. Just breathe."

I looked over August's shoulder at Salem. His eyes were colder than the Chicago wind in winter. But beneath it, there was disappointment. He shook his head, muttering something under his breath before storming off.

I could barely hear anything over my sobs. I felt August's hand gently rubbing my back. His voice was a quiet murmur in my ear. "You're not alone, Paris," he whispered. "I promise. You're going to be okay. I got you."

NIYAH

It was pure chaos outside as we drove to the store. The streets were either completely empty, with nothing but those walkers wandering around, or littered with pandemonium of shrills of terror as people were being attacked. Cars were swerving through the streets, reckless, some trying to dodge the undead, others crashing into anything in their way. And every few blocks, we could see people getting practically eaten alive.

I gripped the steering wheel tight, trying to block out the sounds and the screams that seemed to come from everywhere. Neveah sat next to me, silent and terrified.

When we pulled up to the grocery store, I was relieved to see it wasn't too crowded. A few people were already running out, arms full or carts packed with whatever they could grab. Clearly, we weren't the only ones who had the same idea.

"We gotta move fast," I said to Neveah as we jumped out of the car.

"Okay," she breathed.

"Give me the gun."

She handed it to me, and I slipped it into my waistband.

We both climbed out and met at the hood. Then, holding hands, we rushed inside. The moment we stepped through the automatic doors, my insides twisted. Blood was everywhere. It was splattered on the floor and streaked across the aisles.

Neveah's voice was low, filled with fear. "Momma..."

I didn't want to stop and think about what had happened, so I just squeezed her hand in order to get her to focus. "Come on," I said urgently. "We don't have much time. We have to hurry."

Neveah and I both grabbed carts and started to push them through the aisles as fast as we could. People were running wild, grabbing everything they could get their hands on, like the world was ending.

It felt like it was.

"Neveah, get non-perishables!" I called out. "Get canned goods, meds, and feminine products."

"And tissue and water!" she rushed.

We split up, rushing through the aisles. I grabbed cans of beans, corn, and soup, tossing them into the cart. I got boxes of pasta, rice, and anything else I could find that wouldn't go bad. As I turned the corner, I saw people fighting over the last packs of toilet paper and bottled water. The chaos was too familiar, like when they started talking about a possible pandemic when Covid hit. Only this was worse. *Way* worse.

Neveah was across the store, throwing tampons, pads, and pain relievers into her cart. I grabbed bandages, cold meds, and anything that might come in handy if things got worse. In the frozen food section, I snatched up bags of frozen veggies, some meat—whatever was left—and tossed them into the cart.

The sound of growls came from the next aisle, followed by screams.

"Neveah!" I shouted. "Neveah!"

My stomach dropped.

But suddenly she came racing around the corner with her cart. I breathed a sigh of relief right before a gunshot exploded too close.

"Neveah, hurry!" I yelled, my voice shaking now.

"A walker came into the store," she blurted nervously. "But this guy shot him."

We didn't wait to see what else was coming. With both carts filled to the top, we rushed toward the exit, dodging people still flooding into the store, their faces filled with the same panic I felt in my chest. We ran past them, pushing through the chaos, praying we'd make it home.

☙❦❧

We barely made it back from the grocery store. Every street was chaos—abandoned cars blocking the way, people driving like they had lost their damn minds, running red lights and stop signs. I kept glancing over at Neveah, trying to reassure her with my eyes, but I was scared too. I'd see them—those things—wandering aimlessly or sprinting after their next victim, and it felt like the city was turning into hell right in front of me.

Once we finally pulled up to the house, I parked in the driveway, and we worked fast, dragging the bags of food inside. We'd dumped everything into large garbage bags at the store, knowing we'd need to move quickly. We lugged the bags in, one by one, without talking, without looking at each other, too focused on not drawing attention from those things roaming the streets. As soon as we were inside, I dropped the last bag and immediately went to secure the front door with the security bar.

We couldn't keep Cane's body in the house. So, we both wrapped him in a sheet, trying not to look at his face. We dragged him to the back door, my heart breaking with every inch. Both of us sobbed along the way because it felt so final then.

Cane was dead.

We wanted to bury him, to at least say a real goodbye, but the fear of staying outside too long was too strong. So, we left him there on the back porch. I closed the door, leaning against it for a second, trying to breathe, trying to accept that this was real. But I couldn't. This *couldn't* be it. I kept telling myself this nightmare would end, that we'd get to bury him properly. I wasn't ready to accept that this was an apocalypse, that walkers were actually real.

As I started pulling cans of food from the bags, my ring tone started to blare, startling both me and Neveah. I grabbed it from the counter, feeling my heart racing. The screen lit up with Fable's name.

I instantly regretted answering, as I thought of Cane's body lying on the back porch. "Fable?"

"Niyah," he said softly. He sounded different—like he was trying to act like everything was okay when it was everything but. "I've been calling Cane, but he won't pick up. I know he got bit... What's going on? Is he...?" His words trailed off, and the silence was so damn loud.

"He's gone, Fable. Cane's gone." I choked out the words, feeling like they cut my throat on the way out.

There was a long pause on the other end, a heavy sigh, and then, "Did he...? Did he turn into one of those things?"

My eyes squeezed together tightly as I recalled the sight. "Yeah."

Fable groaned. "*Fuck.*"

"Neveah shot him before he could do anything to us."

More silence took over. Neither of us could find the words— there simply weren't any to explain the unexplainable. I looked over at Neveah. She was still putting up the food, but tears were silently running down her cheeks.

"I'm so sorry, Niyah," Fable finally said. "I can't even imagine what you're feeling right now. I'm *so* sorry."

I swiped at my tears, trying to hold it together in front of Neveah, who kept looking back at me with worried eyes.

Fable's tone shifted, turning more urgent but still tender. "Listen, you and Neveah can't be there alone. I'll come and get you. You're not about to deal with this by yourself."

I shook my head, even though he couldn't see it. "Fable, it's too far. We barely made it back from the store. The streets are insane. Most of them are blocked off, and those things are everywhere. It's not safe for you to drive here."

"I don't care," he gently pressed. "You need to be here with me."

Even in this horrific madness, when he said that, I felt something. But he quickly added, "And the crew. We're all here. We can stay safe together until whatever this is dies down."

"But how are you going to get here?"

"I'll find a way. If I have to walk, I will. I promise, Niyah. I'm not about to leave you and Neveah alone in this."

His words wrapped around me like a warm blanket on a freezing night. "Fable, you really don't have to—"

"I want to," he cut me off softly. "You and Neveah need to be safe, and I want to make sure you are. I'll be there, okay? Just hold on."

The warmth in his words made the weight on my chest feel just a bit lighter. "Thank you, Fable," I whispered, feeling a sense of comfort I hadn't felt since this nightmare started.

"Just hang in there. I'm coming, I swear," he promised again.

"Be careful."

"I will. You two stay inside, lock up everything, and don't answer the door unless you hear me," he instructed.

"Okay," I whispered, feeling some semblance of hope creep in.

"Talk soon, Niyah," Fable reassured me before hanging up.

The call ended, but his words lingered. For the first time that day, a tiny drop of hope warmed me, no matter how impossible the situation seemed.

A FEW DAYS LATER

TARIQ

The last few days had been complete mayhem. None of this shit made sense, even in a place like Chicago, where violence was part of the landscape. People were losing their minds, bodies were dropping everywhere, and those "things" that used to be human were growing in numbers. The news channels kept spinning the same story over and over, saying that the attacks were the result of some new drug making people "act aggressively." But that was bullshit.

Being a Navy man, I'd seen enough to know when things were more than just street-level madness. Though I was medically discharged when I got my Lupus diagnosis, I had an advantage that most people didn't. I was still in contact with Onyx, my best friend, who was actively serving in the Navy. He'd been feeding me information that wasn't making it to the public. The government was scrambling to understand this thing. The official line was that it could be some kind of biological attack, maybe by Russia, hinting at a potential biowarfare strike. The government was scrambling to the point that there was confusion from the top brass down to the foot soldiers. The powers that be weren't even close at having a handle on the situation.

There was no way to test for the infected. They couldn't even tell how it spread. All they knew was that once people turned, it was a fast and violent transformation. So, in order to keep the outbreak maintained, borders were thrown up around the affected areas of Chicago. Onyx said they were being manned by troops who weren't just enforcing a perimeter—they had shoot-to-kill orders. The military was working diligently to let no one in or out of the affected zone. If a person even looked suspicious, they were getting put down. There had even been loud explosions when the military was throwing grenades into large mobs of the undead that approached the border.

Everywhere inside the borders felt like a war zone. We were isolated, cut off from the rest of the city and even the country. I assumed that it was a matter of time before they shut down all communication channels: Wi-Fi, phone lines, television broadcasts—anything that could let word slip out of the zone. If that happened, we'd be completely blind, stuck inside this hell.

I sat on my back porch, gripping my shotgun while smoking a blunt. My eyes locked on the alley, watching the undead stumble aimlessly, their rotten faces lit by the dim light of the moon. I wasn't scared to sit out there. Each time one wandered into the yard, I blasted it, feeling a warped satisfaction as the thing's head exploded.

A few desperate souls had tried to get into my house, mainly the homeless looking for a place to hide. But in this mess, trusting anyone was as dangerous as those damn things outside. I wasn't taking chances. The first few days of this madness, you'd still see people coming out of their homes, maybe trying to convince themselves this wasn't real. That illusion didn't last long. Now it was just the desperate ones—the homeless, the starving—who roamed the streets alongside the undead.

My phone suddenly rang, making me jump. I snatched it from my pocket and looked at the screen.

It was Onyx.

I bolted inside, slamming the back door behind me. Every time Onyx called, I prayed that he had news of when this nightmare would end.

I secured the back door, pushing the refrigerator and dining room table in front of it.

Then I answered the phone. "What's up, Onyx?"

"Tariq, listen," Onyx sounded...*happy*, so I froze, standing in the kitchen with my cell to my ear. "I've figured it out, man. I found a way to get you out of there."

I blinked slowly, waiting to wake up.

"Tariq?" Onyx called out. "Did you hear me? I can get you outta there, man."

"No bullshit? How?"

"I've got a guy, Sam, who's stationed at the border on 35th and King Drive, and he's down to help us. He's going to let you through."

I leaned against the wall, adrenaline rushing through me. "Yo', you serious?"

"*Yes*. I figured it out. You gotta be there early as hell. I mean after midnight but before sunrise. Sam works the night shift and that's the only time he's alone. There's a tunnel near Pier 31, behind the border. But it's hidden and was closed off, but I was able to put a small opening in it. If you can make it to Sam without getting spotted, he'll let you through to the tunnel. You gotta reach the docks by 6 a.m., that's when I'm making the run back to Michigan."

"Man, this sounds risky as hell," I muttered, pacing my small kitchen. "I'm not trying to get shot up."

"We tested it," he told me excitedly. "Me and Sam got his mother, wife, and kids out first, just to be sure. It works, Tariq.

We only have a short window, though. I'm only making three more runs before they change my assignment. Then I won't be bringing supplies by boat anymore. It's gotta be over the next three weeks on a Thursday at exactly 6 a.m. I'll be on Dock B. If you don't make it to me, it's a wrap, because no one has a clue when this shit will be over."

I hesitated, running a hand over my face. "What if I can't make it there by then?"

"You *have* to, bro," Onyx pressed. "The military's on edge, man. They shoot first and ask questions never. But at that hour, most of 'em are asleep or too tired to pay attention. You just gotta move fast and keep your head low."

It was a crazy plan, but it was something. I hadn't felt hope in a while, and this was the small chance I needed. "Alright, Onyx. I'm in."

"Bet. But I need you to..." Onyx's words were suddenly cut off.

"Shit!" I barked as I pulled the phone from my ear. The call had cut off.

I called him back, but I was met with a fast busy signal. Then I heard, "Your call can not be completed as dialed."

"Fuck!" I roared, hanging up.

I dialed him again and was met with the same damn irritating signal. "Your call can not be completed as dialed."

"No, no, no!" I yelled, frantically pressing redial. But it was useless.

The phones were down.

❧

It had been two long, brutal days to get here, and every second felt like hell. Ten miles on foot wasn't supposed to take this long, but between dodging the undead and avoiding scavengers, it had.

I'd spent the first night in an abandoned gas station, curled up with my shotgun like it was a fucking teddy bear. By the second day, I didn't even bother with sleep.

When I finally reached 35th and King Drive, I hid behind a dumpster, keeping low as I scanned the area. I spotted Sam right where Onyx said he'd be. He was a tall, lanky white dude, pacing back and forth with a cigarette between his lips. It was 5:45 a.m. The sky was still dark, a gray sliver of dawn barely touching the horizon.

I took a deep breath, knowing this was it. Either I was getting out, or I was getting shot.

"Yo!" I called out, low but urgently. Then I stepped out from behind the tree, hands raised slightly. "Onyx sent me. I'm Tariq."

Sam's eyes narrowed, and his hand shifted toward his rifle. He looked me up and down with a cold calculating glare. "You been bit?"

"No, man, I swear I haven't," I insisted. "I wouldn't be here if I was."

His eyes locked on me for a few seconds as he studied me. "Show me."

I hesitated, glancing around as if someone could see us. But there was no time for pride. I quickly stripped down, feeling the cool morning air hit my dirty, sweaty skin. It was humiliating, but I wasn't about to ruin my chance over embarrassment. I turned slowly, arms out, proving there were no bites.

Sam's gaze lingered for a second, then he jerked his chin. "Alright. Put your clothes back on."

I dressed quickly, feeling the burn of shame in my cheeks. "So, we good?"

"Yeah, we're good. Go ahead," he muttered, still eyeing me cautiously.

He opened the gate, and just like that, I was on the other side.

"Be careful. Soldiers are securing the fuck out of the premises. If you get caught, you're dead."

I looked back in response to his emotionless warning, but he had already turned his back to me and went back to guarding the border.

As I left the unsafe zone, my eyes stung with tears. I hadn't felt this much hope in days. I never imagined that I could ever get out of this nightmare.

I made my way toward the tunnel Onyx had told me about. It was dark, with the faint sounds of radios crackling in the distance and the occasional scuff of footsteps. Every time I heard a sound, I ducked low, keeping still and barely breathing.

When I finally reached the small opening to the tunnel, I squeezed through, feeling relief and adrenaline flood through me. I sprinted down the narrow passage. The tunnel seemed endless, but then I saw light at the end. I emerged, panting, into the open air.

And there was the pier, lined with abandoned boats. Usually, this spot would be alive with boaters, the smell of lake water, and the low hum of motors getting ready to go out. But now, it was just Onyx, standing tall on Dock B.

I moved quickly, sticking to the shadows as I sprinted toward him. Onyx turned when he heard my footsteps, and we locked eyes. He broke into a run, and we met halfway down the dock, grabbing each other in an excited hug.

"Damn, bro." Onyx let out a long sigh of relief. "I was hoping you made it."

"Man, I thought I was done for a few times," I admitted, trying to catch my breath. "But I'm here. Let's get the hell out of here."

But then I noticed the hesitation in Onyx's eyes. His smile faded, replaced with a reluctant glare that he couldn't bring to my eyes.

I frowned, confused. "What's wrong? What're we waiting for?"

Onyx sighed deeply, looking out onto the water. "What I was trying to tell you before the phones went dead was... I needed you to do something before you came here."

I felt my stomach drop. "What do you mean?"

"I need you to go get Fable. Please, bro," he pleaded. "He's my brother, Tariq. I can't leave without him."

I blinked, trying to wrap my mind around what he was asking. I vaguely remembered Fable from back in the day, when Onyx and I were in high school. Fable was the older one, always in trouble, always in the streets. Meanwhile, Onyx stayed on the right path. He was the good son who joined the Navy. They shared a father but had different mothers.

I shook my head as disbelief took over me. "You want me to *go back* in there and get Fable? Are you serious, Onyx?"

Onyx's expression was unapologetically stern. "I'm very serious. I know it's a lot to ask, but I need you to do this. I can't go myself. I can't go AWOL. I would never be able to get him to safety then. You were the only one I could tell before the phones shut off. He has no idea that I can even get him out. And listen, there is only room for four people on this boat, including me and you. The last time I talked to him, he was quarantined in the house with his crew. But I don't give a fuck who else he is with, keep this shit on the low. I can't have all of them coming here and bringing attention to what I'm doing. I know its going to be hard for him to leave them behind, but I'm not worried about them and I, unfortunately, can't help them all. I'm just worried about you and my brother."

I could see the desperation in his eyes, the kind that only a brother could have.

Though I'd chosen the straight path, I was still a hood nigga. I'd seen things most people couldn't stomach. I'd fought plenty of monsters, real ones, and survived to talk about it. The undead didn't scare me; they were mindless and predictable in their hunger. It was the people with sheer desperation to survive that chilled me. I'd seen what that kind of fear could make a person do, how it stripped away humanity until all that was left was raw, ruthless survival. But I'd lived amongst such ruthlessness all my life. I'd made it through the hood, made it through the Navy, and if I had to make it back through this hellhole to get Fable, I'd do it. This was Onyx, my best friend, the man who risked everything to get me this far. So, I owed him that.

I took a deep breath, nodding slowly. "Alright... What's his address?"

A FEW DAYS LATER

CHAPTER 5

NEVEAH

Sitting by the window upstairs, I stared out through this little hole I made in the wood. It was just enough to see what was happening outside. The world was dead, nothing moving except for those walkers, sprinting up and down the alley like they were hunting for something. The sun was going down, so I could see them. The way they moved made the hairs on the back of my neck stand straight up—arms hanging limp, legs jerking as they ran like they didn't even feel pain. I could hear them too, this low growling mixed with their weird, wet breathing. It sent a cold chill down my spine every time. Sometimes, they'd stop and sniff the air, like dogs, then take off again.

But other than them, the world outside was deserted. No people. No sound. Not even a dog or bird. I hadn't seen anything alive out there for days, just those monsters. And sitting here, watching them, all I could think about was everything I missed. Everything that felt like a whole other life ago.

I actually missed school, even though I used to complain about going all the time. I missed my friends, us sitting at lunch and gossiping about who was dating who, what outfits we were gonna wear to the next party, and who was talking shit online. I missed going to the mall with my girls, taking selfies, and trying on clothes we couldn't afford. I missed sneaking texts to Marcel during class and feeling that little excitement every time he replied. He was a Senior, and I'd had a crush on him since Freshman year. I missed sneaking out to meet him at the park, texting him under the covers when I was supposed to be asleep, daydreaming about what it would be like if I was actually his girlfriend. I was supposed to ask him if he would finally be my boyfriend at homecoming, but now, I didn't know if I would ever see him again.

I missed my daddy. For a few days, I would peer out of the window, looking onto the back porch at him, talking to him. But, by now, there was nothing left of him. What the walkers hadn't eaten, animals had.

Now, my old life felt like a lifetime ago. My life was nothing but boarded-up windows, silence, and the sound of the undead outside, hunting whatever was left. I wondered was Marcel even still alive.

Me and Momma had been stuck in the house, listening to the chaos outside. But it still didn't feel real.

For days after the apocalypse began, we waited for help to come.

It never did.

The government zoned off the affected areas—basically the South Side of Chicago—like we were some kind of experiment. They said it was to stop the walkers from spreading to the rest of the state, but they really just trapped all of us in, like we were disposable.

A few days ago, they canceled all Wi-Fi and phone services. We couldn't watch TV, not even the basic channels. We guessed they didn't want us to call anyone outside the zone, telling them what was really going on. The government was doing everything to keep this quiet, like they didn't want the rest of the world to find out what was really happening here.

Before the Wi-Fi and phone service got cut, people in the affected areas were calling friends and loved ones on the outside, sending pictures and videos of what was happening. But the government and people on the outside of the affected area was explaining it away. No one wanted to believe that this could be real. Every time a video surfaced online, someone would downplay the situation, no matter how many of us confirmed it was real. Then the video would disappear. That's when we knew that whatever was happening was bigger than just us.

The utilities were still on, but we knew it was only a matter of time before they went off too. Nobody was even thinking about paying bills, and the utility companies didn't care that we were trapped in the middle of an apocalypse. We were reluctantly waiting for everything to get cut off. And when they did, we knew everything was going to get even uglier.

We had to board the windows and doors after that first day because a lot of people were desperate to get into anyone's house they could when they were running from those things. Or the walkers would pile up on the doors and windows, that threatened to give in to their weight. Then, we had to worry about scavengers, who were desperate for food and weapons. We couldn't let anyone in. We couldn't trust anybody now. Everyone was out for themselves, and even though I felt bad for the people banging on the door who truly just needed help, we couldn't risk letting someone in who could turn on us.

The scariest part were the sounds outside that never stopped. It was a constant reminder of how close we were to death or turning into one of those things. We constantly could hear the screams, the gunshots, the growling... It was all there, just beyond the walls. Every day, it got worse. And every day, we sat in the house, wondering how much longer we would last.

Though we didn't want Fable and the rest of the crew to get caught by those things, we had been hoping that they made it to us. It was safety in numbers. Plus, we would have felt safer with Fable, Navon, August, and Salem. But every time they tried to come get us, they got turned around by fatigue after fighting so many of the undead while making the two mile walk to come get us. One time, they turned back because it was a mob of ten of those things facing them. Then the phone services when out, so me and Mama assumed they stopped trying.

Suddenly, I heard Momma start to stir behind me. She was thrashing around in her sleep again, mumbling, her face bawled up like she was stuck in a bad dream. We'd been sleeping in the same room ever since this started, out of fear more than anything. The thought of being alone, even for a night, scared both of us.

Her movements were wild, more frantic than usual.

"Momma..." I whispered as I moved towards her.

I tried to shake her gently, but she didn't wake up. Instead, she started to scream.

"Momma!" I whispered louder, panic rising inside me. We couldn't afford to make noise. Sound attracted the walkers, and there were always a few of them roaming nearby. I shook her harder, desperate to wake her up. "Momma, please, wake up!"

Her eyes finally flew open, and she gasped like she'd just surfaced from underwater. She looked around, disoriented, and I could see the fear still lingering in her eyes.

"You were having a nightmare," I whispered as I rubbed her gently, trying to calm her down.

She blinked a few times, taking a deep breath. "I'm sorry, baby," she said, her voice shaking as she sat up. "I'm sorry."

Before I could say anything else, a loud crash came from

downstairs, making both of us jump out of our skin. It was way too loud to ignore. My heart dropped, fear grabbing me instantly.

Momma jumped out of bed, grabbing the gun from the nightstand in one quick motion. She turned to me with wide eyes as her chest rose and fell rapidly. "Stay up here," she whispered through clenched jaws. "Do *not* come downstairs. You hear me?"

But there was no way I was about to stay up here, hiding, while she went downstairs alone. "I'm coming with you.".

"Neveah, I said no. *Stay here*," she snapped through gritted teeth.

But I shook my head and followed her anyway as she crept toward the stairs, as quiet as she could. I knew she didn't want me down there with her, but I wasn't about to let her face whatever was waiting downstairs alone.

TARIQ

We kicked in the window like it was nothing. Boards snapped as Diesel and Trey burst through, guns ready.

After days of walking, hiding, and fighting, I was beyond exhausted. My feet dragged, my throat burned from thirst, and every muscle felt like it had been wrung out. Yesterday, I stumbled upon a camp set up in an abandoned Family Dollar. There were at least twenty people inside, huddled together on makeshift beds of cardboard and blankets.

Diesel and his gang had taken over the Family Dollar after their trap house got overrun by the undead. Since then, he'd been letting additional stragglers into his fortress, but only to put them under his control.

I just needed food and a day or two of rest before I continued to Fable's place. But as soon as Diesel realized I was military, his eyes lit up.

"If you want food and shelter, you gotta earn your keep," he'd told me.

He wanted me to come with him on a few runs for food and supplies. All night, he and his crew laughed as they told stories of robbing whoever Diesel chose. Diesel didn't care who he extorted or how he got what he needed. He got his name for a reason. He was ruthless and always needed more. Every few nights, he hit up survivors, making sure his fortress and crew had more than enough food, guns, meds—whatever he could find.

I was thankful for the good night's sleep and dinner. But I'd woken up tired. I knew I needed more rest if I was going to make it to Fable in time. So, I headed out with Diesel and Trey a little while ago to do what Diesel called "hunting".

I stepped through the busted window after Diesel, scanning the living room. It was a decent spot, boarded up tight, but not tight enough for us. Diesel liked to pick places where people had worked hard to stay alive. He figured, the harder they worked, the more they had.

Diesel glanced back at me with a cruel smirk on his face. "Tariq, check upstairs. See if we got company."

He nodded toward the staircase while he and Trey started rummaging through the kitchen like they owned the place.

I was clutching my gun as I found the stairs. The house was *too* quiet. I knew whoever was here had to be scared shitless, hiding out and praying we'd leave. But that wasn't how Diesel worked.

When I got to the stairs, I could hear soft whispers. It was a woman's voice, probably pleading with whoever she was with to stay quiet. I strained, listening for a second, but then Diesel's voice roared from behind me.

"Come out!" Diesel's bark was mocking and loud, like he didn't give a damn about the undead lurking outside. "You got two choices! Come out and hand over whatever you got, or I'll start making noise. And trust me, it won't take long before them walkers come running. Either way, you gonna lose."

I could hear Trey laughing as he opened cabinets, throwing shit around, looking for supplies. Diesel wasn't bullshitting. He got off on wreaking havoc. He didn't care about survival. He cared about control, and he liked breaking people down.

I stood at the stairs, my finger twitching on the trigger. I didn't want to do this. But if I didn't, Diesel would turn on me just as fast as he did anyone else.

It took a few seconds before two women crept down the stairs, their footsteps so quiet I almost didn't hear them at first. The older one looked like she had just woken up. Her hair was a little messy, and her eyes were still clouded with sleep, but none of that could hide her beauty. Even in the middle of all this madness, her curves were undeniable, and her presence was captivating.

Diesel grinned wide when he saw them, and his eyes lit up like he'd just hit the lottery. "Well, well, well. Look what we got here, fellas," he taunted them with warped satisfaction. "Two pretty ladies."

I stayed quiet as my eyes locked on them while they descended the stairs. When they finally reached the bottom of the stairs, I saw the older one's face spiral with panic. "You broke the fucking window?!" she snapped, looking behind us. "Walkers are gonna come now, you stupid motherfuckas!"

Diesel just shrugged nonchalantly. "Well, then, I suggest you hurry up and give us whatever it is we want, so we can get outta here before your undead neighbors show up." His smile widened, but it was far from friendly.

The older one, who I assumed was the mom, pulled out her gun and aimed it at me and Diesel. Her hands were shaking, but they were steady enough, so I knew she had practice using it.

Diesel didn't even flinch. He just laughed, tilting his head like he was amused by that shit. "You really think that's gonna work out for you? Drop that gun right now, or we'll shoot both of you."

The younger girl's eyes widened. Fear was written all over her face as she glanced between her mom and Diesel. The mom's grip on the gun tightened, but I could see her hesitation. She wasn't dumb, she could see the manic in Diesel's eyes.

She let out a frustrated growl and slowly bent down, setting the gun on the floor, defeat etched in her body language.

"There you go," Diesel coached her with that sick grin on his face.

"What is it that you want?" the mom gritted.

Diesel stared at her, running his eyes over her body slowly. Then suddenly his sick grin deepened. "Yo, Trey, leave that bull-shit alone in that kitchen and come here."

Suddenly, the clanking and thuds in the kitchen ceased. Then Trey appeared inching up the hallway, gun in one hand as he fed himself a Honey Bun with the other.

"Yo', bro, this motherfucka full of snacks..." Trey's words trailed off when his eyes landed on the mom and daughter. His lips slowly began to evilly meet his ears. "Damn, baby," he said as he touched the mom's hair. She flinched and took a deep calming breath, as if she were trying desperately to keep from respond-ing. "You fine than a motherfucka." Then he stepped back, taking his gaze down her body. "And yo' chocolate ass thick as fuck too."

"Nah, nigga, back the fuck up," Diesel barked. "That's mine. You can have the one behind her."

The mom inhaled long and hard as she stepped back, protecting her daughter. "This is my baby. She is a child."

Diesel shrugged. "She look grown to me." Trey sadistically laughed as Diesel told her, "It's been days since I got some pretty pussy, shorty. We're held up with some monsters. They suck some good dick, but they don't look shit like you, baby."

The mom winced as her daughter began to shake and whimper in fear. The mom's dreadful eyes kept bouncing between Diesel and the window.

Diesel looked over his shoulder at me. "Tariq, secure the window while we take these hoes upstairs. Once we're done, you can get you a piece."

"No!" the mom shouted as she took her daughter into her arms.

"Mama," her daughter cried into her chest.

"N-n-n-no! Don't do this to her please. Take me! Just take me!" the mom began to bargain.

Diesel grinned at her, pleased with the offer. "You can handle us both, shorty?"

"That ass big enough for us both," Trey ignorantly added.

As Diesel and Trey kept grinning and taunting, I could hear the low, guttural growling getting closer. They were right outside; probably drawn by the commotion we were causing. Every second that passed, the sound grew louder. And as much as I tried to focus on that, I couldn't get past what Diesel and Trey were about to do. Though I'd just linked with their crew the day prior, Diesel and his gang bragged about what they did to women, and I couldn't just stand by and let that shit happen.

My hand tightened on my gun as I glanced at Diesel, then Trey. Suddenly, I turned and fired. I let off two shots, quick and clean. Diesel's grin dropped as the bullet hit him in the chest. Trey barely had time to react before he dropped too, his body crumpling next to Diesel's on the floor.

The room fell silent, except for the ringing in my ears from the gunshots.

As the two ladies screamed, I saw the relief in their eyes when Diesel and Trey hit the ground. That relief didn't last long, though. Those growls were closer now, and before I knew it, walkers were falling into the window, their decaying hands reaching out, hungry for flesh.

"Go! Upstairs!" I shouted, stepping in front of them as the undead pushed their way inside. Without a second thought, I ushered the ladies toward the stairs, keeping myself between them and the chaos. I admired the older one's know-how to get her gun from the floor before she took off.

"Hurry!" I shouted as the growls and scraping of the hungry, savage walkers filled the house behind us.

NIYAH

We were upstairs in my bedroom, trying to push everything we could against the bedroom door. I could hear the walkers on the other side, their growls getting louder and more determined. The door shook so hard I thought it was going to come right off the hinges. The whole thing rattled like it didn't have much time left, and every slam made my stomach knot with fear.

Tariq was next to Neveah, talking fast, trying to tell us what to do. "Listen, fuck barricading the door. We need to get the fuck out of here."

I cut him off, not even caring what he had to say. "I don't trust you," I snapped, glaring at him. "You just tried to rob me."

"I ain't them," Tariq shot back urgently. "I joined them to survive, but I'm not like them. I didn't sign up for what they were doing. I'm trying to help y'all now."

"Help us? After you broke into my house? Y'all are the reason these motherfuckers are in here in the first place!"

"Momma, please," Neveah cut in, her voice shaking. "We ain't got time for this. We need to figure out what we're gonna do."

Before I could answer, there was a loud crack. I looked at the door, and my blood went cold. One of those things had pushed its arm through, breaking the wood, its rotten hand clawing at the air. Neveah screamed, and I couldn't stop the sound that escaped my own throat.

"Move!" Tariq shouted, shoving us toward the window as more of the door started to splinter.

I looked through it, terrified when I saw at least twenty of the undead trying to force their way inside.

I hesitated, looking down at the window ledge, my heart pounding in my ears. We were on the second floor.

"I can't," I stammered, panic rising. "We're too high up."

"You don't have a choice!" Tariq barked. "Climb out onto the ledge. They're going to tear through that door in seconds!"

I could hear the growls getting louder, the door breaking more by the second. Neveah grabbed my arm, pushing me toward the window.

Before I could even think, Tariq was already pulling it open and helping me through. The moment my knees hit the ledge, the rush of fresh air hit my face, and for a brief second, even in all this chaos, I realized how much I missed it. The smell of the day, the warm breeze—it was something I hadn't felt in weeks, and for a split second, it felt almost normal.

But it wasn't.

None of this was.

I grabbed Neveah's hand as Tariq helped her climb through next.

"Be careful, baby," I told her, breathless. The ledge wasn't wide, and one wrong move could send either of us crashing to the ground below. I pulled her close, trying to keep us steady.

Then Tariq started to climb out. He was halfway through when two of those walkers—growling, snarling, and smelling like death—grabbed his legs, pulling him back into the room. The look on his face was pure panic as he kicked at them, trying to get free, but they weren't letting go.

I froze, anger rushing through me, even in the middle of all this. This man had broken into my house, and his people were about to rape me and my baby. Part of me wanted to leave him right there, to let him deal with the mess he got himself into.

But then Neveah's voice cut through my thoughts. "Momma! Help him!" She reached out, trying to pull Tariq through the window. I saw the desperation in her eyes and felt my own hesitation crumble.

Tariq was fumbling for his gun, but the undead were pulling him harder, their decayed fingers digging into his legs like they were trying to drag him to hell. They were relentless, clawing and snarling, their mouths snapping open and shut as they tried to get closer to him. I could see his face, twisted in fear, fighting for his life.

I pulled out my gun, my hands shaking but steady enough to aim. I couldn't let Neveah see him die like that. I fired twice, the sound piercing through the air. The first walker's head snapped back, its body slumping down immediately, still gripping Tariq's leg. The second staggered, its chest exploding with blood before it finally collapsed.

Tariq gasped, yanking himself free as Neveah and I grabbed his arms and pulled him through the window. We all stumbled back onto the ledge, panting, trying to catch our breath. The sound of the walkers inside grew louder as they stumbled toward the window, their growls turning into high-pitched screeches.

We slammed the window shut together, pushing against the glass like it was the only thing keeping us alive. And then, the walkers hit the glass, hard. Their bloodied, broken fingers clawed at the glass, leaving streaks of red as they banged their heads against it, desperate to get through. Their faces were warped, snarling, eyes wide with hunger, mouths gaping as they snapped at us from the other side.

CHAPTER 6

FABLE

After over a week into this bullshit, the crew was gathered in the living room, trying to figure out what to do about food. With seven people in the house, food was running low. If we didn't do something about it soon, we'd all be starving.

Every day felt like a nightmare we couldn't wake up from. The only thing to be appreciative of was that the crew had each other. There was strength in numbers. But there was no more room for pretending this was anything but an apocalypse. This shit was unreal, and no matter how many of those things we put down, it was still hard to wrap my head around what the fuck we were living through.

But what had been eating at me the most was Niyah. I had no idea how she and Neveah were doing since the phones and Wi-Fi went down. I kept trying to get to her and Neveah, but every attempt had been stopped by the undead. It was becoming clearer that even if I got to her, I might not have been able to even get them back to our camp without possibly losing my life and theirs.

Even in death, I had a deep respect for Cane. He was always a good dude, loyal to those he loved, and I wouldn't ever forget that. But with him gone, it felt like it was my duty to be the one looking out for Niyah now. The feelings I'd kept buried for so many years had only grew in her absence, and without Cane here to protect her, the need to be that man for her burned even brighter. The distance, the silence, not knowing if she was okay had just made what I felt for her multiply. I ached to lay my eyes on her, to know she was alright.

Deep down, I tried to convince myself that they were safer staying put. But, in the back of my mind, I wondered if they were even still alive, if they had managed to survive this long. That thought sickened me and brought me to my knees most nights when I was alone.

"Look, we *gotta* go out for supplies today," Salem said. "Fable, August, you're coming with me."

I glanced over at Navon. I knew exactly why Salem wasn't suggesting him. Navon was in one of his dark moments again. I'd seen it enough times to recognize it. He'd been fighting a hard battle long before this apocalypse came along. Losing his family so young, battling depression alone, and then getting stuck in *this* was crushing him. He had nothing to begin with, and now it felt like this hell was just the universe's sick way of reminding him that his life had never been fair. I could see in the slump of his shoulders and the blank stare that he was beyond tired. He'd run out of steam and hope.

"Navon, you wanna roll with us?" I asked him.

He barely lifted his head. He was staring down at his phone, swiping through photos of life before the undead. "Nah. Y'all go ahead."

"Man, c'mon, we need you," August tried.

He shrugged, keeping his eyes on his phone. "I ain't got it in me today," he muttered.

Irritated, Salem scoffed so loud that all our attention darted towards him, except for Navon's.

"He can just stay here with us," Paris quickly interjected as she eyed me, Salem, and August. Her glare told us silently to get off his back. "We need a guy here anyway in case something pops off."

I nodded. "Bet." Then I looked at Salem and August, saying, "I want to try to get to Niyah and Neveah again. I can't just sit around here and wonder if they're okay."

Meesha looked at me with both concern and agreement in her eyes. "I think y'all should, too," she said carefully. "But... is it really the smart move, Fable? The undead are everywhere, and y'all barely made it back last time. It's getting worse out there, not better."

"I know," I answered. "But I gotta try again. I can't leave them out there, not knowing if they're safe."

Kecia let out a dramatic sigh, then leaned back with a smirk. "Seems like you're a little *too* obsessed with rescuing Niyah, Fable. Just sayin'." She tried to play it off, making her tone casual like it was a joke, but I could hear the jealousy in it.

I shot her a look. "Kecia, it ain't about obsession. It's about doing what's right."

She shrugged, pretending like it didn't bother her. "Mm humph. Whatever you say."

But I could see the fire in her eyes. It was the kind that came from wanting something that wasn't hers to have. And she hated that I wasn't trying to be what she wanted.

"Look," I said, leaning forward. "Niyah and Neveah are out there somewhere, and I won't stop trying. Y'all don't have to come with me, but I gotta do this."

The room fell into an awkward silence. I could feel Kecia's anger and Meesha's worry. But I didn't give a fuck. I was going to get to Niyah and Neveah, no matter how many attempts it took.

"I feel you, bro," Salem told me. "But we'll get to that shit tomorrow. But tonight, we have to get out there and get some food, so we'll have the fucking strength to go rescue the next person."

THE STREETS WERE DEAD SILENT, EXCEPT FOR THE DISTANT growls and the occasional shuffle of something that wasn't human. Me, Salem, and August moved through the neighborhood at night, sticking to the shadows. It was the best way to move now—using the darkness as cover, avoiding the things out here trying to eat us. But it wasn't just the undead we had to worry about. There were scavengers, desperate folks trying to survive, just like us, that were hunting us as well.

As we crept down the block, we didn't talk. We were focused on watching each other's backs. Walking was the safest option. Most streets were blocked off by abandoned cars or barricades people had thrown together, like trees, vehicles, and appliances, idiotically thinking that would stop the undead.

We turned the corner, going down an alley. And that's when August stopped, pointing at a house.

"Yo, that's Old Man Thompson's place," August whispered. "He's been growing food here for years. Y'all remember him, right?"

I nodded. "Yeah, I remember him."

Suddenly, August looked like his mouth was watering. "He has a garden full of shit."

Salem grunted. "You don't think that motherfucka been ran through by now?"

"Nah, if he's still in there, it's food back there. He protected that garden like Fort Knox because he always said Armageddon was coming."

I scoffed at the irony. "Old man was right then."

"So, he definitely probably protecting the fuck out of it now," August insisted.

"Man, we need to try, at least," Salem pressed. "It's getting tight back at the camp."

I nodded, looking at the high fence. Suddenly, it was as if I could smell the fruits and vegetables on the other side.

"Let's make sure it's still food back there first," I told them.

Salem and August nodded in agreement. I took it upon myself to scale the wooden fence. Climbing to the top, I peered over.

Sure enough, there were watermelons, apples, tomatoes—*real* food. It was like hitting the jackpot. Since we'd been holed up at my place, there wasn't much to eat. I was a bachelor who never kept a stocked fridge. Most nights, we were out here, searching for anything to keep us going. We had plenty of guns and ammo. At the beginning of all of this, Navon, Salem, August, and I had risked it all by hitting up our trap spots and cribs for all the guns and ammo we had, but food was a different story.

"You think we can get in?" Salem asked, peering up.

I glanced down at him and then back at the house. "Yeah, we can try, but don't hurt the old man if he comes out. He's a legend in this neighborhood, and we ain't about to take him out just for some watermelons."

Salem smirked, already sizing up the fence. "Yeah ah ight."

I glared down at him. "I'm serious, bro."

He rose his hands in surrender. "You got it."

But I didn't believe this nigga. He was so trigger happy. He was living in a real life video game.

I hopped over the fence first, careful not to make any noise, and landed softly in the garden. August and Salem were right behind me, scaling it like pros. We moved slow, crouching low as we crept through the rows of watermelons and tomatoes. The smell of fresh vegetables hit me, and for a second, I felt a little guilty about raiding Old Man Thompson's garden. But we needed this food, and in times like these, it was about survival, not respect.

But just as we started grabbing what we could—apples, tomatoes, whatever fit in our bags—a bright floodlight snapped on, lighting up the whole yard like it was broad daylight.

"Shit!" I hissed, looking around for cover.

"Grab as much as you can!" Salem ordered lowly.

We scrambled, stuffing food into our shirts and bags, but then shots rang out, loud and sharp, slicing through the air. We ducked immediately, and I saw Salem instinctively reach for his gun.

"Don't!" I grabbed his arm just in time, yanking it down. "I told you, don't shoot!"

"Man, he's shooting at us!" Salem snapped as he ducked behind the bushes with me as more shots roared from the house.

"We ain't killing an old man over some damn tomatoes!" I shouted back.

Another shot whizzed past, just inches from my head. It was too close, *way* too close.

"Let's get outta here!" August yelled, already moving toward the fence as he clung to the bags he'd filled.

We bolted for the fence, scaling it as more gunfire exploded behind us. My heart was in my throat as I reached the top, pulling myself up. Just as I swung my leg over, another shot whizzed by, so close I felt the heat of it pass by my ear.

I dropped down on the other side, hitting the ground hard but not stopping. "Go, go!" I shouted at the others, and we took off running, leaving Old Man Thompson's garden behind, the sound of gunshots still ringing in our ears.

NIYAH

It wasn't safe to stay on the roof. So, we'd been creeping from street to street, looking for shelter. We had knocked on a few doors, but nobody even acknowledged us. But I wasn't surprised. I wouldn't have either.

We'd been moving through the neighborhood for hours. My legs felt like noodles. Every sound made me jump, every creak in the distance felt like a warning.

At one point, I suggested maybe we go to the camp Tariq had come from, since he had killed the men who tried to rob and rape us. But Tariq shut that down quick. "That's not an option," he'd said so seriously that I had to believe him. "That camp's cutthroat. You and Neveah wouldn't be safe there."

So, we kept inching through the dark streets, ears open for the undead, our eyes scanning every shadow.

Tariq led the way, moving like a soldier on a mission, always checking our surroundings, making sure we stayed quiet and hidden. He was focused, ensuring me and Neveah stayed out of harm's way. I wasn't about to admit it out loud, but I felt protected by him. Despite being caught up with Diesel and Trey, I could tell that he wasn't like them.

Suddenly, we heard rapid footsteps coming from an alley nearby. My throat closed, and I felt Tariq tense beside me. Without hesitation, I grabbed my gun, and Tariq did the same. Neveah stayed close to me, eyes darting around to watch for what was coming.

The footsteps got louder, and for a second, I thought it was over. But then, through the darkness, familiar faces emerged. Fable, August, and Salem came sprinting out of the alley, looking just as worn and ragged as we did.

I let out a breath I didn't even realize I was holding. "Thank God," I breathed.

I glanced at Tariq, and I noticed he was relieved too, while wearing this odd smile as he watched them.

It took everything in me to keep myself from yelling their names. Neveah and I ran toward Fable, August, and Salem. At first, they were caught off guard. They halted and lifted their weapons, but for only milliseconds before they realized who we were. August grinned, then opened his mouth to say something, but quickly quieted. Fable's grin went from ear to ear. Even Salem was smiling at Neveah as she darted towards him.

The second I reached them, I hugged them tight. I hadn't realized just how much I missed them, how much I needed to see their faces, to know they were okay, until now.

It was so surreal, seeing them after all this time. The chaos had almost made me forget what it felt like to have people with you that you undoubtedly trusted. It felt like a piece of the old world had come back.

"Y'all good?" Fable asked with his arms around me, looking between me and Neveah. I fell into his chest, surprised and worried at how hard and fast his heart was beating.

"Yeah, we're good now that we found y'all," I said, finally feeling a little weight lift off my shoulders.

The relief on Fable's face was undeniable. He looked at me like I was the only thing in the world he'd been searching for. He held me tighter and longer than he usually would, like he was afraid to let go, like he'd been holding his breath for weeks and could finally breathe again. I felt safe in his arms, like everything that had been falling apart around us didn't matter in that moment. He didn't say it, but I could feel how much he'd been worrying about me, and that alone made me hold on just as tight.

Neveah grinned nervously, hugging Salem before turning to August. "Oh my God, I'm so glad we bumped into y'all."

Fable's eyes locked with mine, and for a second, the world felt normal. He looked so damn good. Better than I remembered, even in the middle of this madness. His arms wrapped around me, and I melted into him, feeling safe for the first time in what felt like forever. I wanted to focus on getting to safety, but I couldn't help the way my heart raced being close to him again. His touch, his smell—everything about him made me feel the safest I felt in a long time.

"You alright?" he whispered in my ear, his breath warm on my skin.

"Better now," I whispered back, squeezing him.

"Man, I was scared I'd never see y'all again," August whispered.

"Hell yeah," Salem agreed. "We were trying to get to y'all. Fable wasn't giving up."

I tried to smother the blush that surfaced as I glanced up at Fable, who hadn't taken his eyes off me.

Tariq cleared his throat gently. "We gotta be quick, y'all. These streets are crawling with the undead."

That's when the other guys finally noticed Tariq standing

behind us. Salem watched him curiously, but it was evident that August and Fable knew him. But while Fable knew him, he still glanced between Tariq and I, eyes burning with curiosity.

Salem agreed with a nod. "Yeah, let's get the fuck up outta here. We still got a lot of ground to cover."

Fable let go of me, stepping back but keeping his eyes on me like he didn't want to lose me again.

FABLE

We made it back to the house after having to take out a few walkers along the way. Every time I killed one of those things, it reminded me how much the world had changed. Everything was so different now, and it felt like it was never going back to normal. But at least we were still alive... for now.

When we stepped through the door, Meesha, Kecia, and Navon were on their feet, relief all over their faces when they saw Niyah and Neveah. I stood back, watching as they hugged and greeted each other. I didn't say much, just watched from a distance, my eyes anchored on Niyah.

Even after all we'd been through, she still looked so beautiful to me. She looked different, but breathtaking. She was forced to be in her natural state now, like most of the women here. No fake hair, no makeup, no lashes. Just her, in the most real way possible.

I found myself staring a little too long, caught up in the way she looked—rare, natural, untouched by the chaos around us. I noticed Kecia catching the way I was watching Niyah. I quickly shifted my gaze, hoping she didn't pick up on what I was feeling.

Kecia wasn't my girl, but being quarantined with her for all this time had made her think she had some ownership over me and this dick. Because of that, I had tried to put distance between us, but on some nights, it was hard to resist the urge to use her body to escape this hell on earth we were all living in.

Having Tariq with us made me feel like I had a piece of my brother with me. And, even though the rest of the crew had gone to a different high school than Onyx and Tariq, Navon and August knew him because they all played basketball back then. So, even Navon had perked up a bit.

We were all packed into the living room, kicking back since we finally had something to be happy about.

Navon leaned back, rubbing his head as he shook it slowly. "Man, who would've thought one day we'd be sitting around dodging dead people instead of dodging bullets and bills?"

Everyone chuckled as Paris agreed, "No, for real! Like I'd much rather be worried about rent than getting my fucking face chewed off today.'"

August shook his head, laughing. "And these walkers, man... They eating niggas like they taste like *chicken*."

"Look, we all used to joke about dying in these streets, but this wasn't what we meant!" I laughed.

"Deadass," Meesha agreed. "If one of y'all turn, just promise me one thing: don't try to eat me. I ain't got enough meat to be worth it. Eat Kecia or Niyah's thick ass."

Niyah jumped in. "Girl, you know they like white meat! So, they getting your light skinned ass first!"

Salem's eyes glinted with a smirk. "Y'all gone be okay if I turn, 'cause I'll be the bougiest walker eva. I'm only chasing niggas that look organic."

The room erupted in more laughter, and for a second, it felt like old times. It was wild how even in the middle of hell, we could find a reason to laugh. And Niyah's smile was orgasmic. I couldn't keep my eyes off of her. I knew that she would soon catch me staring, but I was so open that I didn't even care.

Luckily, Tariq pulled me to the side. "I need to holla at you."

I nodded and followed him into my bedroom. I was glad for the distraction, especially with Kecia watching me like that.

I watched him curiously as he closed the door as if he didn't want anyone else to hear. I leaned against the dresser, crossing my arms. "What's up?"

He smiled as if he had been waiting all of his life for this moment. "Your brother sent me to get you."

My brows curled at the mention of my brother. The last time me and Onyx spoke, he'd told me that the Navy was sending soldiers to the boarders. He'd said he'd do any and everything he could to help me, but I hadn't heard from him since and before the phones and Wi-Fi went down, we heard that the soldiers were shooting any and everything that appeared at those boarders, so I knew there was no way he could help me get out of here.

As Tariq leaned in and started to speak, his voice was low, like he didn't want anyone to overhear what he was about to say. "Onyx has been running supplies to the soldiers at the pier on 31st and Lakeshore."

My brow rose. "Word? You've seen him?"

"Yeah," Tariq nodded as he glanced towards the bedroom door before he continued. "He sent me to come get you. He's figured out a way to get people out on his boat when he comes to drop off the supplies. But he can only come at a certain time, on a certain day."

Hope hit me like a tsunami. It came outta nowhere and damn near knocked me off my feet. This could be it... a way out of this shit.

"You mean there's somewhere to escape to? This shit isn't happening anywhere else in the world?"

I couldn't believe it when Tariq shook his head with such confidence. "No. Only the South Side of Chicago. The military was able to eradicate any potential dangers outside of the unsafe zone before it could spread further."

"When's the next time Onyx will be at the pier?" I rushed.

"This Thursday and next. Those are the only days that he comes and this Thursday, tomorrow, is too soon to make it. So, we only have a week. You have to make it by next Thursday because after that he's being transferred to another assignment. There's only room for four more people on the boat, including myself and Onyx. That's why you can't tell anyone else. If word gets out, it'll be chaos, and nobody's getting out."

The hope that had been flooding me a second ago took a hit. Since it was only four seats, I couldn't even bring my whole crew. My mind raced as I heard their voices through the closed door. How was I supposed to make a choice like that?

"You're telling me I can't tell anyone? Not even my people?" I asked. "We've been through hell together. I can't just leave them behind."

Tariq sighed, understanding my struggle. "I know, man. I wouldn't ask you to do something like this if there was any other way. But Onyx made it clear—this is the only shot, and there's only room for three more people. You, me, and whoever you can fit in that last spot."

I stood there, feeling torn apart. The idea that we could escape this, that it could all be over, felt like a dream I never thought would come true. But then the reality sank in—I couldn't save everyone. The people I cared about, the people who had fought alongside me through this hell, weren't all going to make it.

"Onyx showed me a secret path at the pier," Tariq added, breaking my thoughts. "It'll get us past the soldiers, clean and quiet. But if we don't make that window, it's over. This is it, Fable. It's the last chance."

I nodded slowly as the heavy burden of the decision settled in. As Tariq started to give me every single detail of how we were going to get out, I finally felt hope, but there was also heartache in knowing I'd have to make the hardest choice of my life.

CHAPTER 7

FABLE

We were all still crammed in the living room, trying to make things feel as normal as possible. Most nights, it wasn't hard. When we were all together like this—laughing, talking, playing Spades—it felt almost like the world hadn't completely fallen apart. But then the screams would start, or we'd hear that familiar growl outside, or the desperate pounding on the windows. Those moments reminded us we were living in hell on earth.

Tonight, though, it felt especially normal, like we could breathe a little easier since Niyah and Neveah had joined us. But even with that relief, there was a shadow hanging over everything—the loss of DeShawn and Cane. We didn't talk about it, but I knew we all felt it, especially Niyah. She was smiling and laughing with Paris, catching up like old friends, but I could see that pain in her eyes.

Navon, Salem, Meesha, and August were deep into their game of Spades, arguing over books like the world hadn't gone to shit outside. But it was good to see Navon out of his slump. "I told you, I got six!" Navon shouted, slamming his cards down with a grin.

"Man, you always overbidding!" Salem shot back, laughing. "I should've cut you off three hands ago."

Meanwhile, Kecia was sitting behind Neveah on the couch, running her fingers through Neveah's long, thick curls. "Girl, your hair is so full! I wish mine was like this," Kecia said, admiring it. Neveah giggled, relaxing into her touch.

I was sitting next to Tariq, exchanging stories about what we'd seen out there. His face was serious as he talked about the things Diesel's crew had done to survivors. "They're ruthless, Fable. I've seen them take everything from families, leave 'em with nothing. If Diesel's crew finds out we're holed up here with food and supplies, they're gonna come. And when they do, they're not leaving until they take everything or kill everyone trying to protect it."

I nodded slowly, taking in every word. "We'll be ready if they come. Ain't nobody running up on us taking shit."

Tariq looked at me with hard eyes. "We need to be on the lookout for those niggas. Diesel's crew is thirsty and cutthroat. Their camp isn't far from here. I'm surprised you haven't run into them yet."

"But you said you killed Diesel and Trey, right?"

"Yeah, but it was a few niggas in there secretly waiting for Diesel to die so they could take over."

I didn't respond as my eyes drifted back to Niyah as she laughed with Paris. She was sitting there, looking so damn beautiful. Her laugh, the way she smiled, even the sadness behind her eyes—it all pulled me in. I felt my body relax for the first time since this hell began. There was something about Niyah's presence that made everything feel just a little bit safer, a little bit better.

When Tariq told me what Diesel and Trey did, and what they

planned to do to Niyah and Neveah, rage burned through me like fire. I wanted nothing more than to have those motherfuckers alive in front of me, just so I could tear them apart piece by piece or throw them straight into a horde of the undead. The thought of them laying hands on my girls made my blood boil, but I was thankful as hell that Tariq was there to save them.

Tariq noticed where my eyes were, but before he could say anything, I cut in. "So, Onyx's crazy ass sent you back to find me, huh?"

Tariq chuckled. "Yeah. So, I have to make sure I get you to that pier on time next week."

"I've thought about getting to that pier so many times and stealing a boat. But I know the military is blowing up anything that gets near those borders."

"They *are*," Tariq emphasized.

I nodded, still keeping one eye on Niyah as she turned her head and caught me staring. She smiled softly, her eyes locking with mine for a brief moment before she went back to talking to Paris.

I felt like such a bitch when I smiled back and felt my heart beating steady for the first time in a while.

I glanced over at Tariq, still trying to process everything he'd told me. "Bro, why'd you even come out here? You had safety. Why leave all that to come find me?"

Tariq chuckled under his breath, shaking his head like the answer was obvious. "Onyx really didn't give me a choice. He wasn't leaving without you, and he looked out for me more times than I can count over the years. He had my back in ways nobody else did, and when he asked me to find you, I couldn't imagine telling him no." He leaned back, his eyes scanning the room like he was taking it all in. "Besides, I ain't scared of no fucking walkers. I survived way bigger monsters than some fucking walkers, growing up in the hood."

I let out a small laugh at that, nodding in agreement. "I hear you. The streets are a different kind of beast."

He smirked. "Exactly. I've been running from real monsters my whole life. Walkers ain't nothing but another obstacle to overcome."

NIYAH

The next morning, I woke up with the faint hope that, for just a second, life was normal. My eyes blinked open, and for a split second, the quiet felt peaceful. But then I heard the low growls outside, reminding me that peace was in the rear-view mirror. It irritated me, made the pit of frustration deep in my chest stir.

I looked around the living room, where the rest of the crew was sprawled out, asleep. Everyone was exhausted after staying up until the wee hours of the morning, trying to pretend that the world wasn't crumbling around us. I was careful not to wake anyone as I crept through the room. I stopped for a second, frozen in place as I admired Paris cuddled up under Salem's large frame. I pouted, remembering the way I would spoon with Cane. I missed him so much.

That's when I noticed Fable and Kecia were missing.

I tiptoed through the house, my heart suddenly racing for a reason that had nothing to do with walkers. When I got to Fable's bedroom door, it was open just a crack. I knew I shouldn't, but curiosity pulled me in. I peeked through the door, and my stomach twisted as I saw Fable and Kecia were tangled up in the bed, asleep together.

My heart sank. A jealousy, which I hadn't fully admitted to myself before, hit me harder than I expected. I had known that Kecia was feeling Fable. The way she looked at him, the way she acted when he was around, wasn't hard to see. I guess part of me had been wondering if they were messing around, but I never wanted to dwell on it. I didn't want to admit that it bothered me. But seeing them like that, so close, made it all too clear that they were sleeping together.

I stepped back, leaving the door just as I found it. I couldn't believe how jealous, how heartbroken I felt. I wasn't supposed to care this much. But I did. And now, I couldn't deny it anymore.

I needed some air, to get away from what I just saw, from the way my stomach was still turning over the image of Fable and Kecia together. I remembered Fable had a balcony off the kitchen, so I slipped back there, hoping it would give me a little peace. When I stepped outside, the world felt eerily different. It was quiet, too quiet, except for the random thuds and low growls that seemed to come from nowhere and everywhere at the same time.

I hated myself for feeling jealous about Fable and Kecia. I was still grieving the loss of Cane. It felt so wrong, but I couldn't help it. Seeing them together stirred something up in me. Without Cane, I'd been going through hell on earth completely alone. He was my partner, my strength when things got tough. Now, every day felt like I was carrying this unbearable weight. I could barely process it. I missed him so much that it hurt, and at the same time, I was stuck in this sick, horrific bullshit, feeling something for Fable that I shouldn't. Fable wasn't mine, and he was a close friend of my late-husband, but the ache in my chest when I saw him with Kecia was so real. And I felt so guilty.

I took a seat on the old patio furniture, sinking into the

chair. I brought my knees to my chest and my arms into the long-sleeved shirt Fable had given me so that I could shower. Since Niyah and I had been forced out of our house with nothing, everyone had lent us clothes so that we could shower.

I looked out over the deserted street below, disappointed that everything was still, lifeless. The alley looked abandoned except for a few walkers ambling down it. Their movements were slow, almost lazy, but the way they looked up at me, bloodthirsty and ravenous, sent a shiver down my spine. I knew they couldn't get to me, though. Fable had told me how the crew worked together when the apocalypse started, adding height and traps to the fence to keep them and scavengers out.

Still, looking at those things filled me with nothing but hatred. I hated their existence, hated the fact that they were walking the earth like real-life devils. I stared at them, feeling disgusted, when suddenly, I heard shuffling behind me.

My heart jumped in my chest, and I turned quickly, ready to panic, but then I saw Fable. He stepped out onto the balcony, shirtless, wearing a pair of basketball shorts, and I swear, for a second, I forgot how to breathe. His muscles were tight, skin glowing, and even though I was still mad about what I'd just seen, suddenly, everything was okay.

"Hey," he spoke softly, like he didn't want to startle me. "I didn't mean to sneak up on you."

I shook my head, shaking away the tension. "No, it's fine. I just needed some air."

He sat down next to me, leaning back in the chair, his eyes sweeping the empty street. "I'm glad to see you, Niyah. For real. I never stopped trying to come to get you, but... it was crazy. We couldn't get through."

I looked over at him, immersing myself in the relief. "I know you did. Everything just... fell apart so fast."

Fable nodded. "Yeah, faster than anyone expected. I'm just glad you made it to us somehow. How you holding up?"

I shrugged, not really sure how to answer. "I'm surviving, I guess. It's been... *a lot*. Losing Cane, trying to protect Neveah. It's been a lot, and it doesn't feel real most days."

He sighed, running a hand over his waves. "I can't even imagine what you're going through. Losing Cane like that... I'm sorry, Niyah."

I looked away, swallowing the lump in my throat. "Thanks. It's hard. Every day feels like a fight that I'm losing, but I'm just trying to hold it together for Neveah."

He turned toward me, his eyes locking with mine. "You're strong, Niyah. Always have been. I know it's hard, but you're doing everything you can. That's all that matters."

His words hit me deeper than I expected, and I found myself leaning into them, needing that reassurance. "I guess. It's just... it's hard to see an end to this. I don't know how much longer we can keep going like this."

Fable reached over, gently taking my hand. "We'll make it. I don't know how, but we will. We've made it this far, right?"

I nodded, squeezing his hand. "Yeah. We have."

For a moment, the world outside—the growls, the chaos, the apocalypse—it all felt far away. Sitting there with Fable, I felt a sense of calm I hadn't felt in weeks. But then the image of him and Kecia crept back into my mind, and I couldn't shake the jealousy and confusion swirling inside me.

Suddenly, Neveah's scream echoed through the air, and my heart stopped for a second.

"Marcel!" I heard her shout frantically. Her voice was coming from the front of Fable's house. I gasped, realizing she wasn't inside. Without thinking, Fable and I took off, running back in and through the house.

"Neveah!" I called out, panic rising in my chest.

No answer.

Fable and I grabbed our guns before he carefully opened the front door. My heart sank when I realized the barricades had been removed. The others in the living room were starting to stir, the sudden chaos waking them up.

Fable and I rushed out of the front door and onto the porch where Neveah was standing.

"What the hell are you doing out here by yourself?" I snapped. "Get inside, now!"

She turned to me, her eyes wide but stubborn. "I saw Marcel out of the window! He's down there all by himself!" She pointed down the street, and sure enough, there was a figure standing at the corner.

"Who is that?" Fable asked.

"He goes to school with me!" Neveah said, still calling out Marcel's name like this wasn't a life-or-death situation. "He might need help! Marcel!"

I grabbed her arm, trying to pull her back toward the house. "Neveah, get inside! You know we can't just let people in! He could be bit!"

But she wouldn't budge. "Ma, I know him. He needs help!"

"Be quiet!" I hissed as she continued to scream his name. "You're going to attract the undead!"

But she ignored me, waving Marcel over. "Marcel, come here!"

Before I could stop her, his head snapped up, and he started running toward the house.

My heart sank. "No, no, no!" I grabbed Neveah again, pulling her harder. "He can't come in, Neveah. You know we can't trust anybody!"

"Why can't he come in?" Neveah shot back. "He's my friend."

As we argued, Tariq, Salem, Paris, and Meesha came out onto the porch. Their expressions were full of confusion and concern.

Marcel was getting closer, sprinting down the street like his life depended on it.

"He might be bit!" I yelled, panic and anger bubbling over. "You don't know what's happened to him! We can't take that risk!"

Neveah looked at me, desperation in her eyes. "Ma, I know him. He wouldn't—"

But before she could finish, I cut her off. "This isn't about what you *think* you know. There are rules for a reason, Neveah! We can't trust anybody, not even people we used to know."

As Marcel sprinted toward us, my heart was in my throat. Neveah kept calling his name, her voice filled with hope and fear. But then, out of nowhere, a mob of walkers appeared, shambling from behind cars and out of alleyways, their growls filling the air. Before any of us could react, they were on him.

Marcel screamed, his body hitting the ground as the walkers clawed at him, tearing into him like they'd been waiting for this moment. Neveah's scream pierced through the morning, filled with pure heartache. "No! Marcel! No!" She tried to run toward him, but I grabbed her arm, my own heart breaking for her.

"Neveah, we have to go back inside!" I shouted, trying to pull her back.

She fought me with everything she had, tears streaming down her face, her voice hoarse from screaming. "No! We have to help him! Let me go! Marcel!"

Fable rushed over, gently grabbing her other arm. But she fought against his grip as if he was killing her.

"Neveah, stop!" I spat. "There's nothing we can do!"

But she was hysterical, fighting against both of us, her desperation blinding her to the danger. "No! He needs me! He needs me!" She kicked and screamed, trying to break free, but it was too late. The mob of the undead had torn Marcel apart. His screams faded into nothing but growls and the sound of flesh being ripped.

I could barely hold it together as Fable and I struggled to get her back inside. Neveah was wild, fighting us every step of the way. "Let me go! Let me save him!" she screamed, her voice cracking with grief.

"We have to go, Neveah!" I yelled.

Fable and I worked together, using every ounce of strength to pull her through the front door.

Finally, we managed to get her inside. Neveah collapsed to the floor, sobbing uncontrollably, her body trembling with grief. I knelt beside her, holding her as tightly as I could while her world shattered in front of her.

KECIA

I knew it was gonna be a problem as soon as Niyah and Neveah joined the crew. I had a bad feeling in my gut. Having a teenager in the middle of all this shit was asking for trouble. Neveah had already been defiant and disobedient before the world came to an end. I could see this coming a mile away.

"You could've gotten us all killed!" Niyah snapped, pacing in front of Neveah. "Running out there like that, not thinking! You know the rules, Neveah! And now look at what happened! Yo' lil' friend is gone!"

Neveah was sitting on the couch, tears streaming down her face, trying to talk through the sobs. "Ma, I didn't mean—"

"You didn't *mean?*" Niyah cut her off. "This isn't just about what you *mean.* You don't get to make those kinds of decisions, Neveah! You don't get to put all of us at risk because you want to save someone who might've been bit!"

Neveah sobbed harder, but Niyah still tore into her. "If you had just listened to me, maybe Marcel would still be—"

"Niyah," Fable's voice cut in so calm. He walked up to her slowly. His hand reached out for hers. "Relax."

I watched how gentle he was with her, how careful, like he was handling something fragile. He took her by the hand, and suddenly the whole room shifted. Niyah's breathing slowed as he led her away from Neveah. "Come on, let's step out for a minute," he sweetly coaxed her.

Niyah groaned. "I can't believe she—"

But Fable gently pulled her toward the bedroom. "Come on, let's talk about it in here," he softly commanded.

Neveah wiped her tears as her whole body shook. She tried to catch her breath, stammering, "I-I-I didn't mean to... I thought I could save him," she whimpered, more to herself than anyone else.

I shook my head. This was exactly what I'd been worried about. Having a teenager in the crew was gonna be more drama than any of us needed.

Niyah hesitated, still fuming, but she let Fable guide her out of the living room, her hand still in his. I noticed how natural it looked—him calming her down, leading her away like they had a bond nobody else could touch. He was always soft with her, always careful. It made me feel some type of way, but I bit my tongue, watching them disappear into the bedroom.

CHAPTER 8

FABLE

Niyah paced back and forth in my room. She was pissed.

"That shit was so dangerous. What the fuck is wrong with that girl?" Niyah fussed. "She's been acting out and defying me. She's made this whole nightmare ten times harder on me."

I could see the frustration all in Niyah's face, the way her jaw clenched, the way her hands balled into fists as she tried to calm herself.

"She just won't listen, Fable. She knew that it wasn't safe out there. She saw up close what those things could do to us. Her father changed right in front of her. She had to shoot her own fucking father! But she doesn't care!"

I leaned against the dresser, watching her, trying to find the right words to say. Parenting a teenager is tough enough in normal times, but during an apocalypse is a whole different level of hell. I could see how tired she was, how scared. She loved Neveah, no question, but this situation had her at her breaking point.

"Teenagers are like that," I said softly, walking over to her. "They think they're invincible. They don't get it, not until it's too late. But you're doing everything you can, Niyah. You're protecting her."

She stopped pacing for a second, her eyes fluttering up to mine, still full of that anger, but something else too. Fear, maybe. I reached out, brushing a lock of hair away from her face, just to remind her I was here. That I had her back, no matter how hard this got.

She let out a breath, her shoulders relaxing just a little, but I could still feel the tension brewing in her. I stepped closer, pulling her in for a hug. My arms wrapped around her. I felt her body melt into mine and her breath hitched as she let herself lean into me, like she hadn't allowed herself to let go of the stress until right now.

"I've needed this," she whispered. "Since everything went to shit, I've needed this."

I held her tighter, feeling her grip on me like she didn't want to let go. "I know. Me too."

Just as Niyah was settling into me, the bedroom door swung open without a knock. Kecia barged in. Niyah stepped back from me quickly, putting space between us, and I could see the tension in her eyes as Kecia walked in like she had every right to my personal space.

"I need to shower," Kecia spat, not even bothering to look at Niyah.

I knew that it wasn't about the shower; it was about marking her territory. She was hating, but I didn't care. Kecia was just a fling that had been forcing herself on the dick, something that didn't matter in the long run. She wasn't who I was really thinking about.

Niyah had my heart. She was the one who had been on my mind every second, the one I worried about, the one I cared about. Kecia might have been around, but Niyah was the one I needed.

"Go ahead," I said to Kecia, not giving her the reaction she wanted.

She shot a look at Niyah, but I ignored it, my focus still on Niyah.

Kecia huffed, heading toward the bathroom, and I didn't even glance her way. It didn't matter. Not when Niyah was the only one who really had my attention.

PARIS

"We should hit up the corner store," Salem said.

Fable, Salem, and August had come back with just a handful of fruits and veggies from last night's run, barely enough to get us through another day and we'd devoured it last night.

Meesha leaned back on the couch, shaking her head. "Ain't nothing left in there, Salem. You know that. It's probably crawling with the undead, or scavengers have cleaned it out by now."

Salem wasn't hearing it though. He looked stubborn, like he always did when he had his mind set on something. "We should still go. There's always something left. Maybe not much, but enough to make a meal out of."

I looked over at him, crossing my arms. He wasn't wrong, though. Over the last two weeks, we'd hit up the store as much as we could, and scavengers had been in there, ransacking the place. But every time we went, we managed to find something. Even if it was just a couple cans of beans or some dry pasta, and the girls were always able to make it work.

As they conversed, I looked over at Navon. I felt so sorry for him. He had sunk back deep into one of his lows again. He had been sleeping most of the day. He hadn't showered in days. The stale scent of sweat and misery lingered around him. When he was awake, his eyes looked distant, like he'd checked out of the nightmare we were all living in. I'd seen this cycle before—his high highs followed by crushing lows—but since the undead showed up, it felt like he was drowning faster. He'd slept through most of the day, his mind somewhere else, maybe wishing he was one of the dead, so he wouldn't have to keep fighting.

"I'm coming," I said. I was tired of just sitting around while everyone else was out putting in work. I wanted to do something, to help.

Meesha nodded, sitting up straight. "Me too. I've been cooped up in here too long."

Salem glared at both of us, shaking his head. "Nah. Y'all need to stay here. It's too dangerous out there."

"Salem, we're not helpless," I snapped, standing up to face him. "We know how to protect ourselves. You don't have to coddle us."

August put a hand on his brother's shoulder. "Let them come, man. They can handle it. They know what they're doing, and they need some air."

Salem looked from me to Meesha, clearly not happy about it, but he eventually sighed and backed off. "Fine. But y'all stick close. No running off. We get in, we get out."

I nodded. "We hear you."

It felt good to finally get out of the house, to feel like I was contributing to keeping us alive.

We grabbed our guns. Before all this, Salem had taken me to the gun range a couple of times, teaching me how to shoot. But the last two weeks had given me a lot more practice than I ever wanted. I had to talk Salem into letting me go out with him each time, but I wasn't going to sit around while everyone else fought for survival. But we also grabbed knives and hammers. We tried to use as few bullets as possible, only using them when completely necessary.

We removed the barricades from the front door, then stepped outside into the quiet. The streets had gotten quieter over the past week. There were fewer people outside, the fear of the undead making people stay hidden, like the world had folded in on itself.

As we crept down the street, everyone's eyes were scanning, ears alert to any sign of movement. Suddenly, out of nowhere, a walker appeared growling from inside of a parked car.

My heart jumped into my throat as I screamed, completely caught off guard at the thing snarling with blood caked around its mouth. I lost my balance and fell hard as everyone hollered in shock.

"Shit!" Salem shouted, firing a quick shot that hit the walker right in the head. It dropped, but my leg was already bleeding. I looked down and saw that I'd fallen on some broken glass, the cut deep and nasty, blood pouring out faster than I could even process.

Salem was at my side in an instant, but instead of helping me up, he started fussing. "Damn it, Paris! I told you to stay inside! Look at you now!"

His words stung, but the pain in my leg was worse. "I'm fine," I muttered as I stood up.

Salem grabbed my arm. "You're not fine. You're going back in the house. Meesha, take her back."

Meesha rushed over to help me as my eyes narrowed at Salem. He wasn't like this before. He was always hard and protective, but now there was something darker in him. A cold-ness that made me feel like I was just a liability. I looked up at him as Meesha linked her arm with mine, and I saw that grim, unapologetic expression he wore too often these days. He didn't care about the blood pouring from my leg. All he saw was someone slowing him down.

Over the last few weeks, I'd felt us growing apart, and it scared me. The Salem I fell in love with wasn't this... brutal. I loved him, but the man that I'd fallen in love with was long gone.

And then there was August, looking at me with the compassion my man should have been. The more I pulled away from Salem, the closer I felt to August. He was different, softer in a way that Salem had lost. August made me feel safe in a way that wasn't just about protection—it was emotional. He cared, not just about survival but about how I was holding up through all of this. That connection between us had grown stronger as the days passed, and now it was pulling me in, no matter how hard I tried to fight it.

I loved Salem, but as we got deeper into this apocalypse, I couldn't ignore the bond forming between me and August. And it was tearing me apart, because I didn't know how long I could hold on before something snapped—whether it was between me and Salem or between the three of us.

AUGUST

Once we made sure Paris and Meesha were back inside, Salem and I headed toward the convenience store.

"Man, you need to ease up on Paris," I said, glancing over at Salem. His face was hard, set in that cold expression he'd been wearing more often lately.

Salem scoffed, keeping his eyes straight ahead. "You always trying to tell me how to treat the woman *I'm* fucking. Ain't no room for your soft shit right now. She needs to listen. We're fighting fucking walkers. This isn't the time to be gentle."

I shook my head. "Paris ain't your soldier, Salem, and she's not one of the guys. She's your woman. You can't treat her like she's just another body out here. She's doing her best to survive, just like the rest of us."

He stopped walking for a second, turning to me with that same hard look. "Stay out of it. Paris knows what this is. She knows what I'm trying to do—keep her alive."

"Yeah, but at what cost? You're pushing her away-"

Salem tossed his head back as he laughed physically. "Pushing her away? Where the fuck she gon' go, nigga?! We trapped!"

"You know what the fuck I mean. Just because you think acting tough is the best way to survive this, doesn't mean that you have to be tough with her all the time. You can protect her without treating her like she's just another piece on your chessboard. This ain't the game."

Salem's jaw clenched, and for a second, I thought he was going to snap. Instead, he just turned away, continuing down the street. "Mind your fucking business, August."

I'd watched Salem get harder and harder over time. He had always been cold, a menace in the streets. But now it was like the apocalypse had stripped away any consideration he had left. He was always on edge, ready for war, never letting his guard down. He had fully given himself to this fight, like surviving was the only thing that mattered to him anymore. Somewhere along the way, he forgot about love, about being the man Paris needed.

And I'd seen it in her eyes, the way she'd started to lose faith in him. Paris had always been loving, one of those women who stood by her man no matter what. But lately, she looked...alone, even when she was sitting right next to him. She was too beautiful for that. She was too full of life and love to be treated like she was invisible. I couldn't stand watching the way she looked at Salem now, like she was still waiting for him to show up, to be the man she fell in love with. But he was too far gone.

It hurts seeing someone as beautiful and caring as Paris fade because of the way my brother had changed. She deserved better than feeling alone next to the man she loves.

I didn't push it any further as we reached the convenience store. The last thing I wanted was to start a fight when we had bigger problems to worry about. But I couldn't shake the feeling that Salem was losing himself in all this darkness. I didn't know how long Paris was going to hold on if he kept acting like this.

When we stepped inside the store, it was like walking into an empty shell of what it used to be. The freezers that once vibrated with cold air and stocked shelves of food were now dead. Their doors were wide open, revealing nothing but frost and emptiness. The shelves that used to be packed with snacks, canned goods, and essentials were bare, stripped clean by desperate hands.

Salem cursed under his breath, shaking his head as we moved through the aisles. "Ain't nothing left here."

But we kept moving, hoping for something.

We made our way to the back of the store, into the stockroom, where things looked just as bad. It had been ransacked too, boxes torn open, packaging scattered across the floor like nobody cared about what was left behind. There were a few perishables—some half-rotten vegetables, a couple of loaves of bread, cheese—but it was slim pickings. We wouldn't last long on this, but it was something.

"We can do something with that cheese and bread."

Salem bent down to inspect what was left. "We need to focus on what'll last. We need canned goods, dry food. Stuff that won't spoil."

I leaned against the wall, crossing my arms. "No shit, but there ain't no dry food here. We take what we can get. You're acting like we have options."

His eyes flashed as he stood up, turning to face me. "I'm trying to keep us alive. That means we don't waste time on stuff that's gonna rot in a few days."

"Everything's rotting, nigga!" I shouted. "You think I don't want us to survive? We're both trying to make it, but you can't control every damn thing. We gotta make do with what we find, not what you think we need."

Salem's jaw clenched. "You think I don't know that? I know exactly what this is. But if we don't plan ahead, we're as good as dead."

I shook my head, feeling the distance spiraling between us.

"Planning ahead ain't gonna do shit if we're starving in the meantime."

He didn't respond, just glared at me. We were both on edge, both trying to lead in our own way, but we were getting nowhere. And in the back of my mind, I knew this wasn't just about the food.

PARIS

Niyah worked carefully on my leg, cleaning the cut with precision. I winced as she dabbed at the wound.

"Luckily, you don't need stitches," she muttered as she worked.

I was so glad when she came back with the guys the night before. It was so good to see she and Neveah alive. But I was admittedly happier that we had a nurse in our camp. Luckily, we'd managed to snag a bunch of medical supplies while scavenging.

"This is gonna sting a little," Niyah warned, applying an alcohol-soaked cotton ball on my leg.

I flinched but nodded, my mind elsewhere. "I'm so tired of Salem," I muttered. "He's so rough with me. This life is already hard enough. We're running for our lives, dealing with walkers, scavengers... I need him to be my comfort, not my damn lieutenant."

Niyah glanced up at me, raising an eyebrow. "You've been saying that for a while. You told him how you feel?"

"I've tried," I said, shaking my head. "But he doesn't get it.

It's like all he sees is survival, and I get it, but... I need more than that. I need someone to hold me when things get tough, not bark orders at me like I'm one of his block boys."

She nodded, taping up the bandage and sitting back. "I hear you. But Salem's in survival mode. He's always been like that, even before all this."

I sighed, rubbing my face. "Yeah, but it's different now. I'm losing him. And I'm losing me in the process."

As I spoke, I heard the front door open, and immediately, I tensed up. I could hear August and Salem coming back from their run to the convenience store, and just the sound of Salem's voice made my mood worsen.

August walked into the kitchen first, holding a few meager items in his arms. He dropped what little they'd managed to grab onto the counter.

I sighed, looking at it. "This is it?"

August shrugged, looking just as frustrated. "It's getting harder to find anything. Store's been picked over."

Niyah stood up, taking a quick glance at what they brought back. "It's barely enough."

I looked down at the sad handful of food, my stomach twisting with greed. More than anything, more than wanting Salem to change, I longed for something delicious to eat. Me and the rest of the girls had been able to make what we had taste good with seasonings. But I missed meals that didn't involve scavenging or rationing. I missed the comfort of a good meal—rack of lamb, baked macaroni and cheese, and yams. Just the thought of it made my mouth water, and I felt the ache of missing a life that was long gone.

August leaned down to check on my leg. His touch was gentle, almost tender. The moment his hand brushed my skin, I felt a chill run down my spine. The way his touch affected me, caught me off guard. His touch was so different from the energy Salem had.

I glanced up at him, taking in his tall frame, his basketball build, and the small pool of sweat on his brow. For a second, our eyes locked, and it felt like the whole world outside—walkers, chaos, everything—just disappeared. I knew I shouldn't be feeling this way, but I couldn't help it. I saw something in August that I hadn't felt in a long time.

Just then, Salem walked into the kitchen. His presence snapped me back to reality. He dumped what little he'd collected from the store onto the counter, not even glancing in my direction at first.

"Niyah, August, dip," Salem said bluntly. "I need to talk to Paris."

Niyah and August gave me sympathetic side-eyes as they walked out.

Once we were alone, Salem turned toward me. His expression was hard as always. "You should've listened to me," he sternly told me. "I just want to protect you. I can't coddle you at a time like this. You've got to stay on your p's and q's, or we're both dead."

I sighed, feeling that familiar disappointment wash over me. It was always like this—him lecturing, being rough, never just... loving me. "I get it, Salem. I know we have to survive this. I know what's out there. But I just wish you'd be more gentle with me. I need your comfort, not just your protection. I need to feel like I'm more than just someone you're trying to keep alive. I'm your woman, Salem, not your soldier. I'm terrified too, every day, and all I want is to feel like I'm not alone in this. I need to know that you're still here with me, as my man, not just someone giving me orders. I need your love, not just your strength."

Instead of listening, instead of the yearning in my eyes pulling at his heart strings, Salem's frustration flared up instantly.

He slammed his hand on the counter, making me flinch. "Gentle?" he gritted. "You want gentle when I'm watching people we know get ripped apart by the undead? Ain't nothing gentle about this shit, Paris. What the fuck do you want from me?"

I stared at him, disappointment and heartache seeping into my bones. "What do I want from you? I want a love from you where doors don't slam."

For the first time in a long time, I saw something flicker in Salem's eyes, something that looked like regret. But just as quickly, it was gone, replaced by that same hard, impenetrable, stubborn expression.

CHAPTER 9

FABLE

Dinner wasn't much, but Niyah and Meesha somehow managed to turn the scraps Salem and August brought back into something decent. There was a pot of mushy canned beans, mixed with some wilted greens. Niyah cooked the greens down with a few spices. They added some slightly stale bread, toasted and drenched in butter, and a small portion of boiled potatoes that were soft, but edible with seasoning. It wasn't the kind of meal we were used to, but it filled us up, and that was more than enough these days.

After eating, I needed to clear my head. I headed to my room and peeled off my clothes, getting ready to jump in the shower. The hot water was the only real luxury we had left.

As I stripped in the bathroom, my thoughts drifted to the pier, what it had been consumed with since Tariq told me about Onyx's plan. Onyx was my way out. But Onyx could only take a few people, and my first thought was to take everyone and beg him to make it work somehow. But I knew better. I'd seen what could happen if we overloaded the boat, the risk of capsizing, the chance of getting caught with too many people. All it would take was one mistake, and it'd be over for all of us.

The first names that hit me were Niyah and Neveah. It felt like they were at the front of my mind the moment I thought about that boat. I was considering them first, and that was a problem. My boys and my crew had been with me through thick and thin, fighting this apocalypse like soldiers. We'd survived this long together, and I owed them that same shot at getting out.

But I knew my brother. If he could take more, he would. If he said he only had room for four, that was it. Someone was going to get left behind. It tore at me. How would I pick? Who could I leave in this nightmare while me and Tariq make it back to reality? It didn't sit right with me to think about taking Niyah and Neveah first, like my loyalty to the crew didn't matter. But I wanted them safe, and it was like my mind kept pulling me in that direction, even though I knew I owed everything to my crew.

I didn't know how to make this choice. I couldn't make everyone fit. We couldn't all make it out. And no matter how I sliced it, someone I cared about was going to get left behind. It weighed on me. Each face flashed through my mind, each person who'd fought alongside me, who'd saved my life and stuck with me through the worst of it. But then I'd see Niyah's face, and my gut twisted all over again.

I felt torn, like I had no right to even think about leaving anyone behind, but the clock was ticking, and I had to decide soon.

As I stood in front of the mirror, running the water, I heard the door to my room creak open. My jaw clenched immediately. There was only one person bold enough to come into my room without knocking.

Kecia.

I didn't have to turn around to know it was her. The way she slipped into my space, like she had the right to be there, annoyed the hell out of me.

She slipped into the bathroom behind me, her eyes moving over me in a way that used to get my attention but now just irritated me.

"What's up?" My words were sharper than I intended as I stripped off the last of my clothes.

Her voice was soft and sultry as she stepped closer. "You know what's up."

"I'm good."

"But I'm not."

I turned around, meeting her eyes. "I said no, Kecia."

She crossed her arms as her expression shifted from seductive to angry in seconds. "You've been saying no since Niyah showed up. Ever since she came back, you've been different. You barely look at me, let alone touch me. What's the deal?"

I sighed, frustration causing me to comb my beard with my fingers. "You're getting too attached. I'm not your man, Kecia. You don't own this dick. I don't have to give it to you if I don't want to. If I'm not in the mood, *I'm not in the fucking mood.*"

Kecia's eyes lowered as she studied me. "You weren't in the mood last night either, ironically," she shot back, her voice rising. "Don't play me, Fable."

I didn't owe her an explanation. So, I didn't say anything as I left the bathroom, pulling my clothes back on as I walked out of the bedroom.

As soon as I stepped into the living room, I smirked humorously. Neveah was teaching August some dance, but the nigga had zero rhythm. He was trying, though—his arms flailing off beat, legs all over the place. August was playing the music through a speaker hooked up to an aux cord and his phone. He kept the volume just right to avoid attracting walkers.

Meesha, Tariq, and Paris were on the couch, cracking up like they'd never seen *Friday* before. It was an old DVD I still had lying around, one of the few things keeping us entertained now that Wi-Fi was gone and cable had been a thing of the past even before the apocalypse. Luckily, I still had a DVD player in the attic. Salem, as usual, was posted at the window, peeking through the curtains with his gun tucked in his waistband like he was waiting for something to jump off. Meanwhile, Navon was still knocked out on the couch.

I was worried about my boy. He'd always struggled with depression, but this was the worst I'd ever seen him. It was like he'd given up completely. I kept trying to find a way to pull him out of it, but how do you convince someone not to break when the whole fucking world is falling apart?

As I made my way through the room, I caught Niyah's attention. She was sitting on the loveseat, watching August and Neveah, but when our eyes met, I gave her a little nod, signaling for her to follow me. Without hesitation, she stood up, and we quietly slipped out of the room.

We headed down the hall, through the kitchen, and out the back door. I led her up the metal staircase to the rooftop patio. It had survived the apocalypse, untouched. The string of decorative lights still lined the concrete walls. It almost felt normal up here, like the world hadn't completely gone to shit.

Niyah watched me curiously as I dug behind one of the potted plants, and when I pulled out my stash of pre-rolls, her eyes lit up.

"You're hiding weed up here?" she asked, half-laughing, half-surprised.

I grinned. "Gotta keep it safe. If I left it downstairs, the crew would've smoked it all up by now."

She giggled, shaking her head. "They wouldn't smoke your

stash. I'm sure Navon and Salem went and got their stash when this all went down."

"They did. But this is that good shit."

I sparked it up, took a hit, and handed it to her, but she hesitated.

"I don't know," she said, biting her lip. "If I smoke, it might make me paranoid. The last thing I need is to be even more paranoid at a time like this."

I sat down on the comfortable outdoor sofa. Then I leaned back, giving her a reassuring smile. "Nah, this is the good stuff. Indica. It'll relax you. It won't mess with your head like that."

As she looked at the joint, then back at me, the lights flickered across her face, making her look even more beautiful.

She was still hesitant as she sat next to me. "You sure?"

"Trust me. You're just going to be real relaxed."

After a second, she took it from my hand and brought it to her lips. She exhaled slowly, her eyes meeting mine. "Alright, but if I start seeing things, it's on you."

I laughed softly as she took a hit. "You'll be fine."

Niyah hit the pre-roll a couple more times, her eyes growing a little softer as the indica worked its magic. She leaned back, exhaling slowly, then gave me a side glance that I knew all too well. "So," she started with a slick smirk, "Is this where you bring Kecia?"

I chuckled, shaking my head. I knew what she was doing. She'd already put two and two together when Kecia had been way too obvious about sleeping in my bed.

"Nah," I said, giving her a confident smile. "To be honest, I haven't thought about Kecia since I saw you again."

She took another hit, raising an eyebrow. I noticed her swallow hard, and her body suddenly become stiff. "She was in your bed the other night," she said, ignoring my confession.

I leaned forward, holding her gaze, keeping my tone smooth.

"Yeah, she forced her way into my bed. She likes to do that. And let's be real, who would be mad at sleeping with a warm, willing body during a time like this?" I shrugged.

Her eyes bulged a bit. "Damn, she's just a warm body?"

"I'm being honest. She's aggressive, and a bit thirsty. You know how your friend is-"

"*Meesha's* friend," she corrected. "So, she's not your girlfriend?"

"Nah."

"You just fuck her every night."

"I fuck her every *now* and *then*," I corrected her with a guilty smirk. "But even then, I wanted you. I've always wanted *you*, Niyah, long before you showed up."

That caught her off guard for a second. She looked at me, her eyes narrowing slightly, as if trying to gauge how much truth was behind my words. Then she shook her head with a soft smile.

I leaned over and gently nudged her with my shoulder. "Can I tell you something?"

Her slanted eyes filled with hesitance as she answered slowly, "Yeah. Go 'head."

"I've been into you since high school."

Her jaw dropped slightly, and she blinked at me. "*Really?*"

"I mean it," I insisted. "You were always so fucking dope to me, and smart, beautiful, and funny. I've always loved that shit about you, even back then."

She blushed, but there was disbelief in her eyes. "You're lying."

I shook my head. "Nah, I'm dead serious. Junior year, I had this whole plan to step to you at homecoming, I was going to tell you how I felt. But ..." My voice trailed off, and my mind drifted to a place I hadn't gone in a long time. "My pops died," I finally said, voice low. Those memories clawed at me, but I pushed through them, back to reality. "Everything fell apart after that."

Her face softened, and she seemed to be searching my eyes for something. "I'm sorry, Fable."

I forced a small smile. "It's life. But when I got back to school, Cane was already all hyped up, talking about how he'd snagged you. He was so damn happy."

She looked stunned, almost like she couldn't believe what she was hearing. "So, you just... let him have me?"

"Yeah. He was my boy, but he had no idea how I felt about you. Fair is fair; he got you first. It hurt, but I was a dumb kid. I thought it was better to respect my boy than risk it all for my own feelings. But seeing you with him... that was hard, Niyah. *It's been* hard. Real hard."

She took a shaky breath, eyes glistening. "I had no idea, Fable. I never even thought you noticed me like that."

I let out a humorless laugh. "I noticed everything about you. I could just never do anything about it."

Her gaze softened, and for the first time, I saw something shift between us. Something real.

But then she said, "You're Cane's friend."

"I know," I told her tenderly.

She sighed long and hard. "I miss him."

I nodded. "I know, Niyah. I miss him too. But he's in a better place, while we're stuck in this hell."

She looked down at her hands, at the joint between her fingers burning low. I could see the pain in her eyes, the grief that still sat with her. But I wasn't about to let her drown in it. I leaned in closer, telling her, "And there's nothing wrong with us enjoying one another while missing him."

She looked up at me and our eyes locked. For the first time in a long while, there wasn't just sadness in her gaze. There was something else, something that told me she knew exactly what I was saying.

Niyah was nervous. Her hands were shaky as she passed me

back the pre-roll. She didn't say anything, but I could feel her energy shift. I hit it once more, watching her as she stood and walked over to the railing. Her eyes lifted toward the stars.

I stood up slowly, unsure if I should give her space or move closer. A part of me feared she'd pull away, that she'd run from what I'd confessed. But need kept me going, pulling me toward her. I walked up behind her, my heart pounding a little harder than I'd care to admit.

She didn't run, though. Instead, she leaned back against me, resting her body into my chest. Her warmth and closeness felt so right. I wrapped my arms around her gently, holding her as we stood there under the stars.

"You know," I whispered into her ear, "I've always respected you and Cane's relationship because he was my friend, but deep down, for seventeen years, I've been watching the way you love him, jealous of it, and mad at myself for being jealous at the same time."

She turned slowly in my arms. Looking up at me, her eyes searched mine, like she was trying to figure out if I really meant it. I could feel her walls coming down. She didn't have to say anything. I could feel the pull and need between us.

I leaned down, bringing our faces close, and before she could second-guess it, I kissed her. It was slow at first, hesitant, like we were both unsure of what was happening, but then it deepened. The kiss grew with intensity, and then all the hesitation melted away as if there wasn't shit wrong with what we were doing.

Her hands gripped my arms, and she pulled me closer, pressing my body against hers. The need between us was undeniable, and as we moved together, it was clear that this had been building for a long time. All the unspoken feelings and the moments we ignored came rushing out as we became lost in each other.

I was reluctant to let her go. I never wanted her to leave my arms. But there was so much of her that I wanted to explore. My hands traveled under her shirt as our tongues danced. She let out a small gasp as I cupped and stroked her breasts. My mouth was so pissed at me when I released her tongue. But I gave it something sweeter to taste. I started to kiss her neck as I took her tiny waist into my hands.

My lips moved downwards, kissing tenderly as I knelt before her. My dick dripped with precum at the realization that my tongue was finally exploring her curves. She gasped again as I lifted her shirt, and my mouth found a nipple. I sucked it and then held it gently between my teeth as my tongue played with it. I cupped the other breast with my hand. Each nipple was starting to swell, and her breathing was becoming deeper. Her hands found the back of my head and pulled me into her as my mouth met the other nipple.

Her head fell back as my kisses left her breasts and traveled past her belly button. I slid the leggings down she had been loaned. She kicked her shoes off, and I slid one leg over her foot. She wasn't wearing any panties, so her sweet, brown, pussy lips were glistening in the darkness.

My mouth watered as I spread her legs apart. I started to tongue kiss each of her inner thighs. She moaned softly as my tongue made its way closer and closer to her sex. I could feel the heat coming from it. The scent of her juices was intoxicating me and eventually my tongue slid inside her pussy. My dick got rock hard at the sweet taste of it, at the way it clenched my tongue.

She gasped audibly as I fucked her with the length of my tongue. I reached up her body with both hands as my tongue slid deeply inside her and then made its way to the hood of her clit. I squeezed her breasts, feeling the nipples now pebbling as I started to probe her clit with my tongue, circling it now and then and then sucking on it. She was groaning rhythmically and squirming with pleasure.

Her wetness tasted salty and had the texture of honey.

"*Mmmm*," she moaned, "Oh, Fable..."

I lifted her leg and put it over my shoulder so that I was able to get in deeper, opening my mouth wider and sucking harder, adding pressure with my tongue.

"Fuck, yes," she whimpered. "Shit, Fable. I want you inside of me so bad."

I damn near came hearing her tell me that. I pulled away and pushed my shorts down. My dick was painfully hard. I'd never wanted someone so bad in my life.

I spun her around so that her back was facing me. I pulled her to me and began to kiss the back of her neck deeply. My hands intently explored the curves I'd waited years to be up close and personal with.

She arched her back and reached back for my dick. Then she grasped it gently and guided me inside her. It felt so warm, wet, and tight. Slowly, I pushed myself further in before withdrawing, then pushing inside her again. She lifted one leg onto the railing as my thrust started to increase.

We were moving in rhythm now, slowly at first but gradually picking up speed. She looked back at me with shock and need dancing in those beautiful eyes. She was biting her bottom lip, gasping with each thrust.

I was giving her all this dick. Each and every inch of it.

My own hisses and groans were becoming more animalistic. When I realized how we so easily moved together like a smooth, choreographed dance, I knew this pussy was mine.

Her gasps were louder now. Little cries escaped as she threw that ass back on me. She reached back, digging her nails into my thighs.

I could feel her body tensing as she cried out, "Yes! Fuck me! Fuck... me! Shit!"

I could feel my balls tightening, I was close to the edge. I gripped her shoulders hard.

"I-I'm cumming!!' she breathed.

Her pussy gripped me. Her nails dug into my thigh as she came. It put me over the edge. My dick spasmed, my whole body tensed up, and I released a throaty groan at the same time as she drenched my dick.

CHAPTER 10

KECIA

I stormed through the house, looking for Fable. He wasn't anywhere to be found, and neither was Niyah. My mind was racing, full of anger and jealousy. I couldn't believe he'd rejected me like that and then just disappeared with this bitch. After everything we'd been through, after all the nights we spent together, how could he just toss me aside like I didn't matter?

We weren't in a relationship, but I felt like he was mine. We'd been through this hell together for over a month. We survived side by side, leaning on each other when everything else fell apart. And now he was running off with her.

It felt like a slap in the face, like he was using me this whole time, and I was too stupid to even see it.

I kept searching, my anger rising with every empty room. But I tried to look discreet on the outside so that no one in the house knew what I was doing.

Where the hell are they?

My thoughts were spiraling, each one worse than the last.

He must really like her.

The way he looked at her, the way he spoke to her, was different. He had never looked at me like that.

As I headed toward the back porch, my heart pounded with rage and hurt. When I opened the door, I was hit with the silence of the night, broken only by the distant growls of the undead and the crunching of their footsteps in the alley. I stood there for a moment, fuming, my mind racing.

Where could they be?

And then, the faint smell of weed drifted through the air. I knew immediately that Fable was on the rooftop. My blood boiled even more, because I knew exactly who he was up there with.

I crept up the stairs toward the roof on bare feet. My footsteps were quiet as I tried not to make a sound. My heart was racing, fueled by anger and jealousy, but I didn't want them to know I was coming.

And just as the rooftop came into view, I could see them... fucking.

I couldn't look away. The way he slowly took his time, filling her up, looking into her eyes. He had never fucked me so gently.

I felt like someone had punched me in the gut. My throat tightened with a painful blend of jealousy and heartbreak. I couldn't look for more than a second before pulling back, feeling like I might break if I stayed any longer.

I stepped back and crept back down the stairs as I fought to keep myself together. The ache in my heart was almost too much to bear. Clearly, Fable didn't give an ounce of a fuck about me. He had chosen to fuck her up there, out in the open, in plain sight, for anyone to see, including me.

Without making a sound, I tiptoed back down the stairs, slipping quietly into the house. Inside, I could still hear the conversation and laughter from the others in the living room, but I felt distant from it all. The anger was consuming me, burning hotter than ever, but now there was something else, a deep, aching hate that I needed to feed.

NIYAH

Fable had gone from hitting me from the back on the railing, to on all fours with my knees buried in the faux grass.

That dick was exceptional. It had taken me out of this hell for a little while. The excitement and the exhilaration of finally being with him was the perfect escape that I had needed.

Now, we were lying on the rooftop with his arms wrapped around me. The faux grass beneath us was cool, and I could still feel the aftershocks of the two hours he'd spent in my pussy. My heart was still racing. My skin was still warm from the way he touched me.

But then guilt crept in. Cane's face flashed in my mind over and over again. For a second, I felt disloyal, like I was betraying his memory. Fable was Cane's boy. I felt like I had committed the ultimate betrayal. But then Fable kissed me softly on the forehead, and with that simple touch, the guilt faded. It felt like Cane was telling me it was okay, that he wanted me to feel this again, with someone who cared for me, with someone *he knew* could protect me in this nightmare of a world. Every time Fable pushed a strand of hair out of my face, that reassured me. He made me feel like what we had just done wasn't wrong at all.

We lay there, looking up at the stars, our breaths finally starting to slow. I turned my head, resting it against his chest, feeling his heartbeat beneath my cheek. It was peaceful in a way I hadn't felt in so long.

Suddenly, a warm gust of wind massaged my cheek, smelling of summer. I closed my eyes, reminiscing. "Man, can you imagine what we'd be doing right now if this was a normal summer night?"

Fable chuckled, making his chest rumble under my head. "Probably at one of those festivals in Hyde Park or on a patio at one of the bars we always be at."

"Ooo, I loved the rooftop at Whiskey Business," I swooned longingly. "It was so cute. It's crazy to think about how that was just... life."

Fable slightly groaned. "We took that shit for granted."

I pouted while shaking my head and saying, "I know. Man, I miss that shit so much. It's crazy that life is going on as normal everywhere else in the world while we're stuck here, locked in, fighting for our lives. We're living in this bubble of hell while everything else keeps moving forward. I keep thinking about all the wars I barely paid attention to because they were happening on the other side of the world. Like the people in Palestine... I mean, they were literally stuck in hell on earth, dying by the hundreds. Families were trying to survive without power, without water, and kids were dying. And I was just hanging out and laughing, like that wasn't happening, like people weren't in need, weren't fighting to survive." I exhaled, as the gravity of it all hit me differently now. "And now, it's happening to us. We're trapped. We don't know if we're gonna make it out alive. We don't know if there will be a future for us, for my daughter. The government is just standing by not helping us. It's crazy how you don't get it until it's right in your face, you know?"

Fable nodded with thoughtful eyes as he looked up at the sky.

We weren't so different from any other country at war. We were surrounded by death and fighting for survival. But it was different when it was your own reality, when it wasn't just something you saw on the news or in your social media feed.

Fable stared blankly up into the sky, sighing. "It's crazy to think that just a few states away, motherfuckers are partying right now, enjoying the summer, on yachts and shit, like we aren't stuck in this zone fighting for our lives."

I sighed long and hard, hating the dread that our conversation had suddenly turned into. So, I changed the subject. "Remember Pier 31 on Thursdays? All the music, all those people dancing and vibing... I used to love that shit."

As soon as I mentioned Pier 31, I felt him tense beneath me. Suddenly, his body noticeably stiffened.

Something was off.

I lifted my head, turning to look at him. "What's wrong?" I asked, searching his face.

He hesitated for a second, like he wasn't sure if he should tell me. But then he sighed, running a hand over his beautiful chocolate face before he spoke. "My brother, Onyx, is at the pier."

I sat up a little. My eyebrows furrowed because I could tell by the look in his eyes that there was something more to this.

"Okay," I pressed. "And? He's in the Navy, right? So, he must be there helping with the military at the border. What's the big deal?"

He glanced away for a moment, then turned back to me. "You can't tell anyone. Not yet, not until I figure out what to do."

I slowly nodded as I grew nervous in result of how serious he suddenly got. "I won't say anything. I promise."

He blew a heavy breath, as if he were readying himself. Then he locked eyes with me. "Tariq made it to the safe zone."

My eyes bulged. "Oh my God, did he? How?"

"Onyx has been bringing supplies to the soldiers on the border on his boat."

"He and his boy at the border figured out a way to get people out. They've already tried it, and it worked. They got people out of the unsafe zone, Niyah." Fable sat up on his elbows, looking down on me with eyes that were wide with hope and excitement. "His boy at the border, Sam, agreed to let me and Tariq through. He found this secret tunnel we can get through that leads to the pier so that we can sneak on the boat. He sent Tariq back into the city to come find me so that Tariq can get me to the pier."

I blinked, processing his words. It felt like the world shifted beneath me. "Wait... are you serious?" My voice was barely a whisper. "People are getting out?"

Fable nodded. "Yeah. Well, Onyx got Sam's family out, and he has just one more opportunity to get me and Tariq out before his assignment changes. But there's only so much room on the boat. There is only room for one more person. So, I can't take everyone."

"Fable...Oh my God." I smiled. "You have a chance to get the fuck out of here."

"I know," he groaned. "But it's not that simple. I've got the crew, Niyah. I can't leave them behind, but I can't take everyone either. There's too many of us."

I felt my heart sink a little as the realization of that crashed down on me. *Fable* had a chance to get out, not *us* or *me*.

"Who... who would you take?" I asked quietly, not sure if I wanted to know the answer.

He looked away as his jaw tightened. "That's the problem. I

don't know. I want to take you and Neveah, even though there isn't room for both of you."

I blushed as a slow smile reached my ears. His eyes lit up as they met mine for a second before he continued.

"But my boys and my crew..." He started as he looked back up into the stars. "They've been with me through all of this. I owe them that. But I can't take everyone, and that's killing me."

I didn't know what to say. I could see how much it was tearing him apart, trying to figure out who to save and who to leave behind. And suddenly, the hope I had felt moments ago didn't seem so clear anymore.

I leaned into him again, resting my head on his chest. "You'll figure it out," I whispered, even though I didn't know how we would.

PARIS

The loud banging woke me up out of my sleep. At first, I thought it was just one of those random sounds you hear in the night now—maybe a walker stumbling around outside. But this was different. This was loud and rowdy and was accompanied by taunting voices. Whoever it was wasn't here to sneak in. They *wanted* us to know they were coming.

I sat up quickly, my heart racing as I glanced around the living room. Fable, who had slept out here with us for the first time, was already on his feet, looking alert. Navon, Tariq, August, and Salem were standing up in the dimly lit living room, now wide awake. Meesha jolted out of her sleep. None of us had deep sleep anymore since we were constantly on high alert.

Kecia stumbled out of Fable's bedroom, rubbing her eyes, clearly not expecting this kind of wake-up call.

Everyone exchanged looks. There was an awkward tension in the air between Kecia and Fable, especially since this was the first time he'd slept away from her, leaving her alone in his bed. But nobody had time to dwell on it. There was something worse going on outside.

The noise grew louder, and I could feel the fear rising in my chest. This wasn't the undead—it was people. I turned toward the window, hearing the banging get even more violent. Whoever was out there was trying to break in.

"Shit," Salem muttered, rubbing the back of his neck as he stood at the window, peeking through the curtains. "One of them must have gotten over the gate and let the rest of them in. The gate is wide open. They're gonna attract walkers if they keep this up."

"We secured the house pretty good, right?" Meesha asked, her voice shaking a little as she stood up beside me.

"We did," Fable said, though his expression was tense. "But that doesn't mean they can't get in if they try hard enough."

Tariq, who had been quietly listening, stepped forward. "It's Diesel's crew. I recognize their voices. They're trying to break in."

I felt a chill run through me. Tariq had told all of us how Diesel's crew were ruthless scavengers who took what they wanted, no matter the cost. And now they were at our door.

"How many of them are out there?" Fable asked Salem.

"'Bout ten."

"Fuck," August groaned.

"We can't let them get inside," Salem told us.

"Right," Fable agreed. "If they break through, we're fucked and they're stupid asses are going to let all kinds of walkers in this motherfucka. We need to handle this outside in order to keep the entrances secure and the house safe."

Neveah sat up sleepily. Her eyes were wide with fear as she looked around from person to person. When her eyes fell on me, I gave her a quick, reassuring nod, but inside, I felt the same terror she did.

This was bad.

"They're making too much noise," Fable said as he began to

pace. "If we start shooting, we'll attract more walkers. We have to take them down quietly."

"Weapons?" August's voice was steady, but I could tell he was on edge too.

Fable nodded. "Knives, bats—anything that doesn't make noise. We take them out before they get inside."

The girls, including myself, were told to stay inside. My stomach knotted with anxiety as I watched Salem, Navon, Tariq, August and Fable start gearing up. Salem grabbed a knife. His face was set with that cold, calculated look I'd been seeing more and more lately. Fable's expression wasn't much different. They were focused, ready for battle.

Salem glanced at Fable. "We gotta fuck these niggas up quick and keep them away from the doors."

Fable nodded, turning to the girls. "Stay inside. Stay quiet. We'll handle this."

I swallowed hard, glancing at Neveah, who was now sitting next to me, her small frame shaking with fear. I wanted to tell her it would be okay, but the truth was, I wasn't sure. Tariq had scared the shit out of all of us with his stories about how deadly and ruthless Diesel's crew was.

"Be careful," I whispered, my eyes locking with Salem's as he turned to leave.

I wished I could have that moment with Salem, the kind where I'd hold his face in my hands, kiss him hard, and tell him I loved him. I wanted to beg him to be careful, to promise he'd come back alive. I wanted him to look at me with the same urgency I felt inside, just once, before he walked out that door. But instead, he stood there cold, his eyes distant, giving me nothing. Just a nod, like always, as if this was just another fight, and I was just another woman waiting on the other side of a war he couldn't explain.

Then he disappeared out of the front door with the others.

FABLE

We marched towards the front door like we were headed into battle. Me, August, Salem, Navon, and Tariq all moved like soldiers, each of us knowing what was about to go down. This wasn't the first time we'd faced chaos. But it was the first time it was coming from this many people.

I glanced over at Navon, and his eyes were completely lifeless.

I could hear the banging from outside getting louder. Diesel's crew had scaled the fence and were trying to get through the front door.

The taunting voices of Diesel's crew grew more aggressive. They wanted in. They didn't care about who we were or what we had—they just wanted to take it. My blood was boiling, but I kept my calm because we had to be smart if we were going to take these niggas down.

I turned to the crew. "Keep them away from the door. Do whatever it takes. If they get inside, it's over."

Salem was at the door with his hand on the knob. He turned to us, his eyes scanning each of us, making sure we were ready. I could see that cold look in his eyes—the one that said he was actually eager to handle whatever was waiting on the other side.

"Y'all good?" Salem pressed.

"We good," I answered, nodding. Navon didn't say a word. He just stared ahead without an ounce of emotion in his eyes. The rest of the crew murmured in agreement, tightening their grips on their weapons.

With a deep breath, Salem turned the knob, and the door swung open.

We were met with instant chaos. Diesel's crew came at us hard, swinging bats and knives. The sound of the first blow was sickening, a bat smashing into the side of the doorframe. Navon slammed the door shut, locking it to keep them out as long as possible, as we rushed forward.

A nigga with wild eyes came at me, swinging a knife straight for my throat. I dodged just in time, grabbing his wrist and twisting it until I heard a snap. He howled in pain. I didn't give him any time to recover. I brought my elbow down hard on his face, feeling the crunch of his nose breaking under the blow. Blood splattered, and he dropped to the ground, clutching his face.

To my left, I saw August locked in with two guys, one of them swinging a bat at his legs while the other tried to stab him. August ducked the bat and kicked the guy in the chest, sending him flying back into the fence. But the guy with the knife was fast, lunging at August with wild fury. I could see it coming, but August was quicker. He grabbed the guy's arm, twisting the knife out of his hand and slamming him headfirst into the ground.

Navon was lost in a wild rage, swinging that hammer like a man possessed. He charged at anyone within reach, not even hesitating to put himself in danger. He wasn't just fighting—he was throwing himself into the chaos, welcoming death.

"Navon!" I yelled, trying to get him to stop, but he acted like he didn't hear me. Blood splattered on his face, but he didn't blink; he kept swinging, taking hit after hit, with no fear in his eyes. It was like he wanted this to be the end. I could see it clear as day—he wasn't just reckless; he was done.

Just then, another dude rushed at me with a bat, aiming for my ribs. It clipped my side, sending a jolt of pain through me, but I ignored it and tackled him to the ground. He hit the dirt hard, and I slammed my fist into his jaw, knocking that motherfucker out cold.

Salem was a different beast. I glanced over, and he was handling two of Diesel's men at once. His movements were quick, brutal, and efficient. One guy came at him with a knife, but Salem disarmed him in seconds, flipping the blade and driving it into the guy's side. He let out a choked cry before falling to the ground. Another guy tried to come up from behind, but Salem didn't even flinch. He turned, grabbed the man by the neck, and slammed his head into the brick wall of the house, leaving a trail of blood.

It was all violence and adrenaline with no room for hesitation. These weren't men anymore; they were animals, fighting tooth and nail for what they wanted. We had no choice but to ensure that we completely dismantled them.

Tariq was holding his own, dodging a bat and swinging his own knife, catching one of the guys in the shoulder. The man stumbled, clutching the wound as Tariq knocked the wind out of him by slamming a bat into his chest, sending him sprawling backward.

Every swing, every punch, every crunch of bone was all survival. We were moving as one unit, taking them down, one after another, refusing to let them near the door.

I saw another nigga come charging at Salem with a crowbar, but before I could even yell a warning, Salem sidestepped him and drove a knife deep into his gut. The man let out a guttural scream, his body shaking as he fell to his knees, blood pouring from the wound.

"Finish it!" Salem yelled, his voice echoing through the yard. He turned to me, his eyes wild with adrenaline, blood splattered on his face. "Kill all these motherfuckers!"

The violence was brutal, but it was necessary. This was the world we lived in now. There was no room for mercy, no room for hesitation. We fought because we had to. Because if we didn't, they would take everything from us.

I nodded, wiping the sweat and blood from my brow as I looked around. The fight wasn't over, but we were winning. One by one, Diesel's crew was falling.

CHAPTER 11

NEVEAH

We were all glued to the window, watching the guys outside fighting like it was an action movie. Except it wasn't a movie. This was real life, and I couldn't believe what I was seeing. Meesha was biting her lip, Paris kept gasping every time one of the guys threw a punch, and Kecia was just standing there, holding her breath like I was. I wasn't sure what was scarier—the scavengers or the fact that we could lose this fight and we could all die.

Then, out of nowhere, I heard banging. Like someone was trying to break in through the back. My heart practically stopped. I tapped my mom with shaking fingers as I pointed toward the back door.

She turned her head, eyes wide, and the next thing I knew, Paris, Meesha, Kecia, and my mom were grabbing weapons. No hesitation, no second thoughts. It was like they'd flipped a switch. I tried to calm my breathing, but it wasn't working. I discreetly grabbed a knife and shoved it under my shirt, following them quietly.

When we got to the back door, it was shaking—like *really* shaking. Whoever was on the other side wasn't playing.

Paris whispered, "We can't let them get in here." And everyone just nodded like they were all on the same page.

Meesha whispered, "Y'all ready?"

When everyone agreed, she threw the door open.

Three men stood on the porch, but they weren't ready for us. My mom, Kecia, Meesha, and Paris went at them, swinging bats and knives, and I just stood there for a second, frozen. My heart was racing so fast I thought it would burst. They were handling it, though, and part of me was in awe.

Meesha was the first to swing. Her bat connected with one of the guys' shoulders, but he barely flinched. He was huge, like he could've been a linebacker or something. With one sweep of his arm, he sent Meesha stumbling back, almost knocking her off the porch. Kecia was fast, ducking and weaving like she'd been in plenty fights with men before, but the guy she was up against caught her by the wrist and yanked her off her feet like she didn't weigh anything. Paris screamed and lunged at him with a knife, but he grabbed her by the hair, pulling her so hard I thought he'd rip her scalp off. The men tossed them around like rag dolls, but somehow, my mom and her friends kept getting back up, refusing to let these men get in the house.

I hadn't moved yet. I just watched it all go down like I was stuck in some kind of trance. The fight was chaotic—grunts, metal clanging, wood smashing, and the sound of bodies hitting the porch. I stood there, frozen. I couldn't decide whether to jump in or stay out of it. No one even realized I was there.

Paris and my mom double-team one of the men. They were moving fast, my mom dodging his punches while Paris came at him from the side. And then Paris managed to get close enough and, with a quick, desperate movement, she stabbed him right in the heart. I saw his face twist in pain as he stumbled back, his eyes wide with shock. He collapsed to the ground, and I just stood there, my breath catching in my throat.

But then I saw the gate. The scavengers had broken through, leaving this huge hole in the fence. And that's when one of the other guys realized that I was standing there. He locked eyes with mine. Before I could even blink, he rushed at me, full speed.

My heart shot into my throat as he tackled me. My mom and her friends were too busy fighting off the other two guys to even notice. I fumbled for my knife, my hands shaking like crazy, but he was too fast. He snatched it from me like it was nothing. I panicked. My mind went blank for a split second before I remembered to kick him. I kicked him in the dick, hard. He groaned, rolling over on his back, and I scrambled to my feet.

But he lunged at me again. I didn't have time to think. I took off running, my feet flying down the porch steps, and he was right behind me. I headed straight for the hole in the fence, praying I could get through before he caught me.

I slipped through, my breath coming out in short, sharp bursts. Hearing one of his men grunt out in pain, he turned and ran back to the porch. For a split second, I felt relief. But then, I saw them.

Walkers. There was a sea of them, at least twenty, running straight toward me.

I screamed, but with all the chaos going on, I knew no one could hear me. My feet moved before my brain could catch up, and I ran as fast as I could, away from the house and down the alley.

FABLE

The fight in the front yard was almost over. I watched as Tariq took down the last guy. His blade sank into the man's side, sending him slumping to the ground. Tariq turned his back for just a second, maybe to catch his breath or check on the rest of us, but that second was all it took. The guy leaped up like he had never been hurt, and out of nowhere, he slashed Tariq with what looked like a damn sword.

I saw the blood before I processed what was happening. It poured from Tariq's abdomen, and he collapsed, hitting the dirt with a sickening thud. For a second, none of us moved. We just froze, staring at the blood spilling from him, unable to believe it. Salem, though, didn't hesitate. He lunged at the man like a wild animal, hammering him in the head over and over. His fists were covered in blood until the guy's skull caved in, and his brain spilled out onto the ground.

We all stood there, staring at Tariq's lifeless body. I felt my stomach twist, the reality of what just happened slamming into me.

But Salem's voice cut through the shock like a blade. "Snap out of it. Get the bodies out of the yard before we attract every fucking walker in the city."

We moved like machines, tossing the bodies over the fence, each thud making my skin crawl.

Watching Tariq die felt like a blow to the chest that I never saw coming. He'd come back for me without hesitation, risking everything to get me out of this hell. And now he was gone because of it. Guilt gnawed at me, knowing he could've been safe, but instead, he chose to come back for me. That choice cost him his life. I wanted to honor him in the only way I could. I wanted to be the one to handle his body. It felt like the least I could do for a man who'd given up everything. August helped me lift Tariq's body. We pushed him over the fence, and I prayed that wherever he was now, it was better than this nightmare we were stuck in.

When we finished, I could feel the grief hanging in the air, but there wasn't any time to mourn. We walked back into the house. As we started to board up the front door, we could hear Niyah freaking out a few feet away from the foyer.

Salem looked back at me and nodded his head toward the living room.

I left the guys to secure the house and went in the living room. My eyes bulged when I saw Paris straining to hold Niyah in a bear hug.

"Let me go!" Niyah shouted.

"What the fuck is going on?" I barked.

Niyah was freaking out. Her voice was shaking as she kept saying the same thing over and over. "I can't find Neveah! I can't find my daughter!"

Kecia, Meesha, and Paris were talking over each other to me about the guys who tried to break in from the back. "There were three guys at the back door. We killed them and patched up the hole in the fence they made." Meesha's voice was trembling as she explained, "But Neveah's gone."

Niyah's eyes were wild and panicked. "I'm going to find her," she insisted. "I'm not staying here while my baby's out there."

"You can let her go, Paris. She isn't going anywhere," I demanded.

"Bullshit!" Niyah snapped as she wiggled out of Paris' loosening grasp. "I'm getting the fuck up outta here!"

"We can't just run out there. It's not safe," Salem said, stepping up beside me. "It's walkers everywhere. We wait until it clears up a bit, and then we'll go find her."

Niyah wasn't having that shit, though. She shook her head with her hands clenched into fists. "*You* wait, but I'm going. I don't give a fuck what's out there."

I hesitated, torn between keeping everyone safe and following her into whatever bullshit waited outside of the fence. We had been able to kill Diesel's crew. But the sounds had attracted so many of the undead. They were everywhere, feasting on the bodies we'd thrown over the fence.

Niyah saw that hesitation in me, and I saw the hurt flash across her face.

"I don't need you to choose, Fable," she said quietly with a voice full of pain.

As Niyah spun around, heading for the back door, Paris tried to stop her. Her voice was soft and pleading. "Niyah, please, just wait—"

But Niyah wasn't having it. Her whole body was tense, like a spring ready to snap.

"Move!" she shouted. "If y'all don't let me go find my daughter, I swear to God, I'll let those walkers in while you're all sleeping!"

The room went dead silent. No one knew what to say. I could see the tears welling up in her eyes, and when she spoke again, her voice cracked. "None of you understand. You don't have kids. You have no idea what this is like."

She stormed past them. I wanted to follow her, to say something, but none of us moved. We just watched her walk away.

NIYAH

As I wiped the tears from my eyes, my hands shook while I removed the barriers from Fable's back door. Each piece I moved felt like a betrayal. The hushed whispers from the crew behind me in the living room hit my ears, but I didn't care. They weren't coming with me to find my baby, and that hurt more than anything. I understood why. No one was going to risk their lives for a child that wasn't theirs. But Fable... after the time we spent together on that rooftop, after all the words he'd said to me... he was letting me go out there alone. I felt used, like his words were just a way to get me into bed. That stung deep, cutting through my anger and fear.

The growls of the undead, just on the other side of the fence, filled the air. They were surrounding the house now. They were hungry and restless. But none of that mattered. My baby was out there, and I had to get to her. I didn't care about the walkers. I didn't care about the high possibility of getting killed. I was her mother, and now I understood what that instinct really meant.

I ran through the backyard, my feet pounding against the

dirt. I ran around the dead bodies of Diesel's crew that we had pushed down the porch steps.

When I reached the fence, it looked like a mountain in front of me, but I had no choice. I jumped, grabbed the edge, and tried to pull myself up. My muscles screamed in protest as I struggled. My feet slipped against the wood. I fell back, hitting the ground hard. But I scrambled to my feet and tried again, gritting my teeth, forcing my body up with everything I had. This time, I made it to the top. My arms were burning, and my legs were shaking.

When I looked over the edge, my heart stopped. Most of the walkers were gathered near Fable's house, crowding the vacant lot, their dead eyes staring blankly as they moved slowly, their jaws snapping. Some had ventured into the alley, hunting for more blood. My stomach turned, but I had to make sure none of them were Neveah. I scanned their faces, biting down the urge to cry out, to weep.

I spotted a bush on the other side of the fence and knew that was my best chance to stay quiet. With one deep breath, I leaped down, landing in the bush, the twigs and leaves silencing my fall. Thankfully, I had been so quiet that the undead didn't notice.

Taking a deep breath, I ran. My legs felt like they were moving on their own, faster than I'd ever run in my life.

"Neveah!" My voice was low but desperate as I looked between every house, under every abandoned car, and between the dumpster. "Neveah!"

I heard the footsteps before I saw anything. They were loud and fast. My heart leapt into my throat, but I didn't even hesitate. I drew my gun, the one I never kept on safety anymore. In this world, I had to be ready for anything. I spun around, my finger already on the trigger, ready to fire. I figured it was walkers, or worse, a *group* of them closing in on me. But when I turned, it wasn't the undead.

It was Fable, sprinting toward me desperately. And behind him were walkers running after him. I dropped to a squat, like Cane had taught me a thousand times before, aimed, and fired. The shots rang out loud in the alley, and Fable ducked as he ran toward me, moving fast, but trusting I wouldn't miss.

He trusted me.

Two of the walkers fell as I hit them in the head, but there were still three more. One of them looked like she had once been such a sweet old lady, cooking soul food meals on Sunday evenings. Her long hair was grey, and she was still wearing a moo-moo. The other's pants were sagging so low that it could hardly keep up.

When he reached me, Fable didn't even stop. He grabbed my arm, yanking me to my feet.

"C'mon, baby!" he yelled with adrenaline.

We took off running, my legs burning as I struggled to keep up. Behind us, the growls of the undead were deafening. Their disgusting smell filled my nose, making my stomach churn. I could hear their teeth snapping, as they got closer. They were ready to devour us.

We cut through gangways. Our feet pounded against the pavement, but no matter how fast we ran, the walkers were right behind us.

I was terrified. Each step felt like I was moving further away from Neveah, like I was losing her all over again.

Fable led us toward the neighborhood high school. The fence surrounding the football field was just ahead. He helped me over the waist-high fence, and I scrambled to the other side, but when I turned back, my heart stopped.

One of the undead had grabbed Fable's leg while another

grabbed his arm. He struggled as his face twisted in pain. But he yelled, "Run, Niyah! Go! Keep going!"

"No, Fable!" I cried out.

I couldn't leave him like this. I reached into my pocket. My hands were shaking as I pulled out my knife. Leaning over the fence, I stabbed at the walkers, screaming out in pure frustration and anger. Each strike was fueled by my desperation to save him, to not lose him too. The knife sunk into one of the walker's necks, but the others kept coming, their relentless hunger driving them forward.

I could barely keep my grip steady as I plunged the knife into the first walker's neck again. The blade sliced through its decayed flesh with a sickening squelch. Its grip on Fable's leg loosened just enough for him to kick it off, sending the creature stumbling backward. But the second one was still there, clawing at his arm. Its teeth snapped dangerously close to Fable's skin. I lunged forward, jamming the knife into the side of its skull, feeling the vibration up my arm as bone cracked beneath the force.

The thing went limp instantly, collapsing onto the ground with a wet thud, but my whole body was still shaking. Fable, now free, scrambled over the fence, finally landing on the other side. We were both gasping for air, as we tried to catch our breath. I felt like I couldn't get enough air. Each breath was ragged and sharp in my chest.

But there wasn't time to rest. Just as we started to breathe again, the third walker, crazed and relentless, threw itself over the fence, landing awkwardly but still driven by that warped hunger. Its rasping growl cut through the air as it clawed its way toward us, its eyes locked on Fable and me. We didn't hesitate. We took off running. My legs burned as we sprinted toward the school.

The sound of the walker's snarls followed us, but we didn't look back.

CHAPTER 12

AUGUST

"Fable's dumb as hell for chasing after Niyah like that. We should've never taken in a disobedient teenager to begin with." Kecia fussed as she folded her arms, pacing angrily through the living room.

"We should've gone with him," I said, glancing at Salem. "That was the plan—to stick together."

Salem shook his head firmly. "With all those walkers out there? Fuck no. It was too dangerous. We can't all run off every time someone gets lost out there."

Kecia chimed back in, "Right? Y'all were supposed to get yourselves killed because that girl don't wanna listen? Hell no. Fable wants to chase after some pussy, that's on him."

Salem and I froze. Meesha's eyes bucked while Salem looked confused, furrowing his brows. "Wait, they fucking? I thought he was fucking *you*." He'd said it so casually that some failed not to laugh. I had to bite my lip to keep from losing it, especially with the way Kecia glared at him like he'd crossed some line.

"Shut the fuck up, Salem," Kecia gritted.

Salem shrugged, telling her, "It's a fair question."

Kecia threw a tantrum, growling with frustration. "Yeah, he *was* fucking me. But we're done. If he wants Niyah, he can have her."

"I can't even think about dick at a time like this," Meesha mumbled while nervously playing with her hair that had sweated out into a fro.

"So, this nigga getting *all* the pussy?" I wondered out loud. "That's some bullshit. *Man*, I miss pussy..."

Everyone chuckled, except Paris. She was distant. Her eyes were glazed over like she wasn't even here.

"Gon' out there and get you one of those walkers then, nigga," Salem told me with a deep laugh.

Suddenly, Paris snapped. "Would y'all shut the fuck up?! You sound so fucking heartless! You're cracking jokes when Tariq is dead! Y'all don't even care!"

"I'm sorry, P," I said. "It's my fucked up way of dealing with this bullshit."

But Salem waved her off. "That nigga wasn't my boy. August stop apologizing. You played ball with that nigga a few times damn near twenty years ago."

"Damn, Salem," Meesha replied, cringing.

"The nigga was cool and everything, but let's not act like he was our bestie," Salem argued, which only frustrated Paris more.

She jumped to her feet. Her face was flushed as tears spilled down her cheeks. "Y'all in here laughing and joking about pussy like it's not some real scary shit happening on the other side of these walls! Fable and Niyah could be out there getting killed!"

As she stormed out, the atmosphere in the room finally changed as we took in the words she'd spewed at us.

Meesha threw a sharp look at Salem, narrowing her eyes and flicking her hand toward the hallway, signaling him to go after her. He sighed, moving slower than he should've, like he needed to be convinced to comfort his girl. I watched him get up, feeling that familiar frustration creep in. If Paris was mine, I wouldn't need a fucking signal. I wouldn't have to be told to go support her. Salem just didn't see what he had, and that was becoming clearer every day.

"I should've been the one," Navon suddenly muttered, as if he wasn't talking to anyone but himself. "It should have been me, not Tariq... I don't wanna be here anymore."

Meesha and Kecia glanced at each other, fear creeping into their faces.

Navon's voice grew louder, his pain breaking through in raw, angry shouts. "I don't even know why I'm here! Why the hell am I still here?!"

Nobody moved. It was like we were all watching a bomb about to go off.

"Why couldn't it have been me?!"

Meesha's face paled as she slowly turned to him. "Don't talk like that, Navon," she said softly. "We need you here. You're strong. You can't give up now."

"Strong?" he snapped. "What's strong about living through this bullshit?" His eyes were wild, brimming with tears, but also with a kind of rage that felt dangerous. He clenched his fists like he was ready to hit something, anything.

"Navon, you can't think like that," Kecia tried to intervene. "We've all lost someone. But you have to keep going. We need you—"

"Don't give me that 'we need you' bullshit!" he yelled, standing up suddenly. "I don't need any of this! I'm tired. You hear me? Tired!" He punched the wall, leaving a small dent, but the sound of his hand hitting the wall was drowned out by the sound of his roar.

I stepped forward, moving slowly. "Navon, man... listen to me," I said cautiously. "We all hurtin'. We all wish things were different. But this isn't how it ends for you."

He looked up at me then, tears finally spilling over, his breathing ragged. He didn't even try to wipe them away. "You don't know that. You don't know how this shit will end for any of us, man. And I don't know how much more I got left, August," he whispered, sounding like he was admitting defeat for the first time. "I can't keep doing this. I can't."

I slowly stepped toward him, hands up, trying not to startle him.

"Hey, hey, man, it's alright," I said, keeping my tone steady. I reached for a half-empty bottle of whiskey on the coffee table and handed it to him. "Here, take this. Have a drink and try to relax."

Navon's hands shook as he grabbed the bottle, and he took a long gulp. I stayed close as he drank deeply, his rage giving way to exhaustion. Kecia and Meesha watched him cautiously. Their wide-eyed expressions said they were too scared to move or say anything.

I felt real bad for my boy. I didn't know what else to do, though. Hell, half the time I didn't even know how to keep my own damn self together. We were all one step away from snapping in this mess but seeing him this low hit different.

I kept my hand on his shoulder, feeling the tremble under my palm. I tried to find words, anything to make him believe it was worth holding on for just a little longer. But truth be told, I wasn't sure if I believed it myself. This world had stripped us of almost everything we knew, and what was left felt like scraps.

SALEM

I had followed Paris down the hallway. She broke down right
there in the kitchen, with her back against the counter, shoulders shaking as the tears started to fall. I stopped at the doorway,
my body tense, not really knowing how to deal with this. Paris
had been so fragile since this apocalypse started, but seeing
Tariq's lifeless body had pushed her over the edge.

But before I could say anything, Navon started to snap in the
living room. I stood there listening, making sure August had it
under control.

Soon, it sounded like Navon had quieted again, so I gave my
attention back to Paris.

I stepped forward, trying to figure out what to say. She
looked up at me, her eyes red and swollen, searching for something—anything—from me. But I was never good with this type
of thing. Vulnerability made me... uncomfortable.

I leaned down, wrapping my arms around her, but I knew
they were stiff. I could feel it in the way my arms barely hugged
her. She was trembling, and all I could say was, "It's gonna be

okay, Paris. I got you. I'm not going to let anything happen to you."

But the words felt fake, like I was reading off a script. She buried her face in my chest, but I could feel the way she stiffened too, sensing the disconnect between us. She wanted something I couldn't give, not the way she needed it. And I hated that.

And as soon as the words left my mouth, she exploded. "Something already is happening to me, Salem! Don't you get that?! Whatever you think you're protecting me from, it's already succeeded! *I'm in hell*. Everyday! I'm living it. Every day, fighting the undead, scared out of my mind."

I just stood there, taking it all in as she continued, her words hitting me harder than anything else in this damn apocalypse had.

"You think because you're here, it's enough? Yeah, you're here, physically. But I still feel alone, Salem! I sleep next to you every night, and I'm still alone in this hell, in this *fear*. You're not protecting me from any of the pain or hurt because I'm feeling it. I'm living it."

Her words cut deep, and for the first time, I didn't have a response. I knew she was right, but I didn't know how to fix it.

"You don't get it, Salem," her voice cracked. "Our friends keep dying. We could've *all* just died out there. And you're acting like it's nothing."

I sighed, stepping back, running a hand over my face. "I'm not acting like it's nothing, Paris. But we ain't got time to break down over every loss. That's just how it is. We survive, or we don't. Simple."

Her eyes narrowed with disbelief. "Simple? Is that really all this is to you?" Her eyes searched mine, but I didn't know what she was hoping to find. I couldn't give her what she wanted.

"It has to be simple," I muttered. "Or else we don't make it. I can't be soft out here. You know that."

She pulled away from me completely. Her arms crossed over her chest as she told me, "You're not just hard out there, Salem. You're hard in here. With me. I need you to be... I don't know... something more."

I felt the frustration exploding inside me, but I pushed it down. I wasn't trying to fight with her. I didn't want to lose her, but I didn't know how to do what she was asking. "I love you, Paris. But I don't know how to be whatever it is you need me to be right now."

Her face crumpled as she shook her head. "It can't be this hard. I'm not asking you to change. I just need you to be here... with me. Not just protecting me, but really being here."

"I'm here, Paris. But you know I can't be soft. Not in this world."

Her slanted eyes rolled to the ceiling. Her expression changed to one of surrender, she was giving up... on me. "I don't need soft, Salem. I just need *you*."

She turned away from me, moping away, back down the hallway toward the living room.

I just stood there, feeling like I was losing her and didn't even know how to stop it.

I leaned against the counter, allowing my large shoulders to slump. The only time I ever lost, the only time I ever felt defeated was with Paris.

When I first met Paris, I wasn't like this. I had walls up, but my heart wasn't this cold. My father chose the streets over me. He left me with my stepmom who couldn't stand me. She didn't see me as a kid she needed to care for. She saw me as just an object standing between her and my father. She only put up with me to keep him. My biological mother was no better. She had me just to keep my father, and when that didn't work, she left me on his doorstep like trash. I had to learn early on that I wasn't someone people stayed for. That's when the walls started going up.

But when I first met Paris, I still had some love left in me. I was still soft in some places, still willing to care. Over time, though, things started changing. Every loss hardened my heart, brick by brick. My father and my best friend and right hand were all taken by violence. My mom was taken by Cancer. Then more homies, more people I cared about, were killed or died. They were gone, one by one. The more I lost, the more I shut down.

So, I trained myself to care less. I figured, if I didn't let myself get too attached, it wouldn't hurt so bad when they're taken away. It protected me from the pain of grief that I learned a long time ago was too unbearable to live with.

And once the apocalypse hit, whatever softness I had left, whatever part of me still cared too much, I forced it to die. I felt like I had to become a robot—no emotions, no hesitation—because it was clear from the jump that a lot of us weren't going to make it. No one was coming to save us. The undead were multiplying by the thousands, and every time they killed someone, they just added to their numbers. We weren't just fighting walkers either. The scavengers were so desperate, so thirsty to survive, that they weren't even human anymore either.

We were living in a real-life hell that promised to snatch any one of us at any time. I saw that early on. So, I did what I had to do to protect myself—to protect my heart, my peace. I couldn't let my guard down, not even for a second, not even for Paris, because once I did that, I was done. I would be either dead or broken, and I couldn't afford either. So yeah, I shut down emotionally. I kept myself from caring too much because this world had already taken so much from me. It couldn't take me, too. I refused to let it.

FABLE

Niyah and I were tearing across the football field with one of the undead right on us. Her growls were getting louder, closer. I heard Niyah cry out, and my stomach dropped. I turned back, and she was on the ground. The walker was right there, coming at her fast. So, I doubled back, grabbed her arm, and yanked her up.

But before I could pull us forward, we both froze, hearing Neveah's voice. "Ma!"

We whipped our heads around, scanning the area. Then we saw her face, peeking out from this old shed hidden behind the bleachers. It was damn near covered in vines and moss and blending into the shadows.

"Go!" I shouted, and we took off, pushing our bodies to the limit, racing toward the shed.

We barely made it inside, slamming the door behind us just as the walker crashed into it with this insane force. The whole shed shook, but the door held.

I leaned against the door, panting hard, catching my breath.

My lungs burned like fire, and I could feel Niyah trembling next to me.

As we stood there, trying to pull ourselves together, I looked around. The shed was small and filled with dusty sports equipment, old gym mats tossed in the corner, and rusted tools that hadn't seen the light of day in God knows how long. It smelled like old wood and damp air.

But as I leaned against the door, trying to catch my breath, Niyah was quick to catch hers. It was like the second she got her wind back, she flipped, finding the strength to go off on Neveah.

She was full of motherly fire as she snapped, "What the fuck happened, Neveah? Why did you leave?"

Her bite was enough to put a bit of fear in me, but Neveah didn't flinch. "One of Diesel's crew attacked me. He chased me, so I ran through the hole in the fence."

"You should've been in the gawd damn house! If you'd stayed inside, he wouldn't have been able to chase you! How the hell did you end up here?"

Neveah's words tumbled out as she tried to defend herself. "I didn't want to lead the walkers into the back yard, so I ran in the opposite direction. I was trying to save everyone!"

Niyah blew her breath in the way that women do when they are trying not to lose their shit. Then she laughed so psychotically that I knew that breath didn't help shit. "Save everyone? You're a child! You should've stayed your ass in the house, where a child should be!" She was getting more worked up. Her face was flushed with anger, and before I could say anything, she grabbed Neveah by the arm, yanking her in frustration.

I moved quickly, pulling Niyah back. "Hey, hey, relax. It's alright, calm down," I said, my voice low, trying to soothe her.

And just like that, in my arms, she did. It was like all that fire she had just melted away. She leaned into me, calming down instantly.

I glanced at Neveah, and I could see her watching us, noticing how open her mother was to me.

It was meant for me to wait this long to be with Niyah. All this hell, all this chaos, had brought me here to protect her, to support her when she needed it the most.

Niyah sighed, leaning into my chest. Her voice was quieter now. "I just... I just don't want to lose her," she whispered. "She has to listen to me. I need her to listen to me so that we can survive this."

"I know," I said, holding her a little tighter, feeling like I was exactly where I needed to be. "I know."

"She could have gotten herself killed, *us* killed." I watched Niyah as she started to unravel. Her breaths came in quicker, more ragged. She was so mad at Neveah, and I could see the frustration building up. She couldn't hold it together. "I can't do this. I can't parent her in this shit. She's going to get us killed."

I looked back again, watching Neveah stew in her mother's words.

I leaned in, whispering, "We'll talk about this later, okay? Not in front of her."

But Niyah couldn't calm down. "I need some air," she panted.

I hesitated, looking at the door. We had just barely made it inside. "Niyah..." I started, knowing it was a risk. But her breathing was getting worse. Neveah looked worried too, her eyes wide, like she didn't know what to do.

Gritting reluctantly, I inched towards the door. Then I slowly opened it with the other hand on my gun. I scanned the area outside, listening for any sign of that walker. It was quiet, too quiet, but I didn't see anything.

I looked back, telling her, "You can step outside, but only for a minute."

"Neveah don't fucking touch this door," Niyah hissed.

Her lil' ass had the nerve to roll her eyes slightly before she turned her back on us.

Luckily, Niyah hadn't seen her. Her shoulders were so tense as she stepped out.

"We aren't leaving from in front of the door so she can't go anywhere," I reassured Niyah.

Niyah scoffed as I closed the door behind us. Once we were outside, Niyah took a few deep breaths, trying to pull herself together.

I stayed close to her while watching our surroundings with my piece in my hand, safety off.

"Why'd you tell me to leave you back there, Fable? Why would you risk your life for me?"

I looked at her, wondering where that had come from. But by the looks of her, not only Neveah was making her unravel.

I swallowed hard, looking at her. I leaned against the wall, staring at the ground for a second before answering. "I'd rather risk everything for you than live without you, Niyah. That's just the truth."

She blinked, taken back by what I said. "How? You never even said anything about having feelings for me before. How am I supposed to believe that?"

I sighed, running a hand over my face. "I respected Cane. He was my brother. But that didn't change how I felt about you. I loved you then, and I love you now. And now that I finally have you, I'm not letting that go."

Niyah's eyes softened as she stood there, looking up at me, her eyes glossy, her lips trembling like she wanted to say more but couldn't find the words. I pulled her close, holding her in my arms. She didn't push me away. She didn't resist. And in that moment, I knew it wasn't just important to me to survive the apocalypse. I needed us to survive it together to that we could be together in whatever came next.

"I've loved you since high school, Niyah," I whispered, kissing her forehead. "And that ain't ever gonna change."

She leaned into me, her body relaxing in my arms, and for the first time in a long while, it felt like maybe—*just maybe*—we could have something real in a world that felt so impossible.

CHAPTER 13

PARIS

I sank deeper into Fable's jacuzzi tub, letting the bubbles dance around my skin. The warm water lapped against me like it was trying to wash away all the hell we've been living in. I was so thankful we still had hot water. In the middle of all this chaos, having something as simple as a hot bath felt like a damn blessing. I needed it to calm down, to breathe. But every time I closed my eyes, I saw DeShawn turning, then him eating Legion, and I couldn't stop thinking about Tariq losing his life.

I tried to push it all out of my mind. I tried to focus on the bubbles swirling around me, on the way they hugged my dark chocolate skin. I ran my fingers through my hair, feeling the thick curls slip between my slim, long fingers. I missed the days of protective styles, of wigs and sew-ins. I even missed the quick weave I was trying to hold onto when the walkers first came. I had had that install for two months, and by week two of this nightmare, the tracks were falling out. My natural hair had been a blessing and a curse. It was long, thick, and curly. My 4c hair wasn't easy to manage, but at least it looked good in its natural state.

The warmth of the bath was starting to ease some of the tension in my muscles, but I still couldn't shake the worry in my chest. I was worried sick about Fable, Niyah and Neveah. I couldn't stomach the thought of them out there, in danger, maybe even dying. I was tired of drinking my fears away. I was over smoking weed only for it to make me more paranoid than I already was. I just wanted peace for a moment.

Just as I was starting to relax, the bathroom door creaked open. Salem slowly and cautiously walked in, and stress flooded right back in. I could see that guilty look he always got when he knew I was mad at him. He didn't say anything. He just walked in and sat on the side of the tub.

I tried to ignore him. I closed my eyes and leaned my head back against the edge of the tub, but then I felt him move. I opened my eyes and saw him grab my washcloth off the side of the tub. He soaked it in the bathwater. Then he squeezed some bodywash onto the towel. I reluctantly looked him in his captivating, sage colored orbs as he started lathering up the cloth.

"What are you doing?" I reluctantly asked.

He didn't look at me. He just kept working the towel into a lather. "I'm..." He sighed and allowed his large shoulders to slump. Finally, for the first time in weeks, I watched his wall come down. "I'm trying."

I stared at him, not sure if I should be mad or confused. "Trying what?"

He dipped the towel back into the water, wringing it out slightly before bringing it to my arm, running it over my skin in slow, deliberate motions. "Trying to make things right. Trying to show you... that I care."

I wanted to pull away, but something in his touch made me stay still. I looked at him, *really* looked at him, and saw how tired he was. The hardness in him was still there, but there was something else, too—something softer. That was something I hadn't seen in a long time.

I could tell, in his hard, difficult way, Salem was trying. He had never been a man of words. He showed what he felt for me and his loved ones through actions, through the things he did rather than what he said. So, I stayed quiet, letting him bathe me.

His hand moved the washcloth slowly across my skin. His touch was gentle, despite how rough his hands were. He started with my arm. He ran the warm, soapy cloth over it in slow, careful circles, making sure to cover every inch. His fingers followed behind the washcloth, gliding over my skin, and even though I was still mad, heat rose in me.

Salem moved the cloth down to my other arm, working the same slow pattern. He wasn't rushing. It was like he was trying to say with his touch all the things he couldn't put into words. His brow was furrowed in concentration, like he was trying to make up for all the times he hadn't been there emotionally, all the times he'd been too hard.

When he moved to my chest, my breath caught. He was slow, deliberate, like he didn't want to make a mistake. His hands, calloused and rough from years in the streets, ran over my skin in a way that made me shiver, but not from cold.

He washed my stomach next. Then the cloth moved lower, and I felt my body respond, though I didn't want it to. There was something about Salem that had always pulled me in, even when I was mad at him. His presence and touch did something to me, made me feel both wanted and protected, even in his silence.

For the first time in a long time, I let myself relax in his hands, letting him take care of me in the way only Salem could. I could no longer feel the towel. Now, I felt his large fingers rubbing my clitoris in soothing, gentle circles. I moaned while leaning my head back against the tub. My knees fell apart, giving him full access to what had solely been his for years.

His middle finger slipped into my pussy, and we both moaned in unison. We locked eyes, giving one another a devilish, yearning glare. His finger left my pussy, and I whimpered in disappointment. But I got excited when he left the tub and locked the bathroom door. Then he started to strip, giving me a magnificent show.

Even after all these years, it still caught me off guard just how fine he was. My man had that kind of body that stopped you in your tracks. He was tall, muscular, with a frame built for battle. As his shirt hit the floor, my eyes lingered on his large, broad chest, the kind of chest that looked like it could take on the world. His pecs were solid, the muscles so defined they cast shadows in the dim bathroom light, like they'd been carved out of stone.

His arms were thick and powerful. His veins popped along his skin, telling his story of strength and survival. He had been putting in work with Fable's weights to pass the time, and it was starting to show. Every muscle on him was more defined than before. His biceps flexed as he unbuckled his belt, the muscles shifting under his skin with each movement, drawing my attention like they always did.

When his jeans dropped, revealing those long, cut legs, my breath hitched. His thighs were solid, sculpted from all that running, all that fighting. His calves, too, were built like he could easily outrun the undead. And that V-line, dipping low, that led to a long, thick dick that claimed me... *fuck*.

He stepped out of his clothes with that same quiet confidence he always had. My eyes roamed, tracing every dip and curve of his abs, his obliques, the smooth, brown skin stretched over rippling muscle. He was a man who had been through hell, and his body showed it—hardened by survival, strengthened by the fight. But God, it was beautiful. A body that told a story, a body I still yearned for, even after all we'd been through.

Salem didn't say a word as he stepped closer, his mystical gaze locked on mine, dark and full of that raw intensity that always pulled me in. He didn't need to speak, not when his body did all the talking. And as he stood there, every inch of him bare and powerful, I felt that familiar heat rise inside me, the same way it always did when I looked at him. He was my man—flawed, hard, and complicated—but I still wanted him inside of me like it was the first time.

"Move up," Salem demanded softly but still with that rough edge in it that always made me listen.

I shifted forward in the tub. The warm water swirled around me as I gave him room. Salem climbed in behind me. Fable was a big guy, and he made sure his tub matched that energy. So, Salem and I were able to fit.

I could feel the warmth of Salem's body as he settled in behind me, his legs on either side of mine, and even though we were surrounded by water, the heat coming off him was hotter. As he leaned back, his hands found my waist as he pulled me close.

His lips brushed against my ear. "Turn around." His words were that perfect blend of command and softness.

I didn't hesitate to shift in the water to straddle him. The moment I did, I melted into him, fitting perfectly on his lap. The feel of his strong arms wrapping around me made me feel safe in a way nothing else could. My legs rested on either side of him, and I couldn't help but sigh, loving how I fit into his arms, like we were made for this.

He held me there, his hands running along my back, his fingers tracing slow, lazy circles over my skin as I rested my head against his chest. The water lapped around us, the sound almost soothing, but nothing compared to the way I felt being wrapped up in him.

Then I began to rub my center along his length. It was hard, aiming for my eager center that pulsated for his penetration. I sat up a bit, allowing the head to find its home. I slowly slid down, amazed at how it was still a chore to take all of him in. He was fully inside me, stretching me, until the tip kissed the deepest parts of me. I moaned in appreciation of his penetration. I wrapped my arms around his neck and slowly rode him.

I rode him slowly, and the pressure drove me insane. He grabbed each of my breasts in each hand and started sucking on my nipples. He started to move his hips, fucking me back. His strokes got faster, and I started to moan his name. I rocked my hips back and forth as he pushed himself in deep, spoiling me with his huge dick.

I started bouncing on his dick, as he pumped harder and harder. Water splashed on the floor.

He held me in place, with one hand on the back of my neck and the other arm wrapped securely around my waist. Then he began to fuck the shit out of me. Wet slaps accompanied my moans and his fierce grunting as his balls slapped against me.

"Yes, Salem!" I winced. "Give me all this dick."

He spread his knees, forcing my legs farther apart, until he sunk into me so deep that I felt him hit the back wall of my pussy.

FABLE

We waited until nightfall to make our way back home. The streets had gotten worse over the weeks. The undead had tripled in number. Every corner we turned, we had to be ready for one of those things.

I kept Niyah and Neveah close. Protecting them was an honor. It felt good to be the one to keep them safe. There was something real about the way Niyah clung to me when shit got real. I was into her in a way I hadn't felt before. Even with the world ending around us, I wanted her more than anything.

That said a lot.

I'd been in relationships before. But most of them felt like they were just something to do, like I was pressured into it, or it was just what was expected of me. But Niyah was it for me. I looked at her and saw my wife, the mother of my kids. Even in all this chaos, that's what I saw when I looked at her.

When we finally made it back to the house, I walked up onto the porch. We couldn't ring the bell because the Ring doorbell didn't work without Wi-Fi. We tried to knock gently, though frantically, hoping that someone inside would hear us before the undead did. Neveah's knuckles tapped the window, soft but desperately.

Finally, I heard the barricades inside shifting, and the door opened. As soon as there was a crack in the opening, I rushed Niyah and Neveah inside, shutting the door behind us as fast and quiet as I could. The crew was all in the foyer, relieved.

"Man, I was scared y'all were outta here!" August grinned wide.

"Thank God y'all back," Meesha added with a long, loud breath of relief.

Salem slapped me on the back. "Good to see you, man. I was praying we didn't lose you out there."

I nodded at him, feeling the tension in my body finally release a little. It felt good to be back, to know we made it.

It was good to see Navon woke and alert. He stood from the couch and walked up to me. He shook up with me saying, "Welcome, home, bro."

But as I was about to say something, Kecia came at me fast. She hugged me tighter than she should've, and her embrace lingered too long.

"I don't know what I would've done without you," she whispered in my ear. "I love you, Fable."

I didn't know what to say, so I just kind of pulled back, gently, keeping it nice but distant.

"Glad we're all back safe," I replied, avoiding what she really meant.

But I made a mental note to keep an eye on her. The last thing I needed was more tension in this house, and didn't want to be quarantined in the house with Kecia and Niyah. But, we had to stay with the crew for survival. Numbers mattered, and being out here solo wasn't an option. But I was going to have to put Kecia in her place eventually without causing drama.

NIYAH

I was sitting on the foot of Fable's bed. I had just finished taking a long, hot shower after putting something on my stomach. The heat from the water still clung to my skin.

As I sat there, drying off, the frustration with Neveah was still simmering. No matter what I said, no matter how many times I warned her, she just wouldn't listen. Every day felt like a fight to keep her safe, and every day, she pushed me further away. This world was nothing like the one we used to know, and I needed her to understand that. But she was still so headstrong, so defiant. It scared the hell out of me. The thought of losing her was unbearable. And the worst part was she didn't seem to care. I loved her with everything I had, and I'd do anything to protect her, but she was making it damn near impossible.

I didn't know what to do anymore. She wasn't a little girl I could just send to her room. She was old enough to make her own decisions, but those decisions could get her killed. And the way things were now, I couldn't afford any mistakes. One wrong move, one moment of disobedience, and she could be gone. The world had changed, and if she didn't change with it—if she didn't start listening—we'd both end up in the ground, or worse, as one of the undead. I felt helpless, and I hated it. A mother's instinct was to protect, to nurture, but how could I do that when Neveah was hell-bent on walking right into danger?

At that moment, I missed Cane more than ever. I missed the way that he could get her in line with just a threatening look.

I rubbed lotion over my arms. Then I worked it into my legs. It had been a long, exhausting day. But, shit, *every* day was exhausting now.

As I was drying off, there was a light knock on the door. Before I could ask who it was, I heard his deep, rich voice, and familiar, rough tone. "It's Fable."

A smile tugged at the corners of my mouth. There was something about hearing his voice, especially now, that made me feel grounded and *safe*. It was crazy to think about, but even in the middle of this apocalypse, Fable had given me something I never thought I'd have again—*hope*. He'd gone with me to find Neveah, risked everything, and then he told me how he felt. I never imagined that in the middle of this nightmare, I'd find happiness. Sometimes, I wondered if Cane had a hand in putting us together from the beyond. That thought always gave me a strange sense of peace.

"You can come in," I called out, still smiling as I massaged lotion into my skin.

The door creaked open, and Fable stepped inside. His gaze locked onto me immediately, lustful and intense. I loved the way he stared at me. I liked knowing that even now, in this mess of a world, he wanted *me*. He closed the door behind him and crossed the room, but instead of coming straight to me, he stopped by his dresser. I watched curiously as he opened a drawer and pulled something out.

He walked over and handed it to me. I noticed that his expression was a little softer than usual. I looked down at what he was handing me and froze. It was an Audemar. But not just any Audemar —*Cane's* Audemar. I'd know it anywhere because it was his most prized possession. Once he had finally made it in the game, he'd always said this would be his first purchase, and it was. When I was camped out in our home, I was surrounded and nurtured by so many things that reminded me of him. And when I was forced to leave, I had to leave all of that behind.

My breath caught in my throat as I took it in, the iced-out face glinting under the low light.

Fable sat beside me, close enough that I could feel the body heat coming off him. "It's Cane's," he said quietly. "I kept it safe... until I saw you again. I've been waiting for the right moment to give it to you."

Tears welled up in my eyes before I could stop them. The sight of that watch, Fable's thoughtful intent, it was too much. I ran my fingers over the face of it, remembering all the times Cane used to wear it, how proud he was of it. Tears fell as I felt like Cane was still here with me, watching over us. Maybe he really had wanted this—me and Fable. Maybe he was giving us his blessing from the other side.

"Thank you," my voice cracked. "I—I don't even know what to say."

Fable reached out, wiping the tear that had escaped down my cheek. I tried to blink the rest of them away, but it was too late.

"I miss Cane," my voice trembled. Then I flinched, reluctantly peering at him. "I'm sorry."

Fable's thumb lingered on my cheek for a second longer. Then he gently tilted my face toward his. "Don't be sorry. Never feel sorry for missing him."

I looked into his eyes, and the sincerity there made my heart open even more to him. "I know I can never replace Cane," his baritone told me softly. "And I'm never gonna try. That's not what this is. But I want to be something new for you. A new love. A new beginning. A new chance."

The way he said it, the way his words wrapped around me, it felt like something I didn't know I needed to hear. A new love. A new beginning. I'd never even thought of it that way. I'd been holding onto Cane's memory so tight, afraid to let go. But Fable was right here, showing me that it was okay to hold onto Cane while still making room for something I had been longing for.

He leaned in closer. His forehead rested against mine as he whispered, "You deserve love, Niyah. The kind that makes you feel alive, even in all this shit. And I wanna be that for you."

I couldn't find the words, so I did the only thing that felt right. I closed the gap between us, pressing my lips against his. The kiss was soft at first, tender, but it deepened quickly. It was passionate and full of everything I'd been holding in. His hands found my waist, pulling me closer as I wrapped my arms around his neck.

As we kissed, his hands slid down my body. When he gripped my hips, I purred, giving him the permission he didn't even need to lay me on my back and start to kiss his way down my neck.

He paused briefly at the base of my neck, sucking and gently biting my collarbone. His right hand squeezed my soft, smooth breast, feeling my nipple harden under his palm. He smiled against my skin as his kiss continued to travel down to cover my left nipple with his warm mouth. He suckled gently, savoring my sweet gasps, before taking my nipple between his teeth and tugging, just hard enough that I moaned and I arched my back, silently asking for more.

He switched to my other nipple, and his fingers took the place of his mouth on my right one. He tugged it with my fingers as he sucked my other breast into his mouth and I moaned again as my hand went into his hair.

"Please," I whimpered. "Please, don't stop."

He more than happily obliged. He slid off the bed, coming to rest on his knees in front of me. His strong hands spread me even farther. He growled low in the back of his throat when my pussy was exposed to him. He inhaled long and slow and then moaned as if it was the most savoring scent he'd ever experienced. My breath hitched in my chest as his nose hit my clit, and I felt the hardness of his teeth teasing me.

I whimpered when his mouth finally found me. He spread the lips of my pussy with his mouth, hungry, then slid his tongue from my base to my clit. With another deep groan, he slipped his tongue inside of me and started to feast on my pussy. My clit pulsed every time he sucked it into his mouth, and my hips pressed up against him in time with his movements. I looked down at him, but all I could see were his powerful shoulders between my quivering thighs.

"More," he growled with a mouth full of my sweetness. "Give me more."

"Do you like how I taste?" I panted.

He answered by digging deeper, mouth filling with my juices. He released my knee with one hand and reached under me, pulling me into his mouth even more.

CHAPTER 14

AUGUST

It was really late. The crib was quiet. Mostly everyone was finally able to rest now that Niyah, Neveah, and Fable were back. But I couldn't sleep. My mind was going a mile a minute. And a lot of those thoughts were about Paris. I couldn't shake how upset she'd been lately, how she'd been carrying all this stress and pain around. Salem wasn't making it any easier for her. I knew my brother. I knew the way he was built. He handled things in his own way, but man, it hurt to see how distant he'd gotten from Paris.

She'd left a while ago. She said she needed air. She was up on the roof alone, trying to clear her head. I wanted to check on her, to make sure she was okay, but I was fighting with myself about it. That wasn't my place. She was my brother's girl, and I respected that. But damn, it was getting harder to keep these feelings in check. Every time I saw her looking sad, every time I saw the tears she tried to hide, it shook something in me.

Eventually, I couldn't take it anymore. I had to go up there.

I crept through the house, moving slow and quiet so I wouldn't wake anybody up. I could hear Navon snoring lightly from the floor. Kecia, Neveah, and Meesha's bodies were sprawled out on the couches, trying to get whatever sleep they could in this hell. I stepped over a loose board that I knew would squeak and kept it moving.

As I passed by Fable's room, though the door was closed, I could hear him and Niyah talking in low, hushed tones. I didn't know what it was about, but it wasn't my business. I thought it was bold of him to fuck with Niyah after fucking with Kecia, but it was obvious he had different types of feelings for Niyah. I understood, though. Niyah was everything a man could want in a woman, especially with the way she handled herself through all of this. Kecia was cool, but she always gave off a jump off vibe.

When I got to the roof, Paris didn't notice me at first. She was sitting there, lost in her thoughts, wiping away a few tears. It hurt to see her like that, but I stayed quiet as I walked over.

I sat down beside her. "You okay? You've been out here a while."

She sniffed, brushing another tear from her cheek. "I'm fine. Just tired of ...all of...*this*."

I looked at her, *really* looked at her. She wasn't fine. And something in me, that part that always wanted to take care of her, made me speak up. "You don't look fine. If you need to get something off your chest, I'm here."

She sighed, leaning back against the wall. "I don't know how much longer I can do this, August. I feel like I'm suffocating, and I don't know if... if Salem even sees it."

"He cares, Paris. I know he does. He's just... you know how he is. He keeps everything inside."

"Yeah," she said softly. "But that's not enough anymore."

Hearing her say that, seeing her so broken down was killing me. I wanted to be the one to help her, to be there for her in a way that Salem couldn't. But that wasn't my role. Yet, I was holding myself back with everything I had.

It was getting harder to keep my feelings in check. Seeing Paris up here, so broken, so tired, it tugged at something deep inside me. She had always been strong, always had this light about her, but the last few weeks had been draining that light out of her, slowly. And Salem wasn't making it any easier. I sat next to her, trying to keep my thoughts where they needed to be. But whenever she was around, which was constantly now, it was like all the walls she had built came crashing down.

"It's like... he's right there," she said. "But I feel so alone. Every day, it's like he's slipping further away, and I don't know how to fix it."

"Salem's been like that his whole life. He thinks showing anything other than strength is weakness. But you don't deserve to feel like you're on your own."

Her soft, vulnerable eyes stared right into mine, and I swear I could feel her pain. It wasn't fair. She didn't deserve this. She deserved someone who would see her, *really* see her. And part of me wanted to be that person. But I knew I couldn't.

"I know he's trying," she said, wiping at a tear. "Earlier today, he... he made an effort. And I appreciate it, I *really* do, but I need more than just a moment. I need it forever."

I could see the way she looked at me, like she was searching for something Salem never gave her. She was so close. Her eyes searched mine for something I wasn't supposed to give her. My heart pounded as my hand hovered just inches from hers, wanting so badly to close the distance. But I couldn't.

"You should talk to him, Paris," I said, forcing the words out even though it killed me. "I know he's not easy to deal with, but he loves you. And maybe he doesn't know how to show it, but he's trying in his own way."

She gave me this small smile, like she appreciated what I said, but didn't really believe it. "Thanks, August. For being here... for listening."

As she sat back looking up at the stars, all I could think was how much I wanted to be the one to make her smile like that every day. But that wasn't my place. And as much as it hurt, I wasn't about to cross that line. Not with Paris. Not with my brother's girl.

KECIA

I wasn't asleep when August slipped out of the living room. The way Fable looked at Niyah, like she was the only one he sees, had my rage seething. I knew what was between us wasn't anything serious, but did I really mean that little to him that he would fuck her in my face? I knew that we were just finding comfort in one another during this unrealistically, terrifying time, but I thought I meant at least more to him that I would get an ounce of respect. Sure, we were casual, but he moved on fast, treating her like she already had his heart. They were in their caking while I was lying in the very next room feeling stupid.

It had been eating at me all night, knowing that just last week, it was me in his bed. And now, he was with Niyah, like I didn't even exist. I couldn't take the way they were all over each other. It took every ounce of strength in me to keep my cool.

The green-eyed monster was birthing inside of me and growing hysterically. I stood up and crept through the living room, silent as a mouse. I tiptoed to Fable's bedroom door. I didn't know what I expected to see or why I even wanted to see. I was obsessed at this point.

When I got to the door, I heard them whispering. Though their voices were low, the house was so silent that their words were clear enough for me to hear. My ears perked up when I heard her say, "We can't just leave them."

Then Fable said, "But he can only safely take one other person on the boat."

My blood started boiling right then.

I continued listening, learning with astonishment that Fable knew about a rescue mission at the pier. Fable knew about a way out, a way to safety, and he hadn't said a word to any of us. He hadn't said shit to me or the people who had been fighting along-side him, surviving this nightmare with him, protecting him, and having his back. But he told Niyah. I had been just another piece of his puzzle that he didn't even bother to clue in.

As I backed away from the door, my whole body was trembling with anger.

I was fuming, my mind racing, heart beating fast. Pacing in the dark living room wasn't helping. I couldn't believe that Fable was in there talking to Niyah about a way out of this shit while the rest of us were left out of the loop. He was most likely going to leave all of us to die in this hell while they plotted their little escape. He was going to choose her and her daughter. That was no question. And that left the rest of us here to die.

I needed air and space before I snapped on someone, and Salem wasn't the one I wanted to hear running his mouth if I accidentally woke him up. So, I headed for the foyer, making sure to step lightly.

Just as I started to remove the barricade from the front door, I heard a small voice from behind me.

"Where you goin'?" It was Neveah, sitting up in the dark like some ghost.

"Just going outside for some air," I whispered, glancing back to make sure no one else was up. Last thing I needed was a lecture about going outside or someone trying to stop me.

"Ain't you scared of the undead out there?" Neveah asked.

I smirked, shrugging. "Nah, I've had enough practice killing those things. I ain't scared of the undead anymore."

Neveah's eyes lit up at that, like she was thinking the same thing I was. "Same for me," she whispered back, almost proud.

An idea sparked in my mind, something wicked that made my anger simmer into something more...*devious*.

I smiled, leaning my head to the side. "Wanna go with me?"

Her eyes sparkled with excitement, but then she hesitated. "I would, but my mama will get mad at me."

I raised an eyebrow, as a sly grin spread across my face. "Your mom won't get mad if she doesn't know, will she?"

That got her. She smiled a mischievous grin, and before I knew it, she was on her feet, putting her shoes on as quiet as a mouse. She slipped out the door with me, and I closed it behind us without making a sound.

We stepped into the mildly cool summer air. The world was dark and silent, except for the occasional distant growl or rustle. Neveah seemed jittery at first, but once we got off the porch and into the yard, she started to loosen up. I glanced at her from the corner of my eye, feeling my deceitful wheels turning.

"Your mom's been hard on you lately, huh?" I asked casually.

Neveah looked at me, almost surprised. Then her expression softened, like she was relieved someone finally got it. "Yeah, like... she's been on my ass ever since all this started. She won't even let me breathe."

I nodded, keeping the conversation going as we moved through the yard. "I don't get why she's acting like that. It's not like you're a little kid anymore. You can take care of yourself."

"Exactly!" Neveah burst out quietly, throwing her hands up in frustration. "I'm so tired of being locked in the house. She gets to get out whenever she wants to. I'm so bored. I'm sick of this. She's always under Fable now too, like she forgot all about my dad."

I smirked, feeling anger bubble all over my skin. "Yeah, I've noticed. It's real disrespectful. Your dad just died, and she's already finding you a new daddy. Shit's crazy." I let the words hang in the air, knowing it would stir something up in her.

Neveah nodded quickly as her face bawled up with frustration. "Exactly! She acts like Dad never existed. It's like Fable just swooped in and replaced him. She didn't even care!"

I kept nodding, feeding into her frustration. "It's messed up. I don't know how she could move on so fast, especially with everything that's going on. I wonder..." I paused, locking my eyes on hers. "I wonder if they were messing around before your dad died."

Neveah's face darkened. Her eyes bulged as if the realization hit her. "Oh my God! She probably was!"

"*Ssshh!*" I urged her.

And she immediately quieted. "She was probably cheating on my daddy the whole time!" she whispered harshly. "And she keeps acting like it's all about her. Like I'm not going through this shit- Oops, sorry."

"It's okay." I waved her apology off with a smile. "You can curse in front of me. I won't tell anybody."

She smiled with relief. "Cool. She acts like this shit isn't happening to me too. Like, I miss my friends too, you know? I miss my life, but she doesn't care about that."

I looked at her, pretending to be sympathetic. "Yeah, that's rough. You should be able to hang out with your friends, like she is. You've been through enough already."

She sighed heavily, kicking at a patch of dirt. "I don't even know what happened to my friends. I miss them so much. I miss

Marcel. I think about him every day. I just want things to be normal again."

I nodded, watching her carefully. "I get it, Neveah. I really do. And it's not fair."

The sound of low, deep voices drifted through the night air, catching my attention. I could make out a group of guys talking up the block, maybe scavengers, but maybe not. I turned to Neveah with a sly grin. "Hey, what if those are some cute guys? You wanna go see?"

Neveah's face lit up with excitement. "Really?" she asked, almost bouncing on her feet.

"Why not?" I shrugged, already making my way toward the gate. "They might live on the block. Might be some guys your age to hang with."

I quickly removed the barricades and locks. I pushed the gate open and stepped outside, gesturing for Neveah to follow. She seemed a little hesitant, but the curiosity and excitement pushed her forward. We looked around the block and saw a group of guys standing in a huddle on the corner.

Neveah wasted no time. "Hey!" she called out bold and confidently.

I raised an eyebrow, impressed by how fearless she was around men.

One of the guys turned and waved us over. "Come here!" he shouted.

"We should go meet them," I said, nudging Neveah with a grin.

But Neveah hesitated as her excitement flickered with doubt. "What if they're scavengers... or part of Diesel's crew? I don't want to get... *raped*."

I rolled my eyes. "Relax, we can handle ourselves. Right? Besides, they don't look like trouble." I tugged at her arm, and after a moment of hesitation, she nodded and followed me down the street.

We made our way toward the corner, a few houses away from Fable's. Just as I was about to say something to ease her nerves, a blur of movement shot out from between two parked cars.

It happened so fast.

The walker lunged at Neveah, snarling as it tried to sink its filthy, decayed teeth into her shoulder. She screamed, loud and piercing, as the force of the attack knocked her to the ground. Her body twisted under the weight of the thing, its rotting hands clawing at her, dragging her closer to its snapping jaws.

I just stood there.

Watching.

Its rancid breath filled the air, teeth gnashing as Neveah kicked and punched, trying to fend it off. Her cries for help echoed down the street, but I didn't move.

I didn't want to. She would be one less person to compete with for those seats on the boat.

I stepped back as the walker pinned Neveah down. Its rotten face was inches from her neck. Neveah's hands trembled as she pressed against its chest, trying desperately to keep it from biting her. I slid further back, letting the shadows hide me. I didn't want her to see the betrayal in my eyes.

But then, something in Neveah shifted. With a surge of adrenaline, she shoved the walker to the side just enough to grab her knife from her waistband. Her arm shot forward, and she stabbed it right in the eye. The creature let out a sickening, wet gurgle, collapsing onto her.

Fuck.

I had no choice now. I sprang forward, acting like I had been helping the whole time. I yanked my knife out and drove it into the walker's back, pretending to fight alongside her.

"I got you!" I shouted, trying to mask the irritation that she'd survived with a facade of urgency.

Neveah rolled the lifeless corpse off her, panting. I quickly grabbed her arm, pulling her to her feet. "Come on, we have to get back inside before someone hears us!"

As we hustled towards the house, I looked back to ensure that nobody or nothing was following us. I noticed that the group of guys had vanished. They had most likely ran off when the walker appeared.

Neveah's breathing was ragged as we stumbled toward the gate. I rushed to open it, casting nervous glances over my shoulder to make sure we weren't being hunted.

Neveah limped beside me, clearly rattled by the close call. "Th-thanks," she muttered breathlessly, still clutching her knife.

"Yeah, no problem," I said, pushing her through the gate.

I locked the gate behind us, and we slipped back into the house as quietly as we could, securing the door after shutting it. I could hear that Neveah's breath was still ragged and shaky. Her body was trembling. She barely even looked at me as she slumped against the wall, trying to steady herself.

"Go lay down," I whispered, glancing toward the others, making sure no one was awake to see us sneak back in. "And we don't tell anyone about this, okay? Not a word."

Neveah nodded quickly, too eager to agree. She looked more relieved than anything. Without hesitation, she slipped back under her covers, breathing out in short, nervous bursts. Her hand was still clutching the knife like it was her lifeline. I watched her settle in, the adrenaline finally wearing off as her eyes fluttered closed.

As I watched her, I thought, *I have to be one of those seats on that boat, by any means necessary.*

Every person in this house was now competition.

CHAPTER 15

FABLE

By Saturday, I couldn't take holding in the secret of the pier any longer. The time to be at the pier was getting closer. We only had five days to figure out what to do. With Niyah's help, I decided it was time to tell the others. There was no point in keeping it to myself anymore. We needed a plan so that we could all make it out alive. I refused to leave any of my people behind.

That morning, after the women had made the best breakfast that they could, I gathered the crew in the living room.

"Alright, listen," I started. "I gotta tell y'all something."

Eyes darted towards me, some confused, some already suspicious. I cleared my throat, feeling Niyah's steady, comforting presence next to me.

"Tariq told me that there is a way to get out of here at the pier on 31st and Lakeshore Drive," I explained.

Immediately, everyone perked up. Some sat up straight while other's eyes bucked with hope.

"Onyx figured out a way to get people out of here on his supply boat. He has a guy at the border that will let me through.

There is a tunnel on the east side of the border that will lead to the pier. As long as I can make it without being spotted by any military, I can get on Onyx's boat and he'll take me to Michigan."

"Word?" Salem pressed.

I nodded slowly. "Yeah."

"When is the next time he's coming?" Paris rushed.

"Thursday."

The room exploded with sighs and expressions of relief.

"But," I cut through their excitement. "The thing is. Thursday is his last mission. They are moving him to another department. And...he's only got room for two more people, besides me."

The silence that followed was suffocating. No one said a word for what felt like too long. All I could hear was the sound of bodies shifting on the couch.

"What the hell?" Salem finally broke the silence. "You been sitting on this for a whole week?"

Again, I nodded slowly. "I needed to figure out how to handle it. I'm not trying to leave y'all behind."

Salem scoffed. "Okay, so, Onyx's your brother. *Make* him take all of us. Why is this even a conversation?"

I rubbed the back of my neck. "We can try. But Onyx isn't trying to ruin his job or get himself and us killed behind this. So, I can't promise that he will take all of us, or that he won't turn that fucking boat around when he sees all of us and leave us at that pier. Tariq was firm about only three people being able to go, not including Onyx."

Navon leaned forward. His eyes were wide as if an idea was brewing in his head. "So, what if we grab another boat, steal it, and stay right on his tail. Whoever isn't on Onyx's boat can ride on the other one."

Salem shook his head, shutting that idea down quick. "You

know that ain't happening. The military's shooting anything that ain't their own. No boat's getting through that water without clearance. Everybody knows that. If that's the case, we could have been went to the pier and stole a boat."

Navon sat back, frustrated. The reality of the situation hit harder as everyone started murmuring. As voices got louder, I stood there, feeling the tension rise, like the whole room was about to erupt. I tried to keep my cool, but my mind kept ricocheting between solutions that didn't exist.

Then I caught sight of Kecia, sitting in the corner of the room. Her arms were crossed tight against her chest. She was silent and smug.

"So..." Her taunting, cynical tone sliced through the hysterical noise in the room, "Who are you going to pick, Fable? If Onyx says no and refuses to take all of us, which of us will you choose?"

The room went dead quiet. All eyes were on me. The loving and supportive vibe we used to have was suddenly gone. Now the vibe felt selfish and tense, like everybody was suddenly thinking about themselves.

I shifted, feeling the pressure from all sides. "I'm not gonna have to make that choice," I said, looking each of them in the eye. "We're gonna figure out how to get *everyone* out. We're sticking together, like we always have."

But no one seemed convinced. Not even me.

When Paris spoke up, her voice was quieter than usual. "What if we can't, Fable? What if... you *have* to pick?"

"I *won't*," I pressed harder this time. "I won't do that."

Salem stood, crossing his arms. "You better make sure your brother takes all of us, bro. Ain't nobody gettin' left behind. Not after all we been through."

KECIA

I sat on the couch, arms crossed, stewing in my own anger while everyone else fell back into their normal routine after Fable's little speech. It annoyed me how easily most of them seemed convinced that he'd try to get everyone on that boat. Fable always had this way of making people feel like everything was going to work out, like he had all the answers. But I wasn't convinced this time. There was no way in hell we were all getting out of here. Not with only two available seats. And I wasn't about to be left behind.

I barely registered Niyah walking up to me until she was right in front of me.

"Can we talk in private?" she asked.

My blood boiled just seeing her standing there, acting like she wasn't the reason I most likely wouldn't have a seat on that boat. But I wasn't about to let her see that.

I forced a smile, saying, "Sure."

I got up and followed her down the hall. On the way, I looked back and saw Fable failing at watching us nervously with crazy eyes.

I followed her into the guest bedroom, wondering what the fuck she wanted to talk about. As she closed the door, I caught myself imagining choking her out right then and there. Before the apocalypse, I'd never even thought about killing anyone. Now it was all too easy to picture because I had done it so many times. But I swallowed that thought, smothering that deadly beast inside of me, and waited for her to start talking.

"I just wanted to clear the air," Niyah began so soft and genuinely that she was annoying. "I don't want there to be any beef between us. I know how it might've looked, me coming in and sleeping with Fable so quickly, but I didn't plan for any of this to happen. I just—" She paused, like she was trying to find the right words. "I honestly have been having feelings for him for a very long time. The opportunity presented itself, and I took it."

I kept my face neutral, nodding along, acting like I really understood. "I get it. Girl, you don't have to explain shit to me. Me and Fable were nothing serious," I said, brushing it off like it didn't hurt. "It's obvious that he has always had real feelings for you, and that's cool. It's not a big deal."

Niyah gave me this grateful look, as if my approval actually mattered to her. "Thanks for understanding. I know how it feels when a man moves on, and I never wanted to be that woman doing it so boldly in your face. I'm sorry if I made things uncomfortable."

I shrugged, acting unbothered. "It's fine, really. We're all just trying to survive, right?"

Then, to my surprise, she leaned in and hugged me like we were fucking sister wives or something. I forced myself to hug her back, all the while imagining pulling out my knife and stabbing her right in the back. My fingers twitched, aching for it, but I held it together.

I had to play the long game.

NIYAH

Later that afternoon, everyone was in the living room, passing time like we always did—playing cards, listening to music, and talking shit. Per usual, Neveah wasn't her usual self. She'd been on edge for a few days now. She had been mouthier and more irritable than ever. At the beginning of all of this, I chalked her behavior up to being a hardheaded teenager, dealing with all this chaos like the rest of us. But this was different. She wasn't just being stubborn. She was pushing boundaries, getting cocky and disrespectful, and I couldn't understand where it was coming from.

As I watched her suddenly head for the door, I felt that familiar frustration building up in my chest. I called after her, "Neveah, where the hell you going?"

I instantly got embarrassed. Being quarantined in this house was already difficult. As the days went on, tensions were already high, and with Fable finally telling everyone about the rescue mission, everybody was on edge. I didn't need my hardheaded teenager making shit worse and putting more stress on everyone and our situation.

She didn't even stop. She didn't turn around or hesitate. "To get some air," she spat.

My blood boiled. "The fuck you are. Not without someone with you. You know better than to just step outside like it's safe."

She stopped and turned to look at me. The room went still as everyone watched our confrontation like a ping pong match, as they had been doing all week. I could see the frustration on many of their faces. They were sick of her attitude.

"You think you run this camp like Fable because you're having sex with him?" she spat, crossing her arms. She stared me down like I wasn't the person who brought her into this world.

The room went quiet, *real* quiet, and all I saw was red.

I jumped up from the couch so fast I didn't even feel my feet hit the floor. "Who the hell do you think you're talking to?!" I shouted, storming toward her.

But she stepped back, throwing her arms up, yelling, "I'm tired of being locked in here! I miss my daddy!"

She spun around, yanking the barricades off the door like she'd completely lost her mind.

"Neveah, stop it!" I yelled.

But she was gone, lost in her rage. "I'm sick of being couped up in here!"

She ripped those barricades free, and before I could even grab her, she flung the door open. I chased her, but she was too fast. She rushed towards the gate, flinging off the barricades and opening it.

"I can take care of myself!" she shouted.

And then everything went to hell.

The sound hit me first—the growls, the shuffling feet. The warm air swept in, carrying the stench of death, and then they were there. The undead. Pouring in.

I grabbed Neveah, yanking her back, but it was too late.

Four of the undead came barreling into the yard.

One of the eeriest parts about the infected were how normal they still looked. Beneath all the dirt, blood, and gore, they resembled the people I used to see every day. Some of them wore thick gold chains and diamond earrings, the same kind of flashy jewelry that used to light up parties. They had on designer clothes, fresh Jordans, or new dresses that looked like they came straight off a boutique rack. Others had clothes so new you could tell they'd just turned, their shirts still bright, unstained by time but smeared with fresh blood. Then there were the elderly ones, their skin sagging and pale, eyes cloudy and faces lined with the years they'd lived before this nightmare.

The worst were the kids. Just thinking about it made my stomach churn. Seeing a child lurching towards me, face twisted with hunger, wearing a school uniform or a little hoodie that probably had a cartoon character on it, was more than I could take. Every swing of the bat or pull of the trigger brought a sickening wave of guilt, knowing that these weren't just monsters—they'd once been someone's grandparents, someone's daughter or son, someone's pride and joy.

I grabbed Neveah, pulling her close, trying to shield her. The force knocked us both back, and we hit the ground hard. I could hear Paris and Meesha screaming from the doorway, terrified, high-pitched and panicked.

I was easily able to drag Neveah inside because her body was limp with shock. By the time I got her into the foyer, I saw Fable, Navon, August, and Salem already springing into action, tearing through the front door like soldiers going to war. The weapons they always kept on them flashed in their hands. They didn't hesitate or even blink. They moved like they were born to fight and this was what they had been training for.

Fable was the first to strike. He slammed his machete, that

he'd found during scavenging, straight into the skull of the closest walker, slicing through its head. Blood and gore sprayed the yard. He yanked the blade out as another walker lunged at him, and he swung again, catching it in the neck, nearly decapitating it. It fell to the ground, twitching as black blood gushed from its throat.

Navon was right behind him, his axe gleaming in the afternoon sunlight. He brought it down on the nearest walker, splitting its head open with a sickening crunch. Brains and bone exploded like mashed fruit, but Navon was already onto the next one, kicking it back before burying the axe deep into its head. He twisted the blade, ripping it out, and the thing collapsed at his feet.

Salem was brutal, as always. He moved with uncontrolled aggression with a bat wrapped in barbed wire in one hand and a knife in the other. He slammed the bat into a walker's head, crushing its skull until it was nothing but mush. With the other hand, he stabbed one that came too close, jamming the knife into its eye socket and wrenching it out with a savage twist. The walker dropped, twitching as Salem spat on its corpse.

August wildly swung his crowbar with the kind of force that could knock down a fucking building. He bashed one walker across the face, and its jaw shattered sending its teeth flying in every direction. Then he used the sharp end of the crowbar to stab another through the heart, hooking it and ripping it out, leaving a gaping hole where its heart should've been. The thing gurgled before collapsing, twitching like a broken puppet.

But for every walker they killed, more came. The yard started filling up. The guys were outnumbered. There were at least twenty of the undead now, snarling and groaning, their dead eyes locked on the crew.

"Shit!" I cursed under my breath as I ran inside to grab my weapon.

Paris, Meesha, and Kecia had already armed themselves. I could see the fear in their eyes, but they didn't hesitate. They charged into the yard, swinging bats, knives, and axes at the undead.

Paris was vicious with her bat, swinging it hard into a walker's ribcage, shattering bones with the impact. Meesha was quick with her blade, slicing at the legs of the undead, dropping them to the ground before driving her knife into their skulls. Kecia was silent and focused, slashing at every walker that got too close.

I left Neveah in the foyer and ran to help. My heart dropped when I saw just how many there were now crowding the yard. Their hands clawed at the air, teeth snapping, desperate for flesh. One by one, they tried to push through the crew, but we fought back with every ounce of strength we had.

"Somebody close that fucking gate!" I heard Fable shout as he swung his machete into an undead's neck, nearly severing its head, while Salem smashed a walker's face against the brick wall of the house, turning it into a pulp of blood and bone. Navon's axe cleaved through limbs and torsos, and August's crowbar cracked skulls left and right. But the more we fought, the more they kept coming.

One of the undead lunged at Kecia, knocking her to the ground. I screamed, running toward her, just as Paris bashed its head in with her bat, splattering blood across the grass.

But the undead kept coming, though. They were relentless and determined.

Chaos was everywhere. I could barely think as I pushed through the violence and gore. The smell of rotting flesh was nauseating. My arms ached from swinging my bat. My heart raced as I dodged snapping jaws, but my adrenaline didn't allow me to truly feel any of that. My only thought was getting to that damn gate. I swung my bat hard into the side of a walker's head.

The crack of bone and the splatter of blood barely registered in my mind as I moved.

I was almost at the gate, but another one came at me. Her gray, dead eyes were fixed on my throat. I slashed at it, feeling the weight of the impact in my arm as it crumpled to the ground, twitching. Finally, I was able to get to that gate. I slammed it shut and fumbled with the lock because my hands were slick with sweat and blood. But I was able to twist it until I heard that satisfying click.

I turned back, breathing hard as my eyes scanned the yard.

My heart sank.

We were *still* outnumbered. The crew was doing everything they could to keep the undead off us, but there were just too many.

Then three walkers locked their dead eyes on me.

"Shit!" I hissed under my breath as panic clawed at my chest."

I couldn't take all three. My eyes darted around the yard, but there was nowhere to run, unless I hit the gangway. So, I ran towards it and darted down the narrow space. Turning back quickly, I saw that all three were on my heels.

Once in the yard, I looked around, looking for a safe space to hide. But there was no where to go. And the backdoor was secured shut.

I was trapped.

My hands tightened around my bat. I readied myself, gritting my teeth as they charged at me, and prayed that someone had seen me run back here.

I swung hard at the first one, catching it in the jaw and sending its head snapping back, but the other two were too close now. One grabbed my arm. Its filthy fingers clawed into my skin, and I kicked it back, stumbling. The third one came at me, and I swung again, catching it in the ribs.

In the middle of the madness, I saw movement out of the

corner of my eye. It was Kecia. Relief flooded me for a second. Finally, someone came to help. But then... she turned away. She just ran back toward the front of the house, leaving me to fight off these monsters on my own.

My heart sank. She wasn't just leaving me. She was leaving me to die.

CHAPTER 16

FABLE

We stood there, catching our breath, dripping in sweat, exhausted from taking down all those walkers. Navon leaned against the fence, his chest heaving. August wiped his face with the back of his arm, trying to wipe off the blood splattered across his cheek. Paris and Meesha looked like they'd just come out of a battle for their lives. But Salem didn't look tired at all. He looked like he was ready for round two. He scanned the yard angry and wildly like he wanted more.

I ran a hand over my fade and turned toward the house to get everyone back inside. That's when I realized Niyah and Kecia wasn't with us.

"Where the hell is Niyah and Kecia?"

I spun around, looking at everyone like they had the answer. But everyone was as confused as I was.

"Kecia!?" I barked. "Niyah?!"

Panic slammed into me like a speeding train as my chest constricted instantly.

"Where the fuck are they?" I panicked. I started to move towards the gangway, but just then, Kecia came running out of it, breathless and wide-eyed.

"Where is Niyah?" I rushed.

"She's gone," her words trembled. "Three of the undead chased her to the backyard. I went back to help her but, she.... She got bit."

The world seemed to freeze in place. Everyone's faces fell. Meesha covered her mouth, tears welling up in her eyes. Navon muttered a quiet, "Damn, man," while August just shook his head, disbelief written all over him. Salem, for once, went silent, his cold eyes flickering with rare sympathy.

I felt my whole world cave in. "No, no, no, no," I chanted as I tried to push past Kecia. "I have to—"

But Kecia grabbed my arm, stopping me. "Fable, *no*. It's too late. Do you really want to see her turn? Do you want that to be your last memory of her?"

I froze. Her words hit me harder than any blow I'd ever taken. The thought of Niyah turning into one of those things tore me apart. But I couldn't just leave her out there.

"Just let me handle it," Kecia said softly as her eyes locked onto mine. "You don't need to see what's left of her. Trust me. I'll just let them out of the back gate, so I don't have to hurt Niyah."

My mind raced. Everything inside me screamed to go back, to fight through the undead if I had to, just to see her one last time. But the image of her becoming one of them ripped at my soul. I stood there, torn between rage and despair, not knowing what the fuck to do. I wanted to save Niyah, but if it were true, if there was nothing to save, I couldn't stomach seeing that shit.

I felt like the world collapsed around me. Niyah was gone, just like that, snatched from me after I finally had the chance to love her the way I always wanted to. She was my reason to keep pushing through this nightmare, to protect and survive. And now... she was gone. The image of her turning into one of those things—something I had to shoot down—made me feel sick. I couldn't even process it fully. How was I supposed to go on knowing she was out there, that I'd never get to hold her again, never feel her warmth, never see that fire in her eyes? It was like someone took away my last hope.

I'd waited years, *years,* for the right moment, and I thought we had time. But in this world, time didn't exist. One moment, she was in my arms, alive, breathing, and, now, I didn't even get a chance to say goodbye. I couldn't save her. That's what killed me the most—knowing I couldn't protect her when it mattered most. Everything we were supposed to have was gone, ripped away.

Suddenly, I heard the sound of feet pounding against the pavement, nearing us through the gangway. We all assumed it was one of the undead. We guarded ourselves, ready to defend ourselves and each other. But I turned just in time to see Niyah coming up the gangway, breathless and furious. Everyone breathed out audible sounds of relief as I rushed towards her. I was so relieved seeing her alive. I was breathing again. My heart was functioning like it should. That's when I realized that I could never live without this woman.

I threw my arms around her, but she was so angry that she tore herself out of my grasp. "You left me!" she shouted with her eyes locked on Kecia. "You left me to die!"

Everyone turned to face her, stunned at Niyah's accusations.

"You got bit!" Kecia snapped back. "That's why I left! I saw it happen."

Niyah shook her head, still panting from running. "You saw me? Bullshit! *I* saw *you*! You looked right at me and left me there with three of those motherfuckers! I had to fight them off on my own."

"Kecia, that's what type of time you on?!" I barked. "You just left her to die?!"

Kecia's mouth opened and closed like she didn't know what to say.

"So, you didn't get bit, Niyah?" Meesha asked.

"No!" she snapped as she held her arms out. She turned in a complete circle, showing us that she was unscathed. "They hadn't even come close to biting me when that bitch just ran back the other way! She left me back there to fight those motherfuckas by myself!"

Meesha stepped between us with her hands up. "Y'all, we need to calm down. We're getting loud. Let's just go back inside and figure this out."

I was still fuming, staring at Kecia, trying to figure out what kind of person I'd been rolling with all this time. That's when I noticed Neveah peeking through the front door with wide curious eyes.

"I'm not going back in that house," Niyah snapped, shaking her head. "Not with this bitch! I'd rather fend for myself out there than sleep under the same roof as someone I can't trust."

"Niyah, wait," I said, trying to grab her arm, but she wasn't having it.

"I'm done!" she shouted. "C'mon, Neveah."

Niyah stormed up to the doorway and grabbed her daughter's hand.

Neveah started to cry, pulling back, not wanting to leave. "Ma, I don't want to go! I want to stay here!"

Niyah's face softened for a second, but she didn't give in. "You don't have a choice. We're leaving."

There was rageful fire in Niyah's eyes as she pulled Neveah toward the gate.

Meesha and Paris tried to stop her.

"Calm down and think about this, Niyah," Paris said.

"Right," Meesha agreed.

Niyah's narrowed eyes whipped towards them. "Either Kecia goes, or I do."

The silence that followed spoke volumes, and, with that, Niyah scoffed. "I thought so." She yanked Neveah's hand harder, dragging her toward the gate.

I stepped forward, and she snapped before I could even get the words out. "Don't try to stop me, Fable!"

My eyes locked on her sternly and she finally softened a bit, long enough for me to gently grab her elbow.

"I'm not stopping you, Niyah," I told her. "I'm going with you."

Her body relaxed, like she hadn't expected that.

"Just give me time to grab some weapons and supplies. I'm not letting you go out there alone."

She stood there, fuming, her chest rising and falling with frustration, but she nodded. "Fine."

I nodded and moved quickly towards the front door. I could feel the crew's eyes on me, watching me like I was making a drastic decision.

And maybe I was.

Leaving the crew after everything we'd been through, all the hell we survived, felt wrong, but I didn't have a choice. I wasn't about to let Niyah go out there alone with Neveah, not with how things were getting worse by the day.

Once in the house, I went to my room and grabbed the bookbag I kept under the bed, the one I always had ready just in case. As I walked back to the living room, I could hear Niyah and Neveah arguing outside. It sounded like Neveah still didn't want to go, and Niyah hadn't changed her mind.

The rest of the crew had come back into the house.

Paris stepped forward, watching me with eyes full of concern. "Are you *sure* you want to leave, Fable?"

I didn't even hesitate. "I'm not letting her go out there alone, especially with her daughter."

"Well, then convince her to stay," Meesha pleaded.

I shook my head, listening to Niyah's anger spill in through the windows from outside. "She's not going to listen. So, I have to go with her. I don't have a choice."

Kecia scoffed cynically.

I spun towards her. "Shut the fuck up, Kecia. This is all on you."

Her eyes narrowed, as she snapped back, "I didn't do shit! Niyah's lying on me, and you're just gonna believe her?!"

August cautiously stepped in. "Fable, man... you *really* need to think about this."

"I have thought about it. I'm gonna go with them for now and try to convince her to come back once she cools off."

Taking a deep breath, August nodded in agreement and let it go. Navon and Salem didn't have anything to say. Salem knew he couldn't stop me, and Navon was drowning his depression in a bottle of whiskey.

I moved quickly, gathering weapons, bullets, food—everything we'd need for a day or two.

Once I had everything packed, I took one last look around the house. It felt like I was leaving a piece of myself behind, walking away from the people who had become my family in this hell. But I couldn't stay.

As I shook up with the guys, each of them gave me that look, the one that said they understood, but they didn't like it.

Meesha hugged me, whispering, "Be safe, Fable," like she was afraid this was the last time we'd see each other. Paris held me a little longer than the others, and I could feel her worry. I hugged them all, except Kecia. She was missing, suddenly but I didn't care because I didn't have shit-else to say to her.

As I walked out onto the porch, and my eyes landed on Niyah, everything made sense. I wasn't leaving to abandon my crew; I was leaving to protect my new family.

PARIS

The second Fable left, it was like the glue holding us all together had walked out that door with him. Everyone was restless, pacing, quiet at first, but you could feel the tension, the blame, hanging over all of us.

"This is all Kecia's fault," Meesha hissed as she paced the living room. "What the fuck was she thinking? Is she that jealous of Niyah?"

August nodded in agreement, leaning against the wall with his arms crossed. "Kecia was foul. Kecia's only been around us for what? Two years? She didn't grow up with us, so why would she be loyal to any of us, especially to the chick that took her nigga?"

"Fable was never her nigga," Meesha muttered.

I sat there, watching them, unsure of what to think. I didn't want to believe that Kecia was capable of doing something like that, but then again... she did look way too calm after Niyah came back alive. There was something in the way she acted, like she wasn't surprised. It made me uneasy too.

"If she'll do that to Niyah, what's stopping her from doing it to any of us?" Meesha asked the room. "Every time she gets mad or jealous, she's just gonna try and kill somebody?"

"If what Niyah said is true, Kecia only did it 'cause she was jealous," Salem told her. "She's been solid this whole time. She was just acting like a jealous female."

"So what?" Meesha snapped. "We're supposed to look over our shoulders every time Kecia gets in her feelings?"

The whole crew was on edge. I looked over at Salem, hoping for some kind of answer, but he just sat there, like he was still trying to figure out what was true. It was clear though that nobody trusted Kecia fully anymore.

But Navon was nursing that fucking bottle. He didn't have anything to say, which irritated the fuck out of me. When I hated how overly strong Salem was, I felt like Navon was letting the undead eat him alive without even touching him.

"Navon, put that fucking bottle down!" I bellowed, making everyone jump out of their skin, except him. He didn't flinch or budge. He kept pouring himself a shot, like he didn't even hear me talking to him.

Everyone watched him with glares mixed with concern and disgust. We felt bad for him, but it was hard to put any energy into supporting him when we barely had enough to support ourselves.

Meesha scoffed as she rolled her eyes away from him. "Where is Kecia, anyway?"

August shrugged. "Last I saw, she went out back while Fable was getting ready to go."

Hearing that, Meesha stormed out of the living room, towards the back porch, and the rest of us followed.

Once in the kitchen, we could see Kecia on the back porch, sitting on the edge of the railing, puffing on a blunt. The smoke curled lazily around her head as her eyes locked on the three dead undead still lying in the yard.

"Why the hell did you do that to Niyah?" Meesha snapped as she stormed onto the porch.

Kecia barely glanced at her, exhaling a cloud of smoke. "I didn't do anything. Niyah's lying."

Meesha shot back, stepping closer. "Why would Niyah lie on you like that?"

"Both of y'all said it was three of the undead back here," Salem spoke up. "So, Kecia, why didn't you kill them? Why'd you just leave her? Even if you thought she was already bit, why didn't you at least take out the undead so they wouldn't come back to the front of the house?"

"I didn't want to see her turn," she muttered. "Niyah was my friend too. I wasn't trying to watch her become one of those things. Plus, I figured it was a better chance at killing them if I had some help."

Meesha scoffed, shaking her head. "She wasn't, your friend, not like that."

Kecia's eyes snapped to her. "Are y'all serious right now? Niyah and Fable just wanted to leave so they could get to that boat. Think about it. Now they don't have to convince Onyx of anything. It'll be much easier for them to make it on the boat without us. Think!"

Her words lingered, and I could feel the crew's mood shift. Their uncertainty grew as they started to question everything. She was planting a seed of doubt that some were feeding into. Confusion settled over a few of them. But that didn't sit right with me. I knew Fable. He wouldn't leave us like that.

Meesha's face twisted in anger. "Don't try to flip this on them, Kecia. You left her to die. You didn't even try to help."

Kecia stood up, her eyes narrowing. "Y'all wanna believe whatever makes you feel better. I didn't do shit wrong. Niyah and Fable wanted an excuse to leave, and they got it. They played us." Pausing, she took a long drag of her blunt and inhaled it. The smoke slowly escaped through her nose as she continued, "What y'all need to focus on is staying alive until Thursday. We gotta be at that pier so we can get on that boat. *That's* the focus"

Salem's face hardened as he stepped forward. "You're right. So, we're sitting tight for the next five days, then we make that walk to the pier. But understand this, Kecia..." His threatening green eyes almost glowed with rage. "...if you even *blink* wrong, I'm gonna kill yo' ass."

Offended, Kecia's mouth fell open as Salem walked off, heading back into the house.

NIYAH

It felt like we'd been walking for hours. Fable was right behind me, keeping a watchful eye while Neveah trudged along beside me with an attitude, stomping her feet, huffing every few steps. I understood this wasn't the life any of us wanted, but her attitude was making it harder than it already was. I wanted to smack fire from the heffa, but I had to save my energy to fight fucking walkers.

Every block we passed, the streets were littered with the undead, groaning and dragging their feet, searching for fresh blood. We couldn't even go a full block without having to duck behind a car or into an alley, trying to stay out of their line of sight.

And when that didn't work, we had to take them down, which was becoming more frequent with each step. Two here, three there. Every single one of them smelled worse than the last.

At first, Fable had suggested that we find shelter near his home so that we could easily return once I cooled off. But I quickly let him know that there was no fucking way that I would ever sleep in the same house as that bitch, Kecia. So, he suggested we start moving northeast, slowly making our way toward the pier.

"Can we stop for a second?" Neveah annoyingly whined. "I'm tired."

I didn't bother answering. I just looked over at Fable, who was already scanning the area. He gave me a small nod, and we moved to the side of the street. We crouched behind a car for a moment to catch our breath.

"How much longer are we going to walk?" Neveah muttered, leaning back against the car door, her eyes rolling toward the sky. "Why can't we just go back with the crew?"

"Don't start that shit, Neveah," I hissed. "This is your fault. You let those fucking walkers in in the first place. Disobedient ass. I still wanna slap the shit out of you—"

Fable lay a comforting hand on my shoulder to stop my rant. I conceded, taking a long soothing breath. Neveah rolled her eyes so hard that I hoped they stayed like that.

I took a deep breath, counting to ten in my head to keep from killing my daughter. Fable's hand rested on my shoulder for a moment, grounding me, keeping me calm.

I glanced at Fable, who was scanning the area like always, his gun on ready. He had this silent strength about him that I found comfort in. He'd been the one to keep us all together so far, and I trusted him completely.

"We have to keep going," Fable said quietly, his eyes never leaving the streets. "It's too light out here. We need to find shelter soon, or we're sitting ducks. Let's go." Then he led the way.

I gave Neveah one last threatening look before standing up. I ensured that she followed him before I did the same.

After hours of walking, hiding, and fighting off the undead, my body felt like it was running on fumes. We'd come across a few places that looked like they could be safe—houses with boarded-up windows, a corner store with broken glass, but every time we got close, the people inside made it clear we weren't welcome. They didn't trust anyone, and honestly, I didn't trust them either. We were all fighting to survive out here, and that didn't leave room for hospitality.

It felt like we were running out of options when we found a clothing store. I suggested that we go inside because me and Neveah had left his home with nothing. Fable went in first, like he always did, checking every corner to make sure it was clear. Once he gave the all-clear, Neveah and I followed him inside. It wasn't much, just racks of clothes covered in dust, mannequins knocked over, and a few shelves still standing. But when Neveah's eyes landed on those clothes, I saw a genuine smile cross her face for the first time since we left Fable's house. That smile did something to me. It reminded me of the girl she used to be before all of this. For a few moments, sifting through shirts and jeans felt normal, like we were just on a regular shopping trip instead of trying to survive an apocalypse.

We packed what we could into the bookbags we also found. Fable kept glancing at the door, knowing this place wasn't secure. There were no longer any locks on the doors, and besides, the windows were floor to ceiling. So, there was no way to keep the undead—or worse, other survivors—from coming in. So, it was obvious we couldn't use the store as shelter.

Around the corner, we spotted a block of new housing developments. They looked clean, untouched, like they'd been built just before everything went to hell. One house in particular had a "For Sale" sign in the yard. My heart started to race with hope as we approached it. I prayed with everything in me that no one or nothing was inside.

Fable tried the door. It had been forced open, which wasn't a good sign, but he looked back at us and nodded for us to stay put.

"Wait here," he said as he disappeared inside.

I stood there, holding my breath, gripping Neveah's arm as we waited. The seconds felt like hours. I tried to keep my thoughts positive, but every sound made me jump. I prayed that this was it. That this could be the place where we could finally catch a break, where we could breathe.

Finally, Fable reappeared at the door with a small, satisfied smile. "It's clear. No one's here."

Relief washed over me. Neveah and I rushed past him into the house.

Thankfully, the house was staged. There was furniture, which made it feel more like a home than just another stop along the way. As we walked through the space, Neveah let out this high-pitched squeal that caught me off guard. She was excited, damn near jumping up and down when she found a room with a bed that she could have all to herself.

I didn't share her excitement. Part of me didn't think it was smart for her to be sleeping alone. But honestly Neveah had been getting on my nerves so much lately that I didn't even care at this point. She wanted space and I needed space too. Besides, me and Fable would just sleep in the room right next door to be nearby in case anything went left.

But before I left the doorway, I told her, "Neveah, listen to me. Don't get too comfortable. You saw what was out there. There are walkers every-fucking-where. I can't keep saving you every time you decide to be disobedient." She looked at me like I was ruining her fun, but I leaned in, reiterating. "If you want to act grown, then *be grown*. Think like an adult, Neveah. Your life isn't just your responsibility anymore. Every time you step out of line, every time you do something reckless, someone else has to risk their life to save you. So, even if you don't care about your life, if you care about mine, listen to me and stay put."

TWO DAYS LATER
THREE DAYS TO THE PIER

CHAPTER 17

FABLE

The last two days had been some of the hardest I'd had since this apocalypse started. Back at my house, I still had some luxuries—food, a working stove, hot water. But here, in this vacant house, we didn't have any of that. We didn't have any power or running water.

I'd gone out scavenging the day after we got to the house, thinking I could come back with something that would make this place a little more livable. I spent the whole damn day searching, moving through every street, alley, and corner store that hadn't been looted dry. I was really hoping to find a spot with some hot water, something to at least let us clean ourselves up, but that wasn't happening. The undead were everywhere. I had to dodge and duck so many times just to keep from getting spotted or caught. It was getting way too dangerous to even be out there.

By the time I got back, all I had to show for it was some more snacks—candy, canned tuna, a couple of packs of nuts, bottled water and some energy bars I found in an old gas station. It wasn't much, but it was something. I could see the disappointment on Niyah's face when I came in with that sad haul, but she was so happy that I had come back alive that she didn't say a word.

By now, me, Niyah, and Neveah had already gone through most of the food. Nothing had been enough to truly fill us up. It was just holding us over. I hoped Niyah would get frustrated with how little we had and want to go back to my house, but she wasn't budging. She was done with Kecia, and I couldn't blame her. I felt guilty, leaving my crew like that. We'd been through so much together, but I wasn't about to let Niyah be out here alone. Now, I just prayed we all could make it to the pier in time for Onyx's boat.

Even though things were rough, being here with Niyah made it all feel a little more bearable. We were going through hell—facing things most people in love never have to deal with; starving, running from the undead, always looking over our shoulders, trying to survive. But somehow, it felt like it was pulling us closer. I was falling harder for her, watching her move with so much strength. Most people would've crumbled along time ago, but she was still pushing through.

Seeing Niyah hold it down, even when she was scared or frustrated, made me respect her even more. I admired how she still looked after Neveah, no matter how much Neveah pushed away. There was something about Niyah's resilience that made me want to be better for her. I wanted to protect her, to make sure she was good, not just physically but mentally too. Being with her like this, even in this mess of an apocalypse, just confirmed what I already knew—I wanted Niyah, now and always.

"What are you looking at?" Niyah blushed as she finally noticed me watching her put on fresh clothes. We had washed up with bottled water, a bar of soap, and a shirt we'd ripped up to make washcloths with.

"I'm looking at the most beautiful woman in the world."

JESSICA N. WATKINS

The bedroom was dim, just two candles flickering on the dresser, casting soft shadows on the walls. My eyes kept drifting over to Niyah, her thick frame bathed in that warm glow. The candlelight made her skin look smooth, like velvet, the curves of her body catching the light in all the right places. Her hair, dark and full, framed her face perfectly, resting against her shoulders. Every curve, every inch of her, was just right—thick thighs, wide hips, all of it. She was beautiful, a real woman, soft yet strong.

The candlelight danced across her body, highlighting her curves in a way that made me appreciate her even more. She wasn't just beautiful—she was mesmerizing, the kind of woman that could stop you dead in your tracks.

Niyah giggled as she pulled a shirt over her head. "That's easy to say in a world full of ugly ass walkers." She laughed at her joke as she bent over to grab pants off of the floor, but my dick instantly got hard.

"Unt uh," I grunted. "Don't put those on."

She peered over at me, watching my perverted smirk. "That's why you came up with the idea to wash up with the bottled water."

I chuckled guiltily.

"Nasty ass," she swooned as she padded over to the bed. On her way, her eyes drifted down my naked body and lingered on my dick as it jumped at the sight of her.

She purred as she crawled onto the bed. Her motherly instincts kicked in. She looked over her shoulder, ensuring that the bedroom door was locked. Once she ensured that it was, she turned back to me, lust flooding her slanted eyes.

As soon as her warm, tiny hand grabbed my length, I grew painfully hard.

I hissed like a bitch when she started sucking my dick. I had been watching her for days, unable to touch her. She refused to let me inside of her until she was able to take care of her hygiene. Now even the notion that I was about to be balls deep in that pussy had me nearing the edge.

I started to thrust into her mouth until I could feel my head in her throat. Her nails dug into my thigh as she took all of me in.

"Damn, you look so fucking sexy with my dick in your mouth."

Her eyes watered as she gagged on my steel.

My hand went into her hair, gripping it. She started to orally fuck me faster, causing my hand to tighten on her hair.

"Shit, baby," I groaned.

She took me so deep that I moaned like a bitch. "*Fuuuck*, I'm about to cum."

Then she had the nerve to moan with my dick in her mouth, causing her throat to vibrate around it. Instantly, my cum shot down her throat. She moaned, pleased with the taste of it, making me cum even harder as she milked my dick for every last drop.

She released me and my dick fell out, still hard, still wanting her.

I sat up and laid her down on her back. I started kissing her as I rubbed my dick over her pussy. I slowly slid inside of her. As soon as my tip kissed her cervix, she started breathing heavily. I started moving slowly with each push, waiting for her pussy to adjust to my size.

Finally, I was fully inside. I took my time, wanting her to enjoy this dick as much as I enjoyed her. I gave her slow thrusts while entering her fully and then withdrew slowly until only the tip was still inside of her. I thrust into her again and filled her with my length. Her legs lifted and clamped around the small of my back, and her hands fluttered across my chest. Then I resumed thrusting, harder than I wanted to because that pussy was soaking wet for me.

NIYAH

After we made love, Fable and I lay in bed, catching our breath. My body was relaxed, but my mouth was dry as a desert. I turned to him and muttered, "I need some water."

He nodded, agreeing with me, but neither of us moved for a second.

I giggled. "Who's going to go get it?"

"It's your turn."

I whined and he chuckled as I flung myself upright.

I slipped on one of his shirts and quietly padded out of the room, leaving him behind in the dim candlelight. The house was dark and quiet. There were a few candles scattered around to guide my way. I noticed Neveah's bedroom door was slightly cracked. The soft flicker of a candle was still lit inside. I wanted to check in on her, but I just sighed to myself, not wanting to deal with her attitude right now. She'd been the worst these past couple of days. Her mood had been flipping from annoying to straight up disrespectful. I had just been staying out of her way. The only strength I had left had to be used to get us through the next few days and to safety.

As I reached the bottom of the stairs, I heard a faint sound coming from the kitchen. Fable and I hadn't been able to secure the doors as tightly as we would have liked because we had to use whatever few pieces of wood and pipe that had been left around this new development. My pulse quickened, wondering if scavengers had broken in. My mind immediately jumped to the worst. I tiptoed toward the kitchen, my bare feet moving as silently as possible on the cold floor. When I peeked inside, I gasped out loud. I saw Neveah, standing by the counter, eating like we had a full pantry. My blood boiled instantly. We had agreed to ration the food, but once again, she was doing what the fuck she wanted to.

"Neveah!" My roar bounced off the walls. "What the hell are you doing?! You know that we have to ration this food!"

She froze, mid-bite of a beef jerky, staring at me with that same rebellious look she'd had for days. "I was hungry, Ma."

"We all are!" I shouted as I stormed into the kitchen.

Reaching her, I snatched the jerky from her and threw it onto the counter.

"We barely have enough food as it is! You can't just keep doing whatever you want to do!"

Neveah's eyes rolled as she stomped away. "I'm sick of this! I hate this world! I hate everything!"

"Don't you think I do too?!"

"I miss Daddy! This isn't fair! I can't have anything! You have Fable. You have someone, but what about me? I'm always left alone!"

Her words hit me harder than I expected. For a moment, I felt something shift in me. I was ready to let my guard down, to comfort her. I could see her pain, her fear, her loneliness. But just as I opened my mouth to comfort her, I heard Fable's footsteps on the stairs.

"What's going on?" he asked as he curiously peered into the kitchen.

Neveah turned to him with her face bawled up with anger. "This doesn't have anything to do with you! You're not my father, so mind your business!"

Rage immediately boiled up again. Before I even realized what I was doing, I stepped forward and smacked her across the face. "Don't you ever talk to him like that! Fable has been risking his life every day to protect us, to keep us alive! You have a lot of fucking nerve!"

Neveah's hand flew to her cheek. Her eyes were wide with shock and anger. I could see tears forming in her eyes, but she didn't say another word. Instead, she turned on her heel and ran up the stairs, crying.

I stood there as my body shook with anger and embarrassment. I was still pissed. I moved to go after her, but Fable stopped me with a gentle grip on my hand.

He pulled me closer and into his arms. "Hey, just give her some space."

"All I have been doing is giving that lil' heffa space."

As tears stung my eyes, his head tilted. Sympathy covered his eyes as he kissed the top of my head. "It's okay. You're doing the best you can."

"I don't know what to do with her anymore," I cried. I buried my face in his chest, and my whole body trembled. "I don't know what else to do, Fable. She's hurting, and I can't... I can't fix it. She's my baby, and I'm losing her."

Fable stroked my hair as he softly told me, "You're not losing her, Niyah. She's just... angry and scared. We all are. She'll come around. She just needs time."

I pulled back, looking into his eyes. "But what if time isn't enough? What if I'm failing her? She may never be the same after all of this."

"You're not failing her," Fable said firmly. "You've been doing everything you can."

I clicked my tongue. "Clearly, I'm not."

"Yes, you are. No parent is perfect, and you definitely can't be in times like this. You're keeping her safe and alive. That's what matters."

NEVEAH

I woke up pissed off. My face still stung from the slap Mama gave me last night. I couldn't believe that she hit me, especially in front of Fable, of all people. She wasn't even supposed to be messing with him! She really thought she was in love or whatever, with my daddy's friend. I was so mad she embarrassed me like that. And for what? For speaking the truth? She didn't care about me, didn't care about my feelings, didn't care that I was missing Daddy so much it hurt. It was like she had completely forgotten him and me.

I sat up in bed, hugging my knees to my chest, staring out the window because there was nothing else to do. No curtains were on these windows, so I could see the yard. As my eyes wandered, I saw a puppy in the alley. It was small, like a Yorkie, the type of dog I'd always wanted.

"Oh my gosh!" I quietly gushed. "You're so cute!" I got so excited, and feeling that excitement made me even more happy. I hadn't had anything to be happy about in forever. All I could think about was getting that dog and finally having something to keep me company.

Without thinking, I slipped on my shoes. I moved slowly and quietly, not wanting to make a sound. I didn't want Mama or Fable to catch me because they'd just try to stop me. I crept out of my room and snuck down the hallway. I paused right outside Mama and Fable's bedroom door. I listened for a moment, making sure they were both still knocked out.

Thankfully, I could hear them snoring, so I tiptoed down the stairs. My heart was racing, but not because I was scared. I was excited. Finally, I was going to have something to do, to occupy my time. I made it to the kitchen, slipped out the back door, and ran through the yard, straight for the fence. It was one of those waist-high chain-link fences, which weren't hard to get over. I hopped it easily and looked around the alley to make sure nothing was out there.

Since there was nothing, I spotted the puppy under a parked car in the lot next to the alley. It was such a cute little thing, all soft and fluffy. I crouched down on all fours, feeling the dirt and gravel under my hands as I bent to look under the car. The puppy was there, just wagging its little tail like it was just as excited to see me.

"Hey, little guy," I whispered. "C'mere, c'mere."

The puppy didn't move at first, just looked at me with big, innocent eyes. My heart melted a little. This was the first time in weeks I felt something other than fear or anger. I crawled closer, reaching out my hand slowly, hoping it would come to me.

"Come on, I'm not gonna hurt you. I just wanna take you home—"

Suddenly, I heard low growls and shuffling that was way too close for comfort. My body froze for a second, and a chill ran down my spine. I scrambled out from under the car with my heart in my throat as I straightened up and looked around.

A group of the undead, at least six or seven of them, were emerging from the backdoor of the house I stood behind. They were just a few feet away. Their hollow eyes locked on me the moment I moved. Their rotten smell hit me first. It was the aroma of rotten flesh mixed with dirt and something else, something sickening.

They staggered forward with their mouths open and teeth bared, making that awful growling noise that I'd come to dread.

Then, in an instant, they weren't just staggering. They were sprinting, coming at me full speed. Panic shot through me, as I turned and ran. My legs pumped. My breath was quick and ragged as I raced down the alley. I could hear them behind me. Their feet were slapping against the ground. Those hungry growls were getting closer with every second.

But then, just as I was getting some speed, my foot caught on a chunk of concrete. I went flying forward, hitting the ground hard. Pain shot through my knees and palms as I screamed out in agony. I tried to push myself up, but it was too late.

They were on me.

The first one grabbed my ankle. Its fingers were like ice against my skin. Its face was right in front of mine. Gray, rotted skin hung from its jaw. Its eyes were milky and lifeless, but still full of hunger. It let out a screech, pulling me toward its open mouth. I screamed, kicking and thrashing, trying to break free, but another one grabbed my arm, its jagged nails digging into my skin.

I kicked harder, my free hand frantically searching for anything, but they were too close now. The undead piled on top of me, teeth snapping, growls vibrating through my bones.

The last thing I saw was the puppy, still hiding under the car, before I screamed, "Mama!!! Mama, help *meeeee!*" I screamed until my throat hurt. "Mama, *pleeeease?!*"

CHAPTER 18

FABLE

I t's like we both heard the same terrified scream in our sleep. Me and Niyah shot up at the exact same moment, eyes wide, hearts pounding. She groaned first, running a hand down her face.

"I'm so tired of hearing people get killed," she muttered.

I chuckled, sarcastically, but in agreement. I felt her pain. You don't get used to the random screams. The way they cut through your sleep, those desperate, last-second cries before someone gets ripped apart. It's always there, gnawing at you.

Then we heard another scream so familiar that it damn near stopped my heart. "Mama, *pleeeeease*!"

Niyah gasped as her eyes went wide. "Neveah!"

She jumped out of bed so fast that the sheets flew. I was right behind her as she bolted out of the room, her bare feet slapping against the floor. The panic in her voice was raw, tearing at me as we rushed down the hall to Neveah's room. "Neveah?! Neveah, where are you?!"

Niyah pushed open the door, and I had barely reached the doorway when I heard her scream, "She's not in here!"

Niyah was already turning back, practically flying towards the stairs. I followed, both of us yelling out Neveah's name.

We both damn near slid down the stairs. The living room was empty. Then my eyes grazed the kitchen and locked onto the back door.

The air just left my lungs.

The door was closed but it was no longer barricaded.

"Niyah...," was all I had to say to get her to see it.

"No! No, no, no!" Niyah's scream tore through the silence, filled with more fear than I'd ever heard from anybody. We both rushed to the door, nearly tripping over each other to get outside. She pushed past me and tore it open. We bolted into the backyard. But when we got into the yard, we froze.

It was like my worst nightmare playing out right in front of me.

Neveah's scream was still in the air, but all we could see was a group of undead huddled together, feasting. The sounds of them, the wet tearing of flesh, the way they growled and gnawed was heart wrenching.

Niyah's piercing, high-pitched scream of terror broke through the noise. "*Noooo!*"

My knees buckled. Neveah's body was mangled and covered in blood. She lay limp beneath them. Her eyes, once full of life, were empty, staring at nothing. Niyah dropped to the ground, sobbing uncontrollably. Her hands covered her face as she screamed, her whole body shaking with agony.

I could barely breathe, couldn't move.

"Niyah, we gotta go inside," my voice cracked as I tried to stand her up.

But she was lost, weeping uncontrollably. "No! My baby! Oh God, no!" she wailed, her sobs shaking her entire body. She was broken, *destroyed*, and it was killing me.

Then, out of nowhere, she shot up and bolted toward the fence. I barely caught her in time, grabbing her from behind.

"Niyah, you can't! You can't, baby!" I pleaded, holding her tight.

But she struggled in my arms, desperate, wild with grief.

"I have to help her! Let me go! I have to help my baby!" she screamed as she fought to get out of my grasp. I knew she wanted to help her daughter. I wanted to help her too. But I could see by how lifeless Neveah's legs were and the amount of blood that there was no longer anything to save.

I couldn't let Niyah go. I couldn't let her see that. There was nothing we could do now.

Two of the undead stopped feasting. As they lifted their heads, I saw fresh blood smeared across their faces—Neveah's blood. They looked right at us with their eyes dead. They locked onto us with hunger. They rushed to the fence and started clawing at it. They couldn't climb it, but at any moment, they could throw themselves over it.

Niyah kept fighting against me. Her voice was broken as she sobbed, "Let me help her! Let me help my baby!" Her cries were like knives, cutting deep, but I couldn't let her run to her death.

I bent down, threw her over my shoulder, and took off running toward the house. She kicked and fought against me, screaming and crying, but I held on, not letting her go. As soon as I got to the screen door, I tore it open and rushed inside, slamming it shut behind us. But even then, she tried to push past me. She swung at me, desperate to get out, and I took every hit.

"Niyah, please," I whispered, blocking her with my body, tears welling up in my eyes. Seeing her like this, fighting with everything in her to get back to Neveah, broke me. I could barely hold it together. "She's gone," I whispered, my voice shaking. "She's gone, Niyah."

She stopped for a second, her chest heaving with sobs, her

eyes filled with pain and rage. "No... no... I can't leave her. I can't leave her out there!" she cried, slamming her fists into me. And all I could do was hold her, fighting back my own tears, knowing I couldn't let her go. Not now. Not ever.

Suddenly, Niyah gasped. Her breath was sharp, filled with terror as she stared at something behind me. I froze, my stomach sinking before I even turned around. When I did, my blood ran cold.

The undead were swarming the fence, their rotten limbs reaching over, their decomposing faces gnashing at the air. Their bodies pressed against each other, collapsing forward like a tidal wave of death, piling up against the fence. But then... behind them... I saw Neveah.

Her mangled, broken body, twisted in unnatural angles, was moving. Her arms, once soft and warm, now twitched violently, her fingers clawing at the earth. Her eyes—those once bright, defiant eyes—had glazed over, turning into the cold, lifeless gray of the undead. Blood dripped from the gashes across her face. Her mouth hung open as if she were screaming, but no sound came out. Her head jerked back unnaturally. Then her body jolted, rising, twitching like a puppet on broken strings, until she stood up, no longer Neveah, but one of *them*.

"Niyah, don't," I said, my voice cracking as I turned back to shield her from the sight, but it was too late. She had already seen it.

"No! Oh God, no!" Niyah screamed, trying to push past me. Her hands slammed into my chest as she howled, "That's my baby! That's my baby!" She was hysterical, tears flooding her face. Her sobs ripping through my soul.

I tried to close the door, to block her from seeing any more, but she stood in the way, refusing to move. "Let me go! I have to save her!" she sobbed, her voice hoarse with agony.

"Niyah, it's too late," I pleaded, holding her back. "She's gone, baby. She's gone."

But we both watched, helpless, as Neveah, now fully turned, stumbled toward the fence, her head twitching side to side. Her lifeless eyes locked onto us, her mouth dripping with fresh blood. She moved toward us with the others, her fingers clawing at us, mindless, soulless, and hungry.

Niyah collapsed to her knees, sobbing uncontrollably. "No! Neveah, no!" she screamed, her hands reaching out to her, but Neveah didn't recognize her. She didn't recognize anything anymore.

I knelt beside her, my heart breaking, trying to pull her back. But she wouldn't move. Neither of us could. We were stuck there, watching as Neveah joined the pack of the undead, pushing, snarling, trying to reach us, lost to us forever.

KECIA

I hadn't known that when I talked Neveah into defying her mother in front of everyone and storming out of the house that it would turn into all of this. But, maybe, it had worked out for me, because now, I had a chance to get to Onyx's boat before Fable and Niyah, and, just maybe, I could make it to safety.

So, I had been playing shit real cool ever since they left. I could feel the suspicion, the glances, the way the crew weren't talking to me like they used to. Navon and Meesha had been acting funny toward me, and though Salem seemed like he didn't care one way or another, I knew all that mattered to him was surviving. August was always laid-back, but I couldn't tell if he was actually chill with me or just hiding whatever was going through his head. And Paris was too caught up in her miserable situation with Salem to even look my way. But I wasn't stupid. I knew some of them believed what Niyah said about me, and if I wanted any shot of staying with this crew, I had to make them see that I was on their side. Especially with the pier plan only days away.

"Morning, y'all," I said, trying to sound as cheerful as possible as I strolled into the living room.

Navon didn't even look up from his seat. Meesha glanced at me but quickly looked away. I could tell she was biting her tongue, not saying what she really wanted to. Paris gave me a half-hearted smile, but it didn't reach her eyes.

Only August actually acknowledged me. "What's up, Kecia?"

"What y'all in here talking about?" I asked as I sat on the couch next to him.

"We were just talking about the best, safest way to get to the pier."

"Yeah, we only have two more days," I said. "Y'all need any help with anything? I can start packing supplies if that's what's needed. We don't want to be scrambling last minute."

"Umph," Meesha muttered under her breath, still not looking at me.

But I kept it cool.

Sitting on the floor, Meesha sat up, angling a critical glare at me. "Why you so helpful all of a sudden?"

I smiled sweetly, hiding the irritation bubbling inside me. "I'm just trying to do my part, Meesha. We're all in this together, right?"

She raised an eyebrow dramatically. "Are we?"

I kept my face neutral, even though her tone was testing the hell outta me. "Of course we are. We're all trying to get to that pier and get the hell out of here."

Salem glanced between me and Meesha, clearly not interested in the little back-and-forth. "Enough," he barked. "We need to focus. I don't care about any of this petty shit. We got two days to get to that pier. Anything else is irrelevant."

August looked up at Salem, then over at me and Meesha. "He's right. Let's just get through this. We don't have time for anything else."

I nodded, forcing a smile. "Right. We've got bigger things to worry about. I don't know about anybody else, but I'm a team player and I am loyal."

Paris, who had been sitting quietly this whole time, finally spoke up. "We all need to be on the same page. If there's distrust or tension, it's gonna mess with the plan."

"I'm on the same page as y'all," I said, trying to sound as sincere as possible. "I just want us to make it."

Navon scoffed but didn't say anything, while Meesha kept giving me a side-eye.

"Let's stick together for these next couple of days, okay?" I said, trying to sound like the voice of reason. "We've made it this far. We can't fall apart now. We need each other."

Salem nodded. "Exactly. No more bullshit. Let's just get ready for the walk to the pier."

As the conversation shifted back to the logistics of getting to the pier, I sat back, feeling a little better but still on edge. It was clear they were skeptical of me, but I just had to keep playing my cards right. I'd survive this, just like I had survived everything else. All I had to do was make sure we got to that boat first. And if that meant being extra nice, pretending like I cared about these people's opinions of me, then so be it.

FABLE

After Neveah was gone, Niyah wouldn't even look at me. Her anger was radiating off her body in waves. She blamed me for not letting her reach Neveah. She just lay curled on the couch, crying hysterically for hours, until finally, the sound of her grief faded to silence.

I held my breath, praying she had fallen asleep. Quietly, I crept down the stairs. As I reached the living room, I saw Niyah stretched out on the couch, perfectly still. I was relieved that she was even able to get some rest.

Moving silently, I slipped past her into the kitchen and eased open the back door. I secured it as tightly as possible behind me, pausing only briefly to make sure it wouldn't budge. Then I hurried through the backyard.

Then I began to run down the alley.

My eyes strained in the darkness as I moved from alley to block. When I finally spotted a walker staggering into view, I stopped and waited, until I realized it was a man. I exhaled shakily, then kept moving.

Almost twenty frantic minutes passed before my eyes caught

sight of another walker, stumbling aimlessly along the sidewalk. My heart sank like a stone, as recognition hit me so hard I damn near doubled over. She was young. Her clothes were exactly like Neveah's, and they were filthy and torn from her tragic final moments.

I forced myself forward with tears blurring my vision as I ran toward her. We met in the middle of the empty street. The moonlight casted a perfect light on her now lifeless features. Her vacant eyes met mine, and they instantly transformed to something hungry and vicious.

Instantly, she lunged.

"I'm sorry," I whispered brokenly as I lifted my gun with a trembling hand. Tears streamed down my face as I aimed between those familiar eyes.

I had to close my eyes to pull the trigger. The sound of the gun going off made my knees buckle.

I watched her fall to the asphalt.

I couldn't live with the possibility of Niyah seeing her child like this, or any of Neveah's loved ones having to defend themselves from what she had become.

I stood over her, mourning, frozen in place by all this bullshit. Then I heard the groans and shuffling feet of more of the undead closing in. I snapped out of it and ran, cutting back through the alley.

When I reached the house, I crept in through the back door. I locked it behind me as quietly as I could. I tiptoed into the living room and stood at the edge of the couch, catching my breath while staring down at Niyah. All I wanted was to lie next to her and hold her. But I knew better. Touching her now would only piss her off even more. So I swallowed the ache in my chest and backed away. I crept silently back up the stairs, leaving her to the only peace either of us might get for a very long time.

PARIS

Cleaning up after breakfast, I let the warm water run over my hands, trying to tune out the chaos that had become our everyday life. As I stacked plates on the drying rack, my mind wandered like it often did. It was the only way I could cope now, letting my thoughts drift away from the horror outside and the tension in the house.

Then Salem came through the back door. His expression was stern and focused. "Put on your shoes and come outside." His voice was flat, like it was just another order to bark out.

I turned, wiping my hands on a dish towel. "Why? What's going on?"

His serious glare met mine as if he were impatient. "I want to teach you how to handle weapons better. You need to be on point during the trek to the pier."

I swallowed hard. Of course, it was about survival, not about him nurturing me or us.

He had made an attempt to show me that he cared a few days ago, but that didn't last. The next day, he was back to himself, focused on nothing but staying alive.

He didn't wait for an answer. He just turned and headed back outside. I sighed, tossing the towel onto the counter before heading to the hallway to get my shoes. As I laced them up, I wondered why he couldn't put this much effort into us, into our relationship. He had all the time in the world to teach me how to shoot, how to fight, how to stay alive, but when it came to showing any real emotion, any softness, he was like a brick wall.

Shaking my head, I headed outside. The warm air hit my skin, and I spotted Salem standing in the middle of the yard with a couple of guns laid out on the grass. He turned when he saw me, his face set in that hard expression I knew too well.

"Come on," he barked, motioning for me to hurry up.

I walked over, already feeling the tension building in my chest. "Alright, what do you want me to do?"

He handed me one of the guns, his fingers brushing against mine, but it wasn't a gentle touch. "We need to make sure you can handle this properly. If it comes down to it and we get into some real shit, I want you to be able to handle as many of those motherfuckers that you can."

My eyes traveled to the sky. "Okay."

"Don't roll your eyes at me," he snapped, stepping back. "This is how you stay alive out here, Paris. We have to get to that pier, and I need you on point."

I bit my bottom lip and nodded as I gripped the gun tighter, trying to focus on the weight of it in my hands. Salem started walking me through different drills, how to aim, how to fire. But every time I hesitated, every time I didn't get something exactly right, he was on me.

"Don't hold it like that!" His voice cut through the air like a whip. "You'll break your damn wrist if you don't do it right."

I clenched my jaw, feeling the frustration bubble up in my chest. "I'm trying, Salem!"

"Trying isn't enough!" he shot back, his face hard as stone.

"You need to be ready for anything. You think those things are going to wait for you to get your shit together? Hell nah."

I blinked back tears, my hands trembling as I tried to line up the shot, but all I could feel was how wrong everything felt between us. This wasn't teaching. This wasn't love. This was him treating me like one of his soldiers, and I was sick of it.

"Can you stop yelling at me for five seconds?" I snapped, lowering the gun. "I'm not one of your boys. I'm your girlfriend!"

His eyes narrowed, and for a second, I thought maybe he'd back down. But Salem didn't know how to do that. "I'm trying to keep you alive," he said coldly. "This isn't about feelings, Paris. Stop being weak. This is about life or death. If you don't get it together, you're gonna be dead out there."

His words stung, and I felt a lump form in my throat. "I don't need you to be my drill sergeant, Salem. I need you to be my partner, to actually care about how I feel for once."

He shook his head like I was missing the point entirely. "*This* is how I care, Paris. By making sure you don't die. We're not out here playing house. This shit is real."

I threw the gun down, the sound of it hitting the dirt louder than I expected. "I know it's real, Salem! But that doesn't mean you have to be this hard on me. You don't have to break me just to protect me!"

He stared at me, his face unreadable, but I could see the tension in his jaw, the way his fists clenched at his sides. "I'm trying to *save* you."

I shook my head, tears threatening to spill over. "But you're pushing me away in the process. And I don't know how much more of this I can take."

He stood there, silent, not knowing what to say or maybe not caring enough to say it. All I knew was that I needed more than just survival. I needed him. And he didn't seem to understand that at all.

So, I turned on my heels, walking away from him. "I don't feel like doing this shit right now."

"Paris!" he roared.

That's when the back door creaked open, and August stepped out. He looked between the two of us, eyes narrowing. "Yo', Salem, chill out, man."

Salem's nostrils flared. "Nigga, who the fuck you talkin' to? Stay out of this, August. This ain't got nothing to do with you."

"It does when you're talkin' to her like that," August shot back, stepping closer. His voice was calm, but he was standing on business, which only seemed to irritate Salem more.

Salem's jaw tightened. "She's *my* girl. I'll talk to her however the fuck I want to."

August's eyes hardened, and his tone dropped lower. "Not like this, you won't."

Salem shoved August in the chest, but August barely moved.

"Nigga, I'll beat yo' ass," August warned.

But Salem ignored that and swung on him. It connected with August's jaw, causing his head to snap to the side. But he barely stumbled. He looked back at Salem. Then, without hesitation, he swung back, cracking Salem in the face.

"Stop it!" I yelled, but neither of them was listening. Fists flew, and it became a blur of jabs, blocks, and grunts. I tried to step between them, but they were like bulls locked in a battle that had been brewing for far too long.

August finally got Salem in a hold, pinning his arms behind his back. "Chill, bro."

Salem struggled, breathing hard, but August didn't let go until Salem finally stopped resisting. When he did, Salem pulled away, rage still simmering in his eyes.

Then he suddenly spun around and landed a ruthless punch on August's jaw. The impact was so strong that it knocked August backward. He hit the ground hard.

"Salem, stop it!" I yelled.

Salem's eyes blazed as he glared down at August, then turned his anger toward me. His expression was hard and unforgiving. He shook his head, then stormed back toward the house, slamming the door behind him.

AUGUST

Paris and I sat on the back porch in silence. My jaw throbbed from his punch, but I was too focused on the look in Paris's eyes to care about the pain. She was the one who insisted we stay out here, away from Salem until he and I calmed down.

"Why'd you do that, August?" she asked softly.

I glanced over at her, taking in the sadness that seemed to be a part of her now. "Because you deserve better than that. You don't deserve to be treated like that."

She stared down at her hands, picking at the skin around her nails. "But that will only cause issues between you two."

"I know. But I can't just watch him hurt you. You're amazing. You deserve the world."

The words hung between us. I could see the conflict in her eyes, a mix of longing and guilt. Her lips trembled as she looked at me, and I felt my body lean forward, drawn by something I shouldn't want but couldn't deny. There was pull between us that was stronger than all the reasons we both knew were wrong. Her face was inches from mine, and I could feel the warmth of her breath on my skin. I wanted to kiss her. I'd wanted it for longer than I'd ever admit.

But right when it seemed inevitable, she pulled back suddenly, her eyes wide with regret.

"I can't," she whispered, voice shaky. "I love Salem."

I nodded, feeling the burn of reality hitting me. "I know. I love that crazy ass nigga, too."

We both sat back, letting the moment die between us. The heat faded but the ache stayed. The urge to cross that line was real, but so was the respect we both had for Salem, no matter how much he frustrated or hurt us.

"I've been attracted to you for a while now."

Hearing her admit it out loud felt both surreal and painful. I didn't know whether to be happy or miserable. "Paris..." I started, but she shook her head.

"You're everything I wish Salem could be. You're caring, affectionate. I can actually talk to you. You make me feel seen."

I sat there, stunned by her words. This was the honesty we'd been dancing around for so long. I felt the pull again, the temptation to reach out and touch her, to tell her I could be what she needed.

"But the moment we just almost crossed the line, I realized I can't. I respect Salem too much, no matter how broken things are with him. I can't hurt him like this."

I nodded slowly. "I know."

"He's not perfect, but the flaws he has aren't enough to outweigh the good in him. It's that goodness that's kept me with him all these years."

"And I respect him too. That's why we can't go there. No matter how much I want to."

She gave me a sad, understanding smile. "It's not easy, is it?"

I sighed, running a hand over my face. "No, Paris. It's not easy at all."

We sat in the quiet again, the tension still there, but now layered with a new understanding.

"We keep this between us," I told her.

She looked up at me, nodding slowly. "Promise?"

"Promise."

It was a promise that hurt to make but felt like the only right thing to do.

NIYAH

The next day, I found myself right where I'd been since Neveah was killed—curled up on the couch in the living room, staring at the ceiling. I hadn't slept. I hadn't eaten. My body was numb, but my mind wouldn't stop replaying what had happened. I kept seeing her. I kept hearing her screams, kept seeing those monsters rip my baby apart. Over and over, the sight kept playing in my head like some sick horror movie I couldn't shut off.

Grief sat in my chest, pressing down on me until I could barely breathe. Neveah was *gone*. My daughter, my only child, was gone, and there was nothing left inside me. I had barely survived losing Cane, barely kept it together when I watched him take his last breath. But this? This *broke* me. It shattered whatever was left of the woman I used to be. Now, I felt like nothing but a shell. I was hollow and empty. I couldn't eat. I couldn't sleep. And I damn sure couldn't talk to anyone. Not even Fable.

Especially not Fable.

I didn't care that he was hurting too. I didn't care that he kept looking at me with those wounded eyes, begging me silently to let him in. I didn't care because when it mattered most, when I needed him to let me help my baby, he didn't. He held me back. And now Neveah was dead because I couldn't get to her.

I didn't know if I could ever forgive him for that.

He tried to pull me into bed last night, but I couldn't stand to be near him. His arms felt wrong, and his touch felt suffocating. So, I stayed on the couch, staring up at the ceiling like a ghost, wishing everything would just stop. I didn't cry. I didn't scream. I just... existed, the way people who have nothing left do.

I heard him coming down the stairs. His footsteps were slow and cautious, like he wasn't sure what version of my grief he was about to run into, the version that stayed silent or the version that would lash out. Right now, I didn't even know myself.

He came closer, stopping beside the couch. I didn't bother to look at him.

"Niyah." His voice was so soft and pleading. "You need to eat something."

I stayed silent with my eyes fixed on a crack in the ceiling like it held all the answers to my problems.

"Please, baby, just... just say something. Anything," he begged. The pain in his voice didn't touch me. Nothing did.

"Niyah," he whispered again, his hand brushing over my shoulder. "I know you're hurting, but—"

"Don't fucking touch me," I hissed so venomously as I shook his hand off my shoulder. Hurt covered his eyes as he took a step back. "Don't touch me and stop talking to me."

I heard him exhale slowly as I told him, "Just leave me alone, Fable."

I felt him pull back, could almost hear his heart breaking,

but I didn't care. I didn't have room to care. I was drowning in my own grief, and there was no lifeline coming.

There was a moment of silence before I heard him sigh, long and tired. "I'm sorry," he whispered, voice cracking like he was barely holding himself together. "I'm so damn sorry."

But I didn't respond. I couldn't. The crack in the ceiling had more to offer me than his words did right now.

TWO DAYS LATER
PIER DAY

CHAPTER 19

FABLE

I woke up at midnight. It was time to move. I had planned it down to the minute, knowing it'd take us around four hours to make the walk to 31st and Lake Shore Drive. That's without counting the undead or scavengers we'd probably have to fight off. I wanted to give us more time, especially with Niyah in the state she was in.

I moved quietly around the house, packing up the things we'd need—supplies, weapons, anything I could carry in a bookbag.

My heart was heavy, not just with the fear of what we were about to face but because I didn't even know if she was coming with me. Niyah hadn't said a nice word to me since Neveah died. I wasn't sure if she had eaten, and every time I tried to talk to her, she just shut me down. So, I stayed out of her way, hoping she'd open up again at some point, hoping she'd find her way back to me.

But now I wasn't sure she ever would.

I packed the last of the supplies, then, with a deep breath, I turned toward the living room. Niyah was still lying on the couch, wide awake, staring at nothing. She looked so broken. She was gaunt and lifeless. She hadn't moved from that spot except to use the bathroom, and even then, it was like she was just going through the motions. Seeing her like that was killing me, but I didn't know how to help her anymore.

I slowly and carefully walked over. "It's time to go," I told her cautiously, like I was afraid to wake a sleeping giant. "You coming?"

She didn't answer right away. Her eyes didn't move from the ceiling, but I could see the anger flare up in them. She finally sat up, and her voice was cold as ice. "Of course I'm going. I can't wait to get away from this place... and everything that reminds me of it."

Offended and shocked, my head reared back a bit, but I was speechless.

However, even with the sting of her words, I felt some relief. She was coming, at least.

I stepped back toward the door, giving her space. I watched as she slowly put on her shoes, gathered what little she had, and then she reached for Neveah's bookbag to put everything in. She hesitated before picking it up with trembling fingers. I saw her expression transform to pain. Her shoulders shook as the tears started. I wanted to say something, anything to comfort her, but I knew better. One wrong word and she'd blow up. So, I bit my tongue and waited.

Once she had everything, I led the way to the front door. The cool, night breeze hit me as we stepped outside. The world felt quiet, but it was the kind of quiet that made your skin crawl because you knew it wasn't safe. The fear of what was out there was so overwhelming that I could feel it in my bones.

I glanced back at Niyah. Her face was set in a mask of grief and anger. But, no matter what, I was going to make damn sure she made it to safety, even if she hated me the entire way there.

SALEM

The whole house was tense, and not the usual kind that had become our norm since the apocalypse started. This was different. It was deeper and filled with more fear. The air was thick with it as everyone packed up, trying to prepare for the hell we were about to face.

Paris had barely spoken to me since that fight with August. I didn't feel right going out there with this tension between me and her.

I set down the bag I was stuffing with food and water bottles and headed to the guest bedroom. I pushed open the door quietly, closing it behind me with a soft click. Paris stood by the window, slipping on a shirt. She looked over her shoulder at me, surprised but not saying a word.

I took a deep breath, knowing I needed to say what I'd been holding back for too long. "I can't leave like this, Paris. Not with all this bad energy between us."

She turned to face me fully with an unreadable expression. But I continued, forcing the words out. "I know I haven't been the best to you. Shit, I've been an asshole. But I need you to understand that the way I've been acting isn't about you. It's about me trying to protect myself."

Her eyes narrowed slightly with confusion.

I stepped closer and sat on the bed. "I've lost so many people, Paris. My father, my best friend, and friends in the streets. I survived that. I learned how to keep going, even when it felt impossible. But if I lost you..." I paused, swallowing hard. "If I lost you, baby, I don't know if I'd make it. It would ruin me. So, yeah, I put up walls. It's all I know how to do."

She stayed quiet, soaking it all in. I could see her fighting back tears. "So, what do you want me to say, Salem? That it's okay? That I understand?"

"I don't need you to just say anything. I just want you to know that I'm going to do better," I said. "I know I got a lot to fix, and I'm not making excuses for it. But I'm telling you, I'm done pushing you away because I don't want to lose you, baby. I'm going to get us the fuck up outta here and do better, baby."

She folded her arms. "You don't get to do this now, right before we leave. You can't just flip a switch and expect me to forget everything."

I nodded slowly. "I know. And I ain't asking you to forget. I'm asking you to let me make it right. I'm asking you to give me a chance."

Her shoulders dropped as she let out a long sigh. "I don't want to lose you, Salem," she admitted. "But I'm scared that you'll go right back to being cold and distant."

I stood up and closed the gap between us. "I'm scared too. Scared of what I'll do if I lose you, scared of not being enough. But I'm more scared of living without you."

Tears finally filled her eyes. "Then don't make me live without you," she whispered.

I reached out, touching her face gently. "I won't, Paris. I swear to God, I won't."

She leaned into my hand, and her breath hitched as our eyes locked. I pulled her closer, and my hand cradled the back of her neck as I pressed my lips to hers.

The kiss was full of everything I'd never been able to say. She melted into me as her arms wrapped around my neck.

"I love you, Salem," she breathed between kisses. "I've loved you for so long, even when you made it so damn hard."

"I love you too, Paris," I whispered against her lips. "I've loved you since the day I met you. I just need to learn how to show it."

She pulled back slightly, just enough to look me in the eyes. "I'll teach you."

I gently pressed my forehead against hers. "Thank you, baby."

We'd been walking for hours, but the crew was holding up better than I expected, considering how tired, hungry, and thirsty we all were. The backpacks the guys carried felt like bricks on our backs, even though we'd packed light with just water and whatever food we could ration. We couldn't take too much because anything extra could slow us down.

When we first left camp, it felt like we were marching into battle. Everyone was silent, focused, and determined. We were like soldiers ready to face whatever hell was waiting for us out here. But under all that, I could still see the fear in their eyes. They tried to hide it, tried to act tough, but it was there, just beneath the surface. Except for me. I wasn't scared, not even a little.

I was just determined. I wasn't going to let anything or anybody stop me from getting out of here. The undead, scavengers, military checkpoints; I didn't give a fuck. I was ready to tear down whatever or whoever stood in my way to get to that boat. There was no room for hesitation, no time for second thoughts. If it came down to it, I'd do whatever needed to be done. That was the only way we were getting out alive.

Now, we were heading north on Jeffery Avenue. The quiet streets felt eerie as hell. I scanned every alleyway, every window, keeping my eyes peeled for any movement.

"Salem," August's whispered but urgent voice broke through my thoughts. He was ahead of me with his hand raised, motioning for us to stop. My breath hitched as I glanced up. A pack of the undead, at least thirty of them, stumbled out from around the corner up ahead. They were moving fast, too fast. We had maybe a few seconds to decide before they'd be on us.

"Shit," I muttered, pulling my gun.

"It's too many of them," August said as he froze.

Kecia's eyes widened as she began to panic. "What are we going to do?"

"We can't outrun them, and there is nowhere to hide," Paris said, looking back at me. "Shit!"

I looked around, quickly thinking of where the hell we could hide before they saw us, before they smelled us. But I knew that any sudden movements would put their focus right on us.

But before I could think of anything, Navon turned to face us with the oddest look in his eyes. "Y'all run the other way."

August's eyes narrowed. "What the fuck? What you mean?"

"Get out of here!" he urged as he looked back toward the pack that was closing in on us. "Hurry up!"

"No, man!" I barked, stepping forward, but he shook his head, backing away from us.

"We're almost there. Don't be stupid!" Paris shouted.

"I ain't stupid," Navon said as a weak smile formed his lips. "Y'all keep going. Someone's gotta slow them down."

"We can take them together," I growled.

Navon shook his head. He was more resolute than I'd ever seen him. "No, we can't. It's too many of them, man. You know this. It's not a house behind us for us to run into."

"Don't do this, man," August pleaded. "We're almost there."

We all kept looking over his shoulder, watching the horde inch up the block.

When Navon glanced at us, his eyes lingered on each of us before he turned and charged toward the pack of the undead without another word.

"Fuck!" I barked, lunging for him.

I was able to grab him. August did too. Both of us tried to hold him back with everything we had.

"Navon, no! Don't do this!" August barked.

But Navon was stronger than he should've been in that moment. He was fueled by something bigger than fear and pain. He wrestled out of our grip like a man possessed and broke free, sprinting into the horde.

"No, Navon!" Meesha yelped tearfully.

The sound of gunshots rang out as Navon fired into the horde, dropping two of the undead right off the bat. But there were too many. They swarmed him, bodies piling over his as he fought them off. I watched, helpless and furious, as Navon swung his bat, smashing in skulls left and right, even as more of those undead motherfuckers piled on him.

"Navon!" Paris screamed, but I grabbed her arm, pulling her back.

"Baby, we gotta go." But my own words were weak. My heart was hammering in my chest. I wanted to help my boy, but there was nothing we could do. Navon was already swallowed up by the swarm. His screams rang in the street, but he soon went silent.

For a moment, we just stood there, frozen, staring at the writhing mass of bodies tearing apart the last piece of Navon.

We watched our brother get eaten alive, and I hated every second of it.

"We have to go," I muttered. "*Now* before those mother-fuckers see the rest of us."

Reluctantly, the crew started moving again, forcing our legs to carry us away from the scene, from Navon's death. My fists clenched around my weapon, teeth grinding together so hard I thought I'd break them.

NIYAH

The closer we got to the position at the border where Onyx's friend was stationed, I got more nervous. I wanted to be hopeful and excited. But I couldn't shake the guilt. It sat in my chest, gnawing at me, reminding me of Neveah. I had left her in this nightmare, and nothing would ever make that right. I didn't see how I could ever forgive myself.

Fable walked beside me. His presence was so strong and steady as always, but things between us were still tense. I still couldn't talk to him. Every word felt forced, like we were just going through the motions to survive. He kept his gun in his hand, the same as me, because we couldn't let our guard down.

We were walking east on 35th Street, when we saw two figures stepping out from the shadows. My heart jumped in my chest as we froze. Thankfully, the figures didn't move like the undead. They were human, but they were rough and dirty. They'd obviously been through hell and didn't look like they had shelter. They had eyes that screamed desperation.

The man raised his gun first. "Drop your weapons," he barked menacingly.

The woman stood behind him, watching us with a sneer. Her hand rested on her gun, ready to pull the trigger any second.

I glanced at Fable. My pulse was racing, but he didn't flinch. His grip tightened around his gun, but he didn't lower it.

"Drop them now, or you die here," the man warned again, stepping forward. His eyes darted between me and Fable, but Fable stood his ground. I could see in his eyes that he was calculating his next move.

"You don't want to do this," Fable told them. "Just move around and let us be on our way."

"Where y'all going?" the woman asked us with a taunting smile. "Ain't nothing east but the border and the soldiers shooting anything that comes that way."

"Like I said," Fable gritted. "Y'all don't wanna do this."

The guy's lips curled into a grim smile. "Yeah, I do."

In an instant, it happened. Fable moved faster than I could even react. His gun was up before the guy could blink. A loud crack filled the air as Fable fired, hitting the man in the chest. He fell back, dropping his gun.

Just as his body collapsed, the woman screamed, but Fable was already on her. He swung the butt of his gun across her face, knocking her to the ground before she could even aim. She hit the pavement hard, blood pouring from her nose.

"Let's go," he growled, pulling me by the arm.

My feet were moving before I even realized it, my breath ragged as we took off toward the border. My mind raced as my body wired with adrenaline.

We didn't stop running. Every step was a sprint. Every breath was a struggle, but we kept running. I could hear the snarls of the undead behind us, the sick, wet sounds of their feet scraping against the ground as they gave chase. Fable shot a few of them as we pushed forward. I fired, too, my heart hammering in my chest as I took down a couple with quick shots to the head. But there were always more, coming from the alleys, from behind abandoned cars, from houses we passed. It felt like the whole city was rotting and running after us.

My legs were on fire, but I didn't stop. We couldn't. Not until we reached Sam's station. We were almost there. I could see the faint outline of King Drive up ahead, where the border was. We ran through shadows, dodging the undead as they closed in.

Finally, we made it. Through the darkness, I saw the tall, slim white guy pacing with a shotgun in his hand. He was dressed in army fatigues and the cigarette dangling from his lips as it glowed in the night. He looked like he was as nervous as I was. His eyes darted around the street, watching for any sign of movement.

The border looked like a fortress straight out of a warzone. The gates stretched up high, maybe twelve feet or more, topped with thick coils of barbed wire that glinted under the dim street-lights. Beyond the gates, I could make out makeshift barriers—rows of sandbags stacked like bulky shields, blocking any clear view of what was inside.

Military vehicles, most of them armored trucks with mounted guns, were parked along the side, coated in dirt and grime. The gate itself looked impenetrable, made of solid metal bars welded together, with a massive lock securing the entrance.

Fable slowed us down amongst a group of trees. My legs felt like they were going to give out, and I was shaking so bad I could barely stand.

"Stay here just in case," he told me, breathing hard.

I nodded with my heart in my throat as I watched Fable carefully approach Sam.

Hearing Fable's footsteps, Sam immediately raised his shotgun. "Who the hell's there? Stay where you are!"

Fable raised his hands as he slowly inched towards Sam. "It's Fable Montgomery. Onyx sent Tariq for me."

Sam didn't lower his weapon. He kept it trained on Fable, his eyes narrowing as he took a drag from his cigarette. He looked around as if he were searching for someone else. "Where the hell is Tariq?"

Fable's expression tightened, and even from a distance, I could see the sadness in his eyes. "He was killed by scavengers after he found me."

Sam's face fell. For a moment, he just stood there, processing the words. His grip on the shotgun loosened slightly. "Scavengers," he muttered, shaking his head. "Not the undead?"

Fable shook his head. "No. It was scavengers."

Sam looked down with the cigarette hanging from his lips. The tip glowed faintly in the dark. He glanced back up at Fable with a hard gaze. "You been bit?"

"No," Fable eagerly told him. "I swear."

Sam's eyes lingered on him, searching for any sign of a lie. I wanted to scream, wanted to yell at Sam to hurry up and let us through, but I stayed quiet, watching, waiting, and looking over my shoulder for the undead.

After what felt like an eternity, Sam finally lowered his shotgun. "Alright," he muttered, stepping aside. "Go on."

Fable turned back to me, his eyes locking with mine. "C'mon, baby," he called softly.

I exhaled a shaky breath, the relief hitting me so hard I nearly collapsed. But just as I took a step forward, Sam snapped "Who's that with you?" as he raised his gun again, eyes wide with suspicion.

Fable moved quickly, putting himself between me and Sam. "It's just my girl," he said, calm but pleading.

"Onyx said it would just be you."

"I know. But she's my girl. I can't leave her. She's not bit, I promise you. Just let her through. *Please*. We've been through hell trying to get here. We've been through hell period. It's literally hell out there, man."

It broke my heart to hear Fable plead for our lives.

Sam's eyes bounced between the two of us as his grip tightened on the shotgun again. He looked like he was doing the math in his head, trying to decide if we were worth the risk. Fear crept up my spine as I stood frozen, waiting for him to make a decision.

"*Please*," Fable repeated. "She's clean. I swear."

Sam hesitated as his finger hovered over the trigger.

Then, after a long, excruciating moment, he sighed and lowered the gun once more. "Alright," he muttered.

Both me and Fable let out audible, relieved breaths that we had been holding. Fable reached out, grabbing my hand as we hurried towards Sam.

Sam fumbled for the massive lock. His hands moved quickly. The thick metal clanged as he yanked the chain loose. He shoved his shoulder against the gate, pushing it open with a loud, creaking groan. The gate swung just wide enough for us to slip through.

"Go," he urged, glancing nervously over his shoulder, as if he half-expected someone or something to appear. "Move fast but keep your eyes out for the soldiers on patrol."

Fable and I stepped through the opening together. Once we were through, he pushed the gate shut behind us, locking it swiftly.

As we moved quietly and carefully, Fable glanced at his watch.

"It's five in the morning." He gave me a tired look. His eyes were so heavy with exhaustion. "We should get to the beach and find somewhere to rest until it's time to meet Onyx."

I nodded. My body was aching from the hours of running. I was so worn out that I could barely lift my legs.

As we moved cautiously along 35th Street, I could hear the distant rumble of army vehicles. It had been weeks since I'd heard a car engine. It was music to my ears. Still, my heart pounded like a drum. We had to stay low, ducking behind parked cars and trees. Fable held my hand tightly, signaling when to move and when to stop. The eerie silence of the city was shattered every now and then by distant gunshots or the unsettling, crackling voices of soldiers on their radios.

My breath caught in my throat each time we left the cover of shadows. We darted across intersections when the coast seemed clear. Streetlights sputtered overhead, which made us more visible than I liked. We were exposed, vulnerable, and any wrong move could mean death.

As we neared the lakefront, the air became cooler and had the salty smell of the water. We could hear the low rumble of military vehicles patrolling nearby. I froze when I caught sight of one soldier walking the perimeter. His flashlight swept over the street. Fable pulled me down behind a dumpster. Our bodies pressed against the cold metal as we crouched, holding our breath. The soldier's beam passed just above us, making me close my eyes and pray.

After what felt like an eternity, the soldier moved on. Fable signaled for us to move, and we bolted across the street toward Lakeshore Drive, crouching low as we reached the overpass.

Finally, we made it to 35th Street Beach. There was a restroom just off the sand. The bathroom was disgusting. It was small, grimy, and reeking of pee, but it was a place to hide. Fable locked the door behind us, and for the first time in hours, I let out a breath I didn't even realize I was holding.

I should've been relieved. We were so close to getting out of this hell, so close to safety. But I couldn't feel any of it. All I could think about was Neveah. My daughter was gone. I could still see her mangled body as those things tore into her. No matter how far we ran, I couldn't escape from that.

CHAPTER 20

FABLE

I waited until Niyah's breathing slowed, until the exhaustion finally pulled her into sleep. It took everything in me not to reach out and hold her, comfort her the way I wanted to, but she wasn't fucking with me.

Once I was sure she was out, I slipped out of the bathroom, moving as quietly as possible. The wind off the lake was cool, biting against my skin as I took off running toward the tunnel Tariq told me would lead me to the pier.

I had to make sure this was real. I had to see it with my own eyes. I couldn't let Niyah down again.

But the secret path was just as Tariq had told me. It was hidden, almost invisible in the overgrowth and the rubble. I clawed my way through it, climbing through debris, leaves, and limbs. The tunnel was trash, having been abandoned for weeks.

When I finally emerged on the other side, my knees buckled when I saw the pier and the boats. I couldn't believe it. Tears came to my eyes as they frantically searched for the dock where Tariq said Onyx would be, Dock B.

Finally, I saw Onyx standing there on the pier, talking to a soldier.

I inhaled sharply as my eyes locked onto him, wide, like I was seeing a ghost. I just stared at him, taking him in. This shit didn't feel real.

But I stayed back, watching them from a distance as I hid behind a bush. The soldier finally turned, walking away. I slowly emerged from behind the bush. As if he felt my presence, Onyx spotted me. For a second, I thought he might've frozen in place, but then he motioned for me to stay where I was. He strolled toward me, casual and cool. But as soon as we were close enough, he broke into a run, closing the distance between us and pulling me into a hug.

"Damn, man," Onyx said, squeezing me tight. "I didn't think you were gonna make it."

My breaths were still coming in short bursts from excitement and adrenaline. I held onto him for a bit longer than I probably should have, but it felt good to see him, to know this was real.

He let me go as he started to look behind me. "Where is Tariq?"

My eyes lowered. I couldn't look at him as I told him. "I'm sorry, bro. Tariq didn't make it."

Onyx fell so silent that my eyes were drawn to him. His eyes went glassy, but he didn't let the tears fall. He clenched his jaw so tight that I could see the muscles working, like he was fighting everything inside him just to hold it together.

"The undead?" he forced out.

"No. Scavengers."

"Shit." He doubled over, bracing himself with his hands on his knees. "I sent him back out there."

"Don't blame yourself."

"Fuck!" he roared lowly. Then as if he remembered that I could get killed standing there, he stood upright, looking around with eyes brimming with tears. "We gotta go, but, shit, you're early."

"I had to make sure, bro. Had to see it for myself."

He smiled weakly through his grief. "You saw it. Now let's go. Get on the boat," Onyx said, jerking his head toward the dock. "I can figure out a place for you to hide until I pull off."

I shook my head. "I can't. I gotta go back and get Niyah."

His brows furrowed. "Niyah?"

"My girl."

Onyx frowned, eyes narrowing. "Don't be stupid, man. You're already here. You might not make it back if you leave."

"I just wanted to make sure this was real, bro," I said, glancing back in the direction I'd come from. "But I can't leave her. She's just a few blocks away. I gotta go back for her."

Onyx sighed, running a hand over his face as his eyes scanned the horizon. "You sure about this? What if you get caught trying to go back to get her?"

I gave him a sharp nod. "I'm sure."

"She that important to you? I mean, how can she be if I've never even heard of her?"

It didn't take a second for me to answer, and when I felt how sure I was, I smiled weakly. I would do anything for this woman. "Yea, she's *that* important to me."

He studied me for a moment, then nodded slowly. "Alright but be quick. Don't take too long, Fable. I'll wait as long as I can, but if the soldiers catch on, I'm out. You hear me? I have to pull off at 6 a.m. You have twenty minutes."

"I hear you." I gripped his shoulder, appreciating that he understood. "I'll be back. Just...don't leave without me, man."

He shrugged a shoulder, looking at me like I was the dumbest nigga in the world. "I'll try not to."

I scoffed sadly. "I feel you."

"Don't get killed." Then Onyx gave me a hard look, then turned back toward the boat.

I glanced at the pier, the boat sitting there, waiting for us. Safety was right there. A real chance to survive, to get the fuck out of this hell. But I couldn't take it. Not without her.

I SLIPPED BACK INTO THE BATHROOM AS QUIETLY AS POSSIBLE, but the sound of the door shutting woke her up.

Niyah sat up groggily. "Is it time to go?" She sounded so hopeful, but with the slightest bit of life I hadn't heard in days.

I hated how she looked at me now, like I was some kind of stranger. There was no love or warmth in her eyes, just distance. She hated me. I could feel it in every glance and breath between us. And I hated *it*. I knew once we made it to safety, she wouldn't ever look at me the same again. She might not look at me at all. She'd leave, and that thought hurt more than any walker bite could.

I knew right then that I'd rather be with her in hell than be without her in paradise.

I looked at her, swallowing down the truth. "The secret path is closed off. There's no way to get to the pier without us being seen."

Her face contorted into disbelief. "You're lying," she spat as she scrambled to her feet. She shook her head like she was trying to shake off the lie. "I want to see for myself."

I stepped between her and the door. "I swear to you, Niyah, it's gone. I went myself to make sure because I couldn't sleep. We'd never make it through. I barely got back here without getting caught. It's soldiers everywhere. We have to go back."

Her anger flared, and she started to yell. "I don't believe you!" She shoved me in the chest, fists hitting me. Her voice broke as tears streamed down her face. "Why didn't you let me die with her, huh? Why did you drag me back into this hell?"

Her words sliced through me, each one hitting harder than the last. I could feel her pain radiating off her in waves, and I wanted to fix it. But there was nothing I could do. The only thing I could do was take her to that boat, and that felt like the end of us.

So, I just stood there, taking it, her anger, her grief, her fists, until she collapsed onto the floor, sobbing uncontrollably.

I knelt beside her, my heart breaking. "I'm sorry," I whispered, though the words felt hollow. "I'm so damn sorry. But it's not there, baby. If we go, we're dead. We have to go back. Let's just go back home."

She didn't respond. She just cried until the tears ran dry.

Finally, after what felt like hours, she whispered, "I'm hungry." It was the first time she'd mentioned food since Neveah was killed.

I felt a strange kind of relief wash over me. She was asking for something. She *needed me*. And that wasn't much, but it was something. She was still here, still with me, even if she hated me right now. At least she was depending on me again.

I fumbled through the bag and grabbed an energy bar. After I handed it to her, she opened it and took a slow bite.

"C'mon," I told her. "We have to go."

I cautiously reached for her hand. And surprisingly, she let me take it.

We left the bathroom in silence. Niyah's tears were still fresh on her cheeks. Each step we took toward the border felt like a countdown to nothing. I could see how depressed she was, the hopelessness clinging to her. It broke something in me.

We moved slowly and stepped lightly. I kept checking over my shoulder, making sure we weren't seen. Niyah was crying silently beside me, and it tore me apart. The look on her face was pure devastation, like her spirit had shattered.

Then, the low rumble of an army vehicle came from around the corner. I grabbed her arm and tried to yank her into the shadows with me. But she didn't move on her own. It was like she wanted to be caught.

I whispered urgently, "Don't do this," tightening my grip on her arm.

She looked at me with eyes that were distant and lost. Then she sighed but allowed me to pull her in.

We stood there with our bodies pressed against the wall until the vehicle drove by. When the coast was finally clear, I took her hand and led her toward the street.

Her hand felt so weak. She was so broken. I couldn't take it anymore. I couldn't keep lying. I didn't want to keep her like this. I reached for her hand, and when she glanced at me with hollow eyes, I knew I had to come clean.

"Niyah...I... I was lying."

Confused, her brows curled. "About what?"

"The tunnel. It's there. I saw it. I saw Onyx too."

She stopped in her tracks, yanking her hand out of mine. "What?!" Her voice cracked as disbelief and betrayal flashed in her eyes.

"I'm sorry," I rushed out, stepping closer.

Her face bawled up in anger. She shoved at my chest, trying to push me away. "Why would you do that?!" she hissed as fresh tears welled up.

"I was scared, baby. Not of what's out there. But of losing you. I can't imagine being safe without you. I'd rather be in hell with you than in safety without you."

Her breath hitched, but I could see her walls breaking down.

I closed the space between us and gently held her face. "I'm sorry for not letting you help Neveah." She looked down but I raised her head, forcing her to see the sincerity in my eyes. "But there was nothing you could've done. And I wasn't about to lose you, too."

Tears slipped down her cheeks. Her lips parted as she got ready to finally say something to me without anger in her eyes.

But suddenly gunshots rang out, loud and piercing, coming from the direction of the border. My heart dropped as explosions followed, shaking the ground beneath us.

"Run!" I shouted, grabbing her hand as we took off. The noise behind us was deafening as more shots rang out. The blasts of grenades in the distance made everything shake. I glanced back, and my blood ran cold. Dozens of the undead were coming from the direction of the border.

We pushed harder. We ran for blocks, but it felt like miles. We no longer cared about getting caught. Our feet pounded the pavement as we headed for the tunnel.

Finally, we made it.

"Come on!" I urged, pulling Niyah behind me as we stumbled toward the entrance. We slipped inside, running through the darkness, the growls of the undead joining us in the tunnels behind us.

When we finally burst out on the other side, I could see the pier up ahead, stretching out over the water.

We sprinted for Dock B, hearts racing, legs burning, and off in the distance, I saw Onyx's boat moving away from the pier.

"Onyx!" I shouted, waving my arms desperately.

Niyah joined in, both of us yelling at the top of our lungs. But he couldn't hear us. The boat kept moving.

"No, no, no!" I shouted, frustration and fear blending together as the boat continued to drift. The undead were closing in fast and too close. Desperation took over. I grabbed Niyah's hand again, pulling her toward the edge of the dock.

We didn't think. We just jumped. The cold water hit like a shock, but we pushed through, swimming as hard as we could.

As we surfaced, gasping for air, I saw Onyx finally turning around.

"He sees us!" I choked out, hope surging through my veins as the boat veered toward us.

We kept swimming, our breaths ragged, but the sound of that engine coming closer was the sweetest thing I'd ever heard.

Finally, Onyx's boat pulled up alongside us, and he leaned over, reaching out with both hands. "Get in!"

AUGUST

The closer we got to the border, there were more and more of the undead.

"That's explosions," I told Salem.

"We gotta keep moving," he bit.

Paris' voice was shaky. "Salem, are you sure?"

The girls looked at me for help.

"Something is going on at the border, bro," I told him.

"Then we'll see what it is. C'mon," Salem barked. "We only have twenty minutes before Onyx leaves."

We all regretfully followed with all of our weapons ready.

We made our way down the last block to the border. Each step felt slower than the last, but we pushed forward, cutting down any walker that got too close. I swung my bat with everything I had, its metal crunching against rotting skulls. Paris was right beside me, clutching her knife with both hands, slashing at anything that got near her. Meesha, Salem, and Kecia's grunts and heavy breaths mingled with the guttural growls of the undead.

The closer we got to King Drive, the more they showed up, like they could sense we were almost to safety. They were packed together. They were an unending wave of gnashing teeth and reaching hands. The stench of death was overwhelming.

"Keep going!" Salem shouted, hoarsely. His machete was slick with black, clotted blood. His arm was swinging almost mechanically now, slashing from side to side, cutting a path through the mass of undead.

I could feel my arms getting weaker. My grip on the bat was getting slippery from all the gore.

Finally, King Drive was just up ahead. But what we saw when we looked ahead was a whole new level of hell.

It was like a river, but instead of water, it was filled with the undead. Hundreds of them, all jammed together, clawing, shoving. There were so many that the road itself had vanished under their mangled bodies. It was a writhing, bloody sea of death.

Some of the undead were in army fatigues, their faces twisted in that dead, snarling expression, blood dripping from their decayed lips. The ground was soaked in blood, with bodies—both human and undead—scattered across the streets. It looked like the soldiers tried to take them out, tried to blow up as many as they could, but there were just too damn many.

Paris gasped, covering her mouth, her eyes wide with horror. "We can't get through that," she whispered, shaking her head slowly.

Meesha's voice was barely audible over the growling mass ahead. "How are we supposed to make it across?"

Salem's face was unreadable, but I knew what he was thinking. He'd try anyway, whether it killed him or not.

"Damn," I muttered, my throat tight with dread. "That's... that's too many."

Kecia grew pale as she took a step back. "This is crazy. We'll never make it."

Salem's eyes were blazing as his grip tightened on his machete. "We don't have a choice."

"Nigga, are you crazy?!" I barked.

"So, Navon died for nothing?"

"Look at that shit!" Paris hissed, getting into his face. "It is *impossible*. Navon is not going to be the only person that died for nothing if we don't go the fuck back, Salem!"

"We're too close, baby." He winced, showing the first sign of vulnerability I had seen in my brother in years. "We have to find a way through. We have to."

She gently cupped his beard, locking pleading eyes on him. "We can't, baby. We can't."

We stood there for what felt like hours, staring at that writhing sea of death. It was like watching hope get eaten alive, chewed up by reality. There was no getting across that. Not tonight.

Salem's jaw was clenched and his eyes burned with frustration. He kicked the ground hard, sending dirt flying into the air.

Paris reached out and touched his arm gently. "Let's go back, Salem," she said softly. "We've tried, but we have to live to try again."

For once, he didn't argue. He just nodded, still glaring at the undead like he could will them to disappear. But he turned around, his shoulders dropping a bit, and started walking in the direction we'd come from.

One by one, we followed. Paris held onto Salem's arm. Meesha walked beside Kecia, who looked shell-shocked, her eyes darting around like she expected the walkers to follow us. I trailed behind, my mind replaying Navon's sacrifice over and over again. He'd given us the chance to get this far, and it felt like a betrayal to just walk away now.

But there was nothing else we could do. We weren't making it to the pier that day, and maybe not ever.

The dream of the pier, of getting out of here had been what kept us going. Now, it felt like we had nothing else to hold on to.

NIYAH

We stood there in disbelief as we stepped into the hotel room. Everything felt surreal—clean sheets, room service, even a tiny minibar humming in the corner. After everything we'd been through, it was like stepping into another world.

During the ride across Lake Michigan, we could hear the military talking over the marine VHF radio. The walkers had overrun the border at King Drive. Somehow, they had gotten through the gate. They had reached the beach and were now spreading into other parts of the city. The military was trying to contain the outbreak, but from the frantic chatter, it was clear that control was slipping away.

Luckily, some of the supplies that Onyx brought to the pier were scrubs for the medical staff. So, Fable and I had been able to change out of our wet clothes and into scrubs.

I could hardly believe we'd gotten out. But my heart broke, wondering if Salem, Paris, August, Navon, Kecia, and Meesha were even alive. I knew that they had tried to make it to the pier that day. I wanted to hope, but hope felt too much like betrayal.

When we reached Michigan City, Onyx urgently helped us

off the boat quietly, moving swiftly as he got us to a hotel just off the shore. After checking us in, he handed Fable a stack of cash and told us we would see him soon.

I looked over at Fable, and for the first time in weeks, I saw him really exhale. He dropped his bag and sank onto the king-sized bed, pulling me down with him. We just lay there, side by side, staring up at the ceiling in stunned silence.

I couldn't hold it back any longer. Suddenly, the tears came fast and hard, streaming down my face in waves I couldn't control.

Fable shot up, alarmed. "What's wrong?"

I shook my head, covering my face with my hands as the sobs kept coming. "No... no, nothing's wrong. I'm... *happy*." I giggled excitedly as I tried to dry my tears, but only more of them came flooding down. "I'm so fucking happy." I was choking on my own words, trying to explain. "I lost Cane. I lost Neveah. Our friends didn't make it out. We lost so many people. And I feel guilty, Fable. But at the same time, I'm happy. I'm so damn happy that we made it."

He reached over and pulled me into his arms. "You don't have to apologize for surviving," he whispered. "We fought too hard for this. We would have stayed with the crew. They would have been with us. But you had reason to want to leave."

I pulled back a little to look at him. "No, it's more than that. I'm grateful, Fable. I've never had someone fight for me the way you have." I felt a lump forming in my throat. "I love you, Fable. I've loved you for a long time. I don't know how it happened in all this mess, but I do. And I don't want to spend one more second without telling you that. I'm sorry." I paused, pushing past the lump in my throat. "I was wrong for how I treated you after Neveah... after she was... killed. I was griev-ing, and I just... I needed someone to blame. I wanted to be angry at someone, and it felt wrong to be mad at her." I took a shaky breath, trying to hold it together. "I wasn't fair to you. You've done nothing but try to keep us safe, both me and Neveah."

His eyes grew so soft, filled with that same patience he'd shown since the day me, Neveah, and Tariq ran into him. "You don't have to apologize. I get it. If it were the other way around, I don't know if I could have held it together either."

"No," I insisted, grabbing his hand. "You need to hear it. I know I hurt you, and you didn't deserve it. You've done everything for us—*everything*. I should have been grateful, not lashing out. You were just trying to save me... even when I couldn't save Neveah."

His grip tightened around mine, and I could see his eyes glistening. "I would've given anything to change what happened to her."

"I know," I whispered. "I know you would have."

He pulled me closer, and I wrapped my arms around him. We lay there, just holding each other, the past weeks of chaos, grief, and heartbreak finally settling into some kind of fragile peace.

"Thank you," I murmured against his chest. "For everything."

He kissed the top of my head. "And thank you for not giving up on us."

We stayed like that for a while, just breathing in the quiet of the room and the safety we never thought we'd find.

He leaned in to kiss me with his eyes full of warmth and love. But just as our lips were about to touch, I pushed him back, smiling through my tears. "Unt uh," I teased, my voice playful for the first time in what felt like forever. "You stink. You need a shower first."

He laughed, shaking his head. "*Shiiid*, you do too."

My mouth fell open, and I started cracking up.

"You do," he laughed. "And your hair is still wet, fucking up the sheets. Let me call and ask for some new ones."

My eyes lit up as an idea came to mind. "And you can call room service!!"

His eyes widened cartoonishly. "Fuck yeah."

"Oh my *gaaaawd*." My mouth started to water. "I want a cheeseburger with grilled onions."

"Baby... we ordering every-fucking-thing on the menu."

As he sat up and grabbed the phone, I forced myself to believe that all of this was real. We had made it to safety. The fight wasn't over for the world outside, but for us, it was the beginning of something new.

As I lay there, the gravity of everything I'd been through pressed down on me. The grief, the loss, and the fear felt like scars carved into my soul. I'd seen Cane die right in front of me, I'd watched Neveah turn into one of those things, and I'd faced monsters, both living and undead, that had tried to take everything from me. I'd never imagined that I'd find love amid this nightmare. But somehow, with Fable, I had. He was the only reason I hadn't given up entirely.

I thought about the woman I used to be before this all started: confident, driven, focused on my career and my daughter. I'd been so strong in that old life, but this new world had broken me down to my rawest form. Yet, somewhere in all that destruction, I'd found a different kind of strength—the strength to love again when everything felt so lost. And that was the only real victory I could claim out of this nightmare.

The sound of Fable's voice as he spoke into the phone was a low rumble of a promise that there was still something good to hold onto in this broken world. I wiped away the last of my tears, finally letting a small smile slip through the pain. I didn't know what the next day would bring, but I knew that as long as we had each other, there was still something worth fighting for.

THE END

This is **not** a cliffhanger. Not all characters make it out in a thriller. However, readers **will** get a follow-up on the rest of the crew.

Other Books by Jessica N. Watkins:

THE GIRL FROM ENGLEWOOD (STANDALONE)
PROPERTY OF A SAVAGE (STANDALONE)
WHEN MY SOUL MET A THUG (STANDALONE)
SAY MY FUCKING NAME (STANDALONE)
I'LL KISS ALL YOUR WOUNDS (STANDALONE)
PROPERTY OF A LEGACY (STANDALONE)

PROPERTY OF A RICH NIGGA (COMPLETE SERIES)
Property of a Rich Nigga
Property of a Rich Nigga 2
Property of a Rich Nigga 3
Capo (Prequel)

A RICH MAN'S WIFE (COMPLETE SERIES)
A Rich Man's Wife
A Rich Man's Wife 2

EVERY LOVE STORY IS BEAUTIFUL, BUT OURS IS
HOOD SERIES (COMPLETE SERIES)
Every Love Story Is Beautiful, But Ours Is Hood
Every Love Story Is Beautiful, But Ours Is Hood 2
Every Love Story Is Beautiful, But Ours Is Hood 3

WHEN THE SIDE NIGGA CATCH FEELINGS SERIES
(COMPLETE SERIES)
When The Side Nigga Catch Feelings
When the Side Nigga Catch Feelings 2

IN TRUE THUG FASHION (COMPLETE SERIES)
In True Thug Fashion 1
In True Thug Fashion 2
In True Thug Fashion 3

SECRETS OF A SIDE BITCH SERIES (COMPLETE
SERIES)
Secrets of a Side Bitch
Secrets of a Side Bitch 2
Secrets of a Side Bitch 3
Secrets of a Side Bitch – The Simone Story
Secrets of a Side Bitch 4

A SOUTH SIDE LOVE STORY (COMPLETED SERIES)
A South Side Love Story
A South Side Love Story 2
A South Side Love Story 3
A South Side Love Story 4

CAPONE AND CAPRI SERIES (COMPLETE SERIES)
Capone and Capri
Capone and Capri 2

A THUG'S LOVE SERIES (COMPLETE SERIES)
A Thug's Love
A Thug's Love 2
A Thug's Love 3
A Thug's Love 4
A Thug's Love 5

NIGGAS AIN'T SHIT (COMPLETE SERIES)
Niggas Ain't Shit
Niggas Ain't Shit 2

THE CAUSE AND CURE IS YOU SERIES (PARANORMAL
COMPLETE SERIES)
The Cause and Cure Is You
The Cause and Cure Is You 2

HOUSE IN VIRGINIA (COMPLETE SERIES)
House In Virginia 1
House in Virginia 2

SNOW (COMPLETE SERIES)
SNOW 1
SNOW 2

GET NOTIFIED

Want to be notified when the new, hot Urban Fiction and Interracial Romance books are released? Text the keyword "JWP" to 22828 to receive an email notifying you of new releases, giveaways, announcements, and more!

JESSICA WATKINS PRESENTS
IS ACCEPTING SUBMISSIONS

Jessica Watkins Presents is the home of many well-known, best-selling authors in Urban, Interracial, and IR and AA Paranormal Romance. We provide editing services, promotion and marketing, one-on-one consulting with a renowned, national best-selling author, assistance in branding, and more, FREE of charge to you, the author.

We are currently accepting submissions for the following genres: Urban, Interracial, and IR and AA Paranormal Romance. If you are interested in becoming a published author and have a FINISHED manuscript, please send the synopsis, genre and the first three chapters in a PDF or Word file to jwp.submissions@gmail.com. Complete manuscripts must be at least 45,000 words.

Made in the USA
Monee, IL
29 March 2025